CPE 8/06

This book should be returned to any branch of the
Lancashire County Library on or before the date shown

In Pursuit of Anna

He'd seen her lying on the deck, glistening all over with oil, her breasts lolling to the sides, the nipples hard.

'They're always like this, aren't they?' he asked, his fingers tweaking the stiff points. 'You're always ready to be fucked.'

'By you, yes.' Maggie moved back, her breath coming in little pants. Her eyes were glazed as she stared at his moist cock. She eased her hand underneath the elastic of her bikini bottom and sighed. 'Christ, it's like the tropics down there.'

'Turn around.'

She did, presenting her full, rounded ass to him. Derek pulled the bikini over her hips, his prick twitching at the sight of her velvety pussy. He slipped his fingers into her, his urge fuelled by her responding moan. He grasped her hips, yanking her towards him as he drove forward. Maggie squealed with pleasure when he filled her and began pumping, like driving a paddle into a churn filled with sweet butter. Her body bounced in rhythm with his thrusts, her breasts dangling. Derek gritted his teeth and slipped his hand between her legs.

'Oh, yes,' Maggie gasped. 'Rub it ... fuck, Derek ... make me come. Oh, please.'

By the same author:

The Captivation
The Transformation
The Naked Truth

In Pursuit of Anna
Natasha Rostova

CPP	CLN
CBA	CLO
CFU	CMI
CIN	CPE 8/06
CKI	CRI 2/07
CLE	CSA
CLH	CSH 03/08
CLHH 9/07	

BLACK LACE

Black Lace books contain sexual fantasies.
In real life, always practise safe sex.

First published in 2006 by
Black Lace
Thames Wharf Studios
Rainville Road
London W6 9HA

Typeset by SetSystems Ltd, Saffron Walden, Essex
Printed and bound by Mackays of Chatham PLC

ISBN 0 352 34060 6
ISBN 9 780352 340603

Prologue

Anna Maxwell grasped the bottle and pushed a few bills across the bar. Not much more where that came from, she thought grimly. A crush of bodies pressed in on her from all sides amid the rising smell of alcohol and sweat. The walls of the club throbbed with energy.

Anna caught a glimpse of herself in the mirror behind the bar as she turned away. Her pageboy haircut was a butter-tinted blonde thanks to an over-the-counter dye, her eyes lined with heavy black liner, her lips crimson red just the way she liked them. She was wearing jeans torn at the knees and a black T-shirt with the sleeves rolled up to reveal one of her tattoos.

Her father would say that she looked like a demented Cinderella. He would think she was slumming in clubs like this one, that she was acting like a tart for flirting with roughened men. He would say that she was no better than her mother, that she was a disgrace to his name.

Not that she gave a flying rat's ass what her father would say or think.

She moved to sit behind a table in a darkened corner of the club. One guy had told her last night that she was as pretty as a doll, but that had been a clumsy attempt to slide his way under her skirt. As it turned out, she'd let him; he was good-looking in a beefy sort of way and proved to be surprisingly adept with his fingers.

Anna tilted her head back and took a long swallow of beer. The central dance floor was filled with people twisting and gyrating to the heavy beat. A few coloured lights pulsed over the crowd. Anna shifted against the vinyl seat as the pulsing centred between her legs. Usually she preferred dank bars with jukeboxes, sawdust on the floors and burly men playing pool, but she'd been in the mood tonight for loud music and crowds. Both of which were working their magic.

She caught the eye of a tall, thin young man who was making his way towards her. Anna's gaze swept over him. Shaggy brown hair, tailored trousers, dark polo shirt. Good Lord, loafers! Probably a college student looking to get laid.

'Hey. You alone?' he asked.

No points for creativity, Anna thought. She nodded anyway and moved over so that he could sit beside her.

'I'm Todd,' he said, holding out his hand.

'I'm Anna.'

His grip was good, firm and not sweaty. 'Care to dance?'

'Not right now.'

'I'm a student at USC,' he said.

'I figured.'

'Yeah? What do you do?'

She looked him in the eye. 'I'm a fugitive.'

Todd seemed bemused.

'From justice,' Anna said. 'You know, on the run.'

Todd stared at her for a minute, then laughed. 'Is that right?'

'Uh huh.' Anna took another swallow of beer. 'You could be arrested for aiding and abetting if you hang around me.'

'I'll take my chances. Sure you don't want to dance?'

Anna shrugged and pushed the bottle away. 'OK.'

She slid out from behind the table and went to the dance floor. She turned towards Todd, wrapped her arms around his waist, pressed her pelvis against his. Coloured lights spilled over her like a melting rainbow. His body was solid, if a little angular. The beat of the music began to pound in her blood. Anna closed her eyes and forgot.

1

'She's a fucking eel.'

A thick folder landed in front of Derek Rowland with a thud. Attached to the front cover with a paperclip was a tattered mugshot. Derek plucked the photo from the clip and looked at it. A woman in her mid-twenties with dark, ruffled hair, her expression defiant. Her hard gaze was a marked contrast to her features. Her heart-shaped face and thickly lashed brown eyes looked as if they belonged to a classic movie star like Clara Bow rather than an accused felon.

'An eel, huh?' Derek asked.

'Yeah. Slippery and wet.' Gus Walker chuckled at his own joke. He brought his cigarette to his mouth and took a drag. 'She skipped three weeks ago. Her bail piece and bond are in the data folder. Bring her in and I'll give you twenty per cent.'

Derek raised an eyebrow. 'You want her bad.'

'You would too. She stole a shitload from her father. He's the one who had her arrested.'

'What's he do?'

'Richard Maxwell. Owns Jump Start Computers up in San Jose.'

'She's Daddy's little rich girl?'

'Probably could have been,' Gus replied. He rubbed his left eye with tobacco-stained fingers. 'Instead she stole from him, got arrested, and skipped bail. There's a good bit of info about her there. I want her back. She owes me.'

'Is there a co-signer?'

'Her sister.'

3

'Then she's responsible.'

Gus frowned. 'What the fuck do you care who's responsible? I want that little twat back. If I don't pay that surety company back, it's going to screw up my future business. I can't afford that.'

'Has anyone else gone after her?'

'Not yet.'

'If her father lives in San Jose, what was she doing in LA?'

'She was working at a branch of her father's company. He has houses both here and in the Bay Area. He's up there now.'

'You talk to him yet?'

'That's your job. You want it or not?'

'Sure.' Derek tucked the folder underneath his arm and stood. 'I'll be in touch.'

He left Gus's office and headed out to the parking lot. The asphalt radiated waves of heat. Traffic moved sluggishly past on Wilshire Boulevard, cars emitting puffs of exhaust into the air. Derek walked past the ninety-nine-cent store, dry cleaner and Vietnamese take-out joint that comprised the rest of the strip mall. He slipped on his sunglasses as he approached a grey SUV illegally parked at the kerb.

A woman sat in the driver's seat, her head bent as she worked at a BlackBerry. Her long brown hair was pulled back into a sloppy knot, her tanned arms contrasting with the crisp white of her T-shirt. She glanced up when Derek opened the door.

'Oh, hey. How did it go?'

'Good. Seems interesting.'

'Hold on. I'm just checking my email. Waiting for a tip.' She concentrated on the BlackBerry again. 'Ah ha. Good. He's willing to meet with me.'

'Who's "he"?' Derek asked.

'You know that girl who jumped a week ago? This is her ex-boyfriend.'

'Sounds like he wants revenge.'

'I don't care what he wants, as long as he helps me find her.'

She slipped the BlackBerry into a worn-out backpack and started the car. One would never know by looking at Freddie James that she was one of the most promising new bounty hunters in the business. She had a freshly scrubbed look about her – big brown eyes, a sprinkle of freckles across her nose, not a hint of makeup. Derek knew well that Freddie's somewhat innocent, girl-next-door appearance concealed a fiery core. Like chocolate wrapped around a spicy liquor centre, sweetness with a bite.

'What've you got?' Freddie asked as she turned with a squeal of the tyres on to Wilshire and headed west.

The sun was beginning a slow descent into the smog-laced horizon, splashing light against the windows of the numerous hotels, high-rise office buildings and apartments that bordered Los Angeles' busiest street. Innumerable cars stretched over the four lanes, lining up in front of a cacophony of traffic lights blinking red and green.

'A woman who skipped three weeks ago,' Derek said. 'Wealthy father. I'll pay him a visit.'

He pulled out his cell phone and punched in the number for his information analyst. A voice mail system responded on the other end. Derek spent several minutes relaying names and numbers to the machine, cursing when he had to repeat something.

'Damn computers.'

'Any leads?' Freddie asked after he had snapped the phone closed.

'Not yet. Do you have a job?'

'Just my fraud girl.'

'Anything after that?'

'No. I almost had a job from David, but the bastard wanted a fuck first.'

'I told you to stay away from him.'

'And I told you I can take care of myself around men like him.' Freddie scratched her nose. 'You should know by now that I don't fuck for work.'

'So he didn't give you the job?'

'No, I threw it back at him. He said he'd still give it to me, but it ticks me off that he'd even think of propositioning me.' She slammed the brakes as the car came to a red light behind columns of traffic at the junction of Wilshire and Westwood Boulevards. 'He sure as hell wouldn't do that to you.'

'Hope not.'

Freddie sighed. Derek knew that sigh well. It contained Freddie's boundless desire to be the best combined with her constant frustration over the inevitable sexism of the business.

He watched the mob of people traversing the crosswalk. Office workers and UCLA students walked rapidly across the street, manoeuvring around each other with the finesse of those accustomed to sharing space with others. The village of Westwood spread out to the right, a disordered combination of bars, restaurants and shops with the UCLA campus at one end and the massive grey-and-white-striped bulk of the Armand Hammer Museum at the other.

'I've been wanting to see that,' Freddie said.

'What?'

'That exhibit.' Freddie nodded towards a series of banners attached to the street lamps that lined Wilshire. The banners were emblazoned with the Hammer logo and the title *The Beauty of the Wicked*. 'Artist named Hanson Jangliz. They say his work is exotic and perverse.'

'Sounds worth the price of admission.'

'You'd think so.'

'I didn't know you were into exotic perversion,' Derek said.

Freddie tossed him a look. 'There's a lot about me you don't know.'

'Yeah? Like what?'

'Maybe stuff I don't want you to know.'

'Yeah? Like what?'

Freddie grinned. 'I'm going to maintain an air of mystery.'

'I always did like women of mystery.'

'You just like women, period,' Freddie said.

'You know me well, my friend.'

The lines of traffic began inching forward. Freddie pulled down the sunshade to block the western descent of the sun.

'I don't know,' she said. 'Maybe I'll take David's job. I'm bored enough. He's a bastard, but he's harmless.'

'You can work with me, if you want,' Derek said.

He'd never wanted a partner, but Freddie had been the sole exception in his fifteen-year career as a bounty hunter. They had met two years ago when a bondsman reneged on an agreement with Derek and gave his case to Freddie. She had just been starting out in the business and decided that she'd be his partner for a while.

Ticked off that she'd taken his case, Derek hadn't been at all agreeable, but he soon discovered that Freddie's determination could surpass his reluctance. He'd even developed a grudging admiration for her persistence. Their friendship hadn't been fast, but, over time, it had grown strong and dependable. Derek trusted no one else the way he trusted Freddie. They often still worked as partners, splitting both the work and the fee, but Freddie was becoming increasingly determined to work alone.

'You're going after a boring little rich bitch?' Freddie shook her head. 'Thanks, but David's skip is a biker wanted for attempted murder. I'd rather go after him.'

'I'll bet you would.'

Freddie swerved around the corner at Barrington

Avenue and pulled up to a car-repair shop. 'When're you going to get a reliable car?'

'When you get a respectable job.'

Freddie snorted derisively. 'Don't hold your breath. Need me to wait?'

'No.' Derek eased his long frame out of the car and bent to look at her. He knew she could take care of herself, but he'd never stop feeling protective towards her. 'Thanks for the ride. And stay away from David.'

Freddie gave him a weary smile, revealing perfect white teeth. 'Thanks for the warning, but, for the millionth time, I'll be fine.'

'And, for the millionth time, I still want you to be careful.'

'I always am.' Freddie pushed the gear shift into drive. 'Keep me posted, OK?'

Derek nodded. He approached the garage where several vehicles waited with their hoods up like gaping mouths. A repairman told him that it would be about twenty minutes before his car was ready. Derek went into the air-conditioned office and sat down on a plastic chair to wait. He opened the folder Gus had given him.

After a few minutes of scanning the paperwork, he learnt that Anna Maxwell had been arrested for embezzling nearly half a million dollars from her father through a fake vendor account. She was arrested at her Hollywood apartment, then posted bond through Gus before jumping bail and disappearing. By now, she could be anywhere.

Derek stuffed the papers back into the folder when the receptionist called his name. He paid the bill, collected his keys and went out to his 1966 Mustang. He gave the hood of the car an affectionate pat before getting behind the wheel.

He eased right on to Santa Monica Boulevard and the 405 heading south. Rush-hour traffic clogged the freeway like bacon grease in an artery. Derek turned up the radio as he inched towards Redondo Beach. Somewhat to his surprise, he was looking forward to tracking down little Anna Maxwell. Maybe he could extract more cash from her father by bringing her in.

When he reached the Queen Marina, he parked in the lot and walked on to the dock. The sun hung low on the horizon, illuminating the fishing boats and pleasure cruisers that bobbed in the water. The marina was located a good distance from the horseshoe-shaped Redondo Beach Pier, which was lined with shops and restaurants and regularly crowded with people. Although Derek would prefer an entirely isolated place to dock, the marina was small enough to afford him a degree of seclusion.

As he approached his boat, Derek felt a familiar loosening of tension.

'Derek!' A female voice carried over the water.

Derek lifted his hand to shade his eyes from the sun. A woman in her mid-forties stood on the deck of an Atkins Ingrid double-ender. Bronzed and solid with muscle, she wore a blue bikini and white wrap. She lifted her hand towards him.

'I'm grilling steaks tonight,' she called. 'Come on over.'

Derek did a quick debate in his head, since he wanted to start staking out Anna Maxwell's latest address. Still, there was plenty of time. And Maggie always offered him more than just steaks.

'Sure,' he agreed. 'Give me half an hour.'

He stepped on to the deck of his sailboat, a 35-foot fibreglass yacht that he'd owned for more than ten years. The familiar rolling sensation of the water was an erotic surge.

Strips of fibreglass cloth, buckets of epoxy resin and enamel paint, sanding tools and paint rollers were piled around the deck of *Jezebel*. After he'd finished caulking the hull-to-deck joints, Derek planned to repaint the deck and topsides of the boat as what he hoped would be his final project. He had already spent countless hours over the last three years replacing *Jezebel*'s rigging, fixing the bilge pumps and testing the steering system. Once he had enough money to overhaul the diesel engine and purchase new sails and a mast, he might be able to plan an actual date to start his journey.

He went below deck, where he had gutted the two sleeping berths to make room for one centreline queen-sized berth. There was a navigation station with a chart table, a small galley with a propane stove and enough stowage room in the forepeak area to hold food, medical and clothing supplies, the mainsail cover, wind-vane blades, rolled charts and a solar panel. There were plenty of other supplies he needed to fully outfit the yacht, but at this point he had more time than money.

Derek pulled a tattered leather suitcase from one of the lockers, figuring he might as well pack for his trip tomorrow. He tossed in a few changes of clothes and shaving gear. After a moment's consideration, he took a .45 semi-automatic from the bottom drawer of the dresser and packed it as well. Didn't seem that Anna Maxwell was dangerous, but you never knew when it came to women.

Derek checked the metal boxes of gear that he kept stacked in another locker. He decided against taking any surveillance or recon equipment since he expected to return to LA within a day or two. He took a quick shower and changed into shorts and a clean shirt, then dragged a brush through his dark hair.

He snapped the locks on the suitcase and went to put it in the trunk of his car before joining Maggie on her boat. He'd never been interested in socialising with other live-aboards, but Maggie had proven to be easy company. A divorced free spirit, she gave only as much as she was willing to give and took whatever he was willing to offer. Every so often, she helped him relax, unwind, forget about everything except her.

'You look incredible,' he remarked as he climbed on to the deck.

'So do you.' Maggie smiled and kissed his cheek. She smelled like coconut tanning oil. A gold chain glistened around her neck. 'Come on. It's almost ready.'

Derek followed her to the bow, his gaze skimming over long, muscular thighs that could grip his hips like a vice. Anticipating that very embrace, he sat down in one of the beach chairs. A charcoal grill sizzled with two thick porterhouse steaks and skewers of onions and bell peppers. Without needing to ask what he wanted to drink, Maggie handed him an ice-cold bottle of beer.

Yeah, Derek thought as he took a long draught. She was a good woman.

Maggie lowered herself into a chair across from him, rubbing a hand through her short, brown hair. Her skin was beginning to show the leathery wear of too much sun and wind, but it suited her adventurous spirit. She gave him another smile, her eyes crinkling at the corners as she lifted a bottle to her lips. One strap of her bikini fell over her arm, baring the swell of her breast.

'I haven't seen you around much these past few weeks,' she remarked. 'You've been busy working?'

'Yeah, lot of people jumping bail these days,' Derek said. 'Must be the heat.'

'The heat does have an effect on people,' Maggie observed. She tossed one leg casually over the arm of the chair, exposing the juncture of her thighs. The fabric of her suit wedged up between the lips of her pussy, making it look deliciously plump. Derek thought he might not make it through dinner, porterhouse steak or not.

He looked away from Maggie and out to sea. 'I'm going up to the Bay Area for a few days tomorrow. Keep an eye on things for me, would you?'

'Sure.' Maggie rose to check the steaks. She forked them on to two plates and handed one to Derek. 'Is it for work or pleasure?'

'Work. You're my pleasure.' He winked at her.

'Oh, you!' Despite her disparaging look, Maggie's cheeks flushed. 'Is Freddie going with you?'

'No, she's got her own job.'

Derek didn't miss the minor undertone of jealousy in Maggie's voice. Derek had never bothered telling her that he and Freddie had never fucked – not because he didn't find her attractive, but because they had some sort of unspoken rule against it. They were good friends, allies in the trenches. He'd trust Freddie with his life, but he wouldn't sleep with her. Derek hadn't told Maggie that because he didn't discuss Freddie with anyone.

'What kind of job?' Maggie asked.

'Same kind I've got.'

He cut into the juicy steak, which was grilled to perfection. Tender and flavourful. No doubt, Maggie could cook. They stopped talking as they ate. The sun continued to sink into the horizon like a deflating beach ball. Maggie supplied him with another cold beer when she noticed him finish the bottle. Derek washed down the last of the steak with a groan of satisfaction.

Maggie pushed aside her plate and lifted her arms, closing her eyes against the breeze coming in off the water. She stretched her legs out in front of her.

'Delicious,' she murmured.

'Uh huh.'

Derek gazed at her, at the half-circles of paler skin revealed by the bikini top that inched downward. Her waist was pleasantly thick, her stomach tight with muscle. Hard as acorns, her nipples pressed against her top. Derek's penis swelled as he thought about stripping her down.

He reached out to take her hand, tugging her to her feet. Maggie's eyes fluttered open. She gave him another lazy smile and stood in front of him, her hands on her hips. The white wrap slipped to the deck. Maggie started to push the straps of her bikini over her arms, but Derek shook his head.

'Leave it on.'

'Whatever you say.' Maggie sank to her knees and slid her hands over his thighs as she insinuated herself between them. Her hands went to the buttons of his shirt as she leant in to press her mouth against his. She tasted like salt. Derek's head filled with the smell of coconut oil. Maggie unfastened his shirt, murmuring approval low in her throat as she rubbed her hands over his hair-roughened chest. She slid her mouth over his jaw and lower, nibbling at the tendons of his neck, her tongue wet.

Derek stroked his hands over her bare shoulders and arms. Her skin was hot, always hot, as if she drank the sun, as if she burnt from the inside out. Her mouth moved over his chest as her hands went to the fly of his shorts. With expert fingers, she unfastened the buttons and pulled the shorts over his hips. Her eyes widened slightly as his erection pushed lewdly against his underwear.

'God, Derek,' Maggie breathed. 'You're so fucking fantastic.'

She eased his clothes off, then cupped him in her hand and lowered her head between his legs. Her mouth closed around his prick. Derek muttered a half-hearted curse under his breath and leant his head against the back of the chair. Like being enclosed by hot honey. She worked her tongue as if it were powered by a motor, sliding it over the shaft, tickling the tip, her hands working at the swollen sacs below. Derek watched her face become flushed with arousal, her breath steaming against his cock.

He threaded his hands through her hair, pulling her closer, then moved to grasp the stretchy straps of her bikini top. He twisted the straps around his hands and pulled them over her arms as she continued to suck on him. Her breasts sprang free, weighty and round, nipples like plump, juicy raisins. Derek's groin tightened further at the sight. Her tits were paler than the rest of her, but tanned enough to indicate that she had a penchant for sunbathing topless. He'd seen her lying on the deck, glistening all over with oil, her breasts lolling to the sides, the nipples hard.

'They're always like this, aren't they?' he asked, his fingers tweaking the stiff points. 'You're always ready to be fucked.'

'By you, yes.' Maggie moved back, her breath coming in little pants. Her eyes were glazed as she stared at his moist cock. She eased her hand underneath the elastic of her bikini bottom and sighed. 'Christ, it's like the tropics down there.'

'Turn around.'

She did, presenting her full, rounded ass to him. Derek pulled the bikini over her hips, his prick twitching at the sight of her velvety pussy. He slipped his fingers into her, his urge fuelled by her responding moan. He grasped her hips, yanking her towards him as he drove forward. Maggie squealed with pleasure when he filled her and began pumping, like driving a paddle into a churn filled with sweet butter. Her body bounced in rhythm with his thrusts, her breasts dangling. Derek gritted his teeth and slipped his hand between her legs.

'Oh, yes,' Maggie gasped. 'Rub it ... fuck, Derek ... make me come. Oh, please.'

He splayed his fingers over her clit, feeling her body tense with desperation. Her back was slick with sweat, her muscles moving with tight grace underneath her skin. Derek spread one hand over her back as he continued working her, as her bottom slapped back against his hips, as his cock drowned in her heat. She came hard, her whole body arching, a squeal emerging from her throat. Her sheath convulsed around him, squeezing out his own orgasm. He thrust into her with a final groan.

They both collapsed on to the deck, breathing heavily. Maggie's hand fluttered over his chest. She took his softening erection lightly in one hand, milking the final sensations from him.

'Am I ever glad we've become such good friends,' she murmured.

'Me too.' Derek kissed the top of her head. Although he would have liked to lie there with her for the rest of the evening, he moved to stand. 'Sorry, Mags, but I've got to go. Have a job to start tonight.'

'I figured.' She didn't appear annoyed by his abrupt departure, but, then, she never was. In fact, she was sometimes the one to cut things short once they'd both had their fill of each other. Of course, she was also often game for another round. Or two.

Maggie twirled the wrap over her naked body and pulled herself to a sitting position. 'Drive safely. I'll watch your boat for you.'

'Thanks. Freddie might stop by.'

'Then I'll watch out for Freddie, too.'

'See you soon, Mags.'

Derek buttoned his shorts and headed out to the car. After a steak dinner and sex, he should've been replete enough to sleep for a while. Instead, he was oddly alert. As he eased back on to Wilshire, his mind went to his latest target. He hadn't gone after a woman in a long time – at least, not a fugitive one. He wondered if Anna Maxwell would be an easy mark or a challenge. He categorically hoped for the latter.

Should she or shouldn't she? Anna couldn't decide. She'd danced herself sweaty, her heart was throbbing like a piston, and her skin was hot – usually enough of a combination to eclipse her misgivings – but Todd was just so damn bland. Moreover, he danced like a hyperactive praying mantis, all gangly arms and legs flailing about uncontrollably. If he screwed the way he danced, she was in for an absurd liaison.

Anna pushed her way off the dance floor. Todd was right behind her, his hand on her lower back. She reached the door and turned towards him, raising her voice to be heard above the din. 'I've got to go. Thanks.'

'Go? Hey, I thought we were –'

'You thought wrong. See you around.'

After collecting her jacket, she left the club. The cool evening breeze brushed against her face with a refreshing kiss. She took a deep breath, collecting the air in her lungs. Under other circumstances, she might have given Todd what he'd been expecting, but she really wasn't in the mood for dullness right now.

When it came to men, Anna preferred the roughened type – the off-duty cops and firefighters, the dock and construction workers who frequented dives. She liked the kind of men who wore boots and faded jeans, who sat backwards in chairs with their legs spread and their arms resting on the chair back. She liked the men who exuded sexuality while being entirely unaware that they were doing so. She liked them for their calloused hands, whiskered jaws, hairy chests. She liked their bulk hovering over her. And she liked how they could make her feel.

Todd, with his gawky movements and loafers, was a sweet but insipid shadow of that kind of man.

She glanced at her watch. Two a.m. Not too late to look for one of her men to satisfy the urgency that had been building inside. She climbed into her car and slammed the door. Aw, hell. She was tired. And she really should conserve her energy.

Anna drove through the darkened streets back to her shoebox-sized apartment off Fairfax. Consisting of only six units, the building was small and ugly with peeling paint and an unkempt garden. She'd taken the place because it was semi-furnished and the landlord hadn't bothered to do a credit check or even make her sign a lease. He didn't seem to care about her background as long as she paid her rent on time and in cash. To cement his indifference, she'd paid him a month's rent in advance.

She went up the exterior stairs. The sounds of lascivious moans emerged through an open window. Anna muttered a sound of annoyance as she let herself into her apartment. Her downstairs neighbour was a low-income stripper who turned tricks on the side for extra cash. Charmaine had suggested that Anna could make good money doing the same thing, but Anna knew she'd never be that desperate. She let a man into her bed only if she wanted him there.

She closed the windows and turned on the wall-unit air conditioner to drown out the sound of Charmaine's over-the-top squeals. She flopped down on the torn sofa and surveyed her surroundings. Two open suitcases rested along a wall, overflowing with clothes. Aside from that, she hadn't taken anything with her from her last apartment, which had been a far more decent place in Hollywood. She figured the less she took, the harder time they'd have finding her.

Anna's stomach rumbled. She went to peer into the refrigerator and extracted a leftover burrito. She removed the plastic wrap and stuck it in the microwave. She knew Gus Walker would want to find her. Badly. He'd probably hit the roof when she missed her court appearance.

Anna pulled the lukewarm burrito out of the microwave and ate it with her fingers. Despite the injustice of her situation, she felt guilty for leaving Gus in the lurch. Her father was another matter. She still couldn't believe the bastard had her arrested.

Realising she was beginning to sink into self-pity, Anna brushed off her hands and went to take a shower.

Whatever her father thought, she'd prove him wrong. That was the reason she skipped bail to begin with. She would find a way to prove him wrong or, at the very least, she'd go down fighting.

2

'You want it?' David Parker asked as he rifled through a filing cabinet in his office. He was good-looking in an unkempt way, his brown hair tousled, his beard scraggly. 'The job, I mean.'

Freddie rested her hands on her hips as she surveyed him. 'How much?'

'Ten per cent.'

'Don't insult me. Twenty.'

'Fifteen.'

'Done.' Freddie held out her hand. 'Give it to me.'

David's mouth twitched. 'We are talking about the skip's info, aren't we?'

'Nothing but.' Freddie leant over, placing her hands flat on the desk as she looked him in the eye. 'Look, Parker, you'd better be giving me this job, because I'm good. I'm a black belt. I have a sniper's accuracy at fifty yards. I know ten different ways to incapacitate a man. You may want to fuck me, but don't you ever dare fuck *with* me.'

Something flashed in his expression, but Freddie couldn't tell if it was respect or irritation.

'I might be a bastard, Freddie, but I'm not stupid. I'd only give you a job if I thought you could do it. Contrary to what you might think, I want my money back more than I want you.'

'Then give me the file.'

He handed over a worn manila folder. 'Be careful. He's dangerous.'

'So am I.'

Freddie pivoted on her heel and walked out of the

office. She hated constant warnings that she be careful, as if she weren't experienced enough to know that. Even Derek could rarely talk shop without some kind of veiled or explicit warning about the dangers involved. And he knew better than any man how competent she was.

She glanced at her watch and headed back to her Sixth Street apartment in Santa Monica. Trees lined the adjacent boulevard leading directly to the waterfront. She loved the West Los Angeles location, which was close to the beach and the bustling activity of the pedestrian-only Third Street Promenade between Wilshire and Broadway. There were plenty of restaurants, nightclubs, bars and theatres to always provide her with something to do, but unfortunately she rarely had time for entertainment. Still, it was nice to have plenty of options.

Freddie turned into the parking garage, her gaze catching sight of a familiar Mustang parked along the opposite street. Rather than take the elevator to her apartment, Freddie walked out through the open garage door.

'Hey.' Derek crossed the street to greet her.

Dressed in his standard working gear of worn jeans and a T-shirt, he still managed to look as if he were in command of the very air around him. He walked with a deceptively casual stride, one that concealed his sense of vigilance. Combined with his dark hair and tall, well-built frame, he drew attention just by strolling down the sidewalk. His features were strong and symmetrical – dark grey eyes that could appear stone cold, a sharp jawline and a mouth that was beautifully shaped. He never showed any awareness of his appearance, unless one counted his uninhibited dalliances with various women. Other than that, Derek's arrogance sprang from his success at his job. He was unequalled and he knew it.

It wasn't the first time that Freddie had noticed Derek's good looks with a hint of irritation. His appearance could only ever serve as an advantage, whereas hers seemed consistently to be a liability. She didn't think her looks were anything special, but, in her line of work, most men seemed to think she was fair game.

'What's with the frown?' Derek stopped before her.

Freddie shook her head. 'Nothing. I just got back from David's. I took the job.'

'There's the reason for the frown.'

'It'll keep me busy,' Freddie said. 'What're you doing here?'

'Wondering if you want to have lunch,' Derek said. 'I'm driving up to San Jose tonight, but I have the afternoon free. I'm waiting to hear from John about my skip's credit activity.'

'I can't. I'm meeting an informant in half an hour.' Freddie tilted her head back to look at him, taking note of the increased relaxation of his posture. 'So who was it?'

'Who was what?'

'The woman you had sex with last night.'

'Damn, Freddie. Go be a psychic instead of a bounty hunter.'

Freddie grinned. 'Let me guess. Maggie.'

'She made me a steak dinner.'

'You don't have to defend yourself,' Freddie said. 'Or her, for that matter. How was it?' She laughed at Derek's surprised expression. 'The steak, I meant.'

'Tender and juicy. And the steak was good, too.' Derek gave her his own lopsided grin and reached out to chuck her under the chin. 'I'll call you when I get back. Stay out of trouble.'

'You too.'

Freddie turned and went into the building, pausing to collect her mail. She was unable to prevent an image of Derek and Maggie, bodies naked and writhing, from appearing in her mind. Her heart skipped a beat. She was uncomfortably aware of a rustle of jealousy over the fact that Derek always seemed replete with sexual satisfaction, while Freddie had been hungry for it longer than she cared to remember.

Pushing the thought from her mind, she nodded a greeting at her neighbour as she entered her apartment. Windows lining the living room provided plenty of light. She had decorated the place with ocean colours of cream and blue that complemented the splashy prints she'd hung on the walls. Airy curtains billowed gently in the breeze of the open windows. Bookshelves lined the walls, topped with potted plants and framed photographs. Her apartment was her haven, a place to which she invited almost no one.

Freddie unclipped her hair, letting the long cinnamon-coloured mass fall around her shoulders. Since becoming a bounty hunter, she had considered cutting her hair under the assumption that a short, no-nonsense haircut might earn her more respect from bondsmen and other agents. She'd never been able to go through with it, choosing instead just to wear her hair up or hidden under a baseball cap. Unless it helped her complete a job, she didn't use feminine wiles among her peers, but she wasn't above such tactics when it came to informants and other contacts.

She changed into shorts and a tank top, pausing to slip her feet into a pair of sandals before heading back outside. She walked to the Third Street café where she had arranged to meet Gavin Vincent, her latest bail jumper's ex-boyfriend.

Pedestrians clad mostly in shorts and T-shirts strolled down the street, meandering in and out of the myriad shops, restaurants, art galleries and movie theatres. The sun beat down ceaselessly, heat mixing with the aroma of salt from the bay. Topiary sculptures, fountains and palm trees lined the promenade. The music of Peruvian bamboo panpipes and quena flutes drifted from a group of street performers.

Freddie manoeuvred around several pushcarts displaying silver jewellery and hand-blown glass objects. As she neared the café, her gaze landed on a young man who had the look of a surfer. He had a mop of sun-cooked blond hair, tanned skin and a pair of biceps that any woman would be hard pressed not to admire. Since Freddie wasn't 'any woman', however, she tried hard not to admire anything about him.

Dressed in shorts and a T-shirt, Gavin Vincent was stretched out like a seal, his sandal-clad feet resting on another chair, sunglasses nested in his thick hair. He was eating an ice-cream cone with evident enjoyment.

'Mr Vincent?' Freddie stopped beside the table.

He looked up, his eyes sliding with unabashed appreciation over her body. 'Yes.'

Freddie held out her hand. 'Freddie James.'

'Well.' His hand enclosed hers, warm and dry. His smile flashed like a half-moon against his tan. 'This is a pleasant surprise. Have a seat.'

Freddie pulled out a chair on the other side of the table, aware that he was still studying her.

'Care for an ice cream?' he asked. 'I'm having vanilla, but they have a dozen other flavours.'

'No, thanks. I just want to find out what you know about Barbara.'

'Yeah. She's whacked.'

Freddie almost smiled. 'That's not very helpful. Has she contacted you?'

'Yeah, probably three times.'

'Any idea where she might be?'

'First time, she said she was at a Motel Six out in Covina. I don't know where she went after that.'

'What did she tell you?'

'She wanted me to wire her some money.'

'Did you?'

'A little. I don't mind helping her out.'

'She's a fugitive, you realise.'

'Yeah, I know she's messed up, but she's not a bad girl. She just got . . . derailed, you know?'

He took another lick of his ice cream. Freddie thought he must smell like sand, surf and sweat. She shuddered, imagining inhaling such a potent cocktail. Too bad all informants didn't look like him. The female agents, not to mention some of the more enterprising men, would probably be willing to repay him in any number of ways.

'Did she . . .' Freddie told herself to focus on the task at hand. 'Did she tell you why she was arrested?'

'I assume she stole something. She was something of a klepto.'

'She wrote quite a few bad cheques. Her court date was set for last week.' Freddie's eyes narrowed. 'Sure you haven't seen her?'

Gavin flashed her a grin. 'If I have, are you going to arrest me?'

'I'm not interested in you. I'm interested in her.'

His eyebrows rose slightly. 'Really? Then I'm very interested in your being interested in her.'

Freddie successfully projected an aura of disdain, even as an unexpected quiver of excitement went through her. She tried to suppress it, telling herself that she was only interested in getting the job done, that she wasn't becoming ridiculously entranced by the sight of Gavin Vincent licking creamy drops from the cone.

'You've seen her, haven't you?'

'OK, once,' Gavin confessed. 'I went out to Covina to bring her the money. She said she was heading to Las Vegas.'

'Do you know if she's there?'

'No idea. Haven't heard from her since Covina.'

'What's she planning to do in Vegas?' Freddie asked, staring at the movement of his tongue. It was swirling around as if it were a living creature.

'Dunno.' Gavin's lips closed over the top of the scoop. 'Get a job as a cocktail waitress, I guess. She doesn't have what it takes to be a showgirl.' His gaze slid over her again. 'Unlike you.'

Freddie felt his gaze as if it were physically hot. She cleared her throat and looked away from him. 'A showgirl is not something I have ever aspired to be.'

'Did you aspire to be a bounty hunter?'

'Bail-enforcement agent,' Freddie corrected.

'Sorry.' Gavin gave her a sheepish grin, his mouth wet with vanilla ice cream. 'How'd a girl like you get to be a bounty – uh, bail-enforcement agent, anyway?'

It certainly wasn't the first time Freddie had been asked that question. She did a quick debate in her head about whether or not to give Gavin the full story, but then she figured it couldn't hurt. She'd never made much of an effort to conceal her past, primarily because there was little that needed concealing.

'Well, my father once did time for armed robbery,' Freddie said. 'He was always skirting the edge of the law. I had this idea that I'd never be like that. After college, I spent a lot of time doing odd jobs. A couple years ago, I was working as a security guard over at LACMA. Guarding art collections wasn't exactly exciting, so I decided to apply for police academy. I heard about fugitive recovery from a fellow applicant and thought it sounded more interesting. I took some courses, went on a few cases, then had a reluctant partner while I was finding my way.'

'Someone was reluctant to partner with you? Couldn't have been a man.'

Freddie almost smiled. 'Derek is a man, all right. He's one of the best agents in the business. I latched on to him like a barnacle. Well, first I stole a case from him. He still hasn't forgiven me. I was just starting out and met a bondsman who had offered Derek a case. Then he reneged and gave it to me.'

'Why'd he do that?'

'I sweet-talked him,' Freddie admitted. She wasn't

exactly proud of that. She'd quickly learnt that sweet-talking bondsmen and other agents would garner her little respect, no matter how many fugitives she recovered. 'And I said I'd do it for much less than Derek wanted. I still needed the money, not to mention the experience. I brought the skip in two days later. Derek was grudgingly impressed. I knew I could learn from him, so I decided I'd be his partner for a while.'

'I guess he didn't like that.'

'No. He didn't want anything to do with me. He kept trying to shake me, but I turned up everywhere he went. Finally he gave up and dealt with me. Learnt more from him in a few months than I could've learnt in a year on my own.'

'Good for you.' Gavin popped the last of the cone into his mouth and crunched into it. 'Frankly, this Derek dude sounds like something of an ass. If you wanted to latch on to me like a barnacle, I sure as hell wouldn't try to shake you. Well, not in a bad way.'

He flashed her another engaging grin. A shockingly graphic image appeared in Freddie's mind, one involving her fastened against Gavin, her knees grasping his hips as she bucked on top of him.

She unfolded her bare legs from their crossed position. The material of her shorts stuck to her inner thighs, indicating that she'd got hot from more than just the sun. Over an ice cream, no less. She wondered if she could come up with some sort of mathematical equation about the degree of a woman's arousal being proportionate to the coldness of the food she watched a man eat. If Gavin sucked on a cube of ice, she'd probably melt right into a puddle.

'If you hear anything from Barbara,' she said, 'I'd appreciate a call.'

'I don't have your number.'

Freddie took a business card from her pocket and slid

it across the table to him. She stood. 'You can also still reach me by email.'

'I'd rather call. Do I get a reward if I help you bring Barbara in?'

'The reward of having a clear conscience.'

Gavin rolled his eyes. 'You haven't always been such a Girl Scout, have you?'

'I prefer to stay on the right side of the law, yes.'

'Oh, come on, Freddie. Being bad is a lot more fun than being a Girl Scout, isn't it?'

'I wouldn't know.'

'Want me to teach you?'

Jesus, Freddie thought as her entire body surged. Judging by her reaction to him, one would think she hadn't had sex in months. She did a quick calculation in her head.

Well, what did you know about that? It *had* been months. Eight months, to be exact. Eight and a half, if she didn't count the last fling she'd had with her ex-boyfriend. Which she didn't, considering it had been based on nothing but her own poor judgement as well as her desire not to admit that Derek had been right. He hadn't approved of that boyfriend from the beginning, which made the collapse of the relationship all the more difficult to bear.

She shook her head as if to clear her thoughts. 'Being bad, as you so delicately put it, is not on my agenda.'

'Now that', Gavin said as he looked her over, 'is a shame.'

His hot eyes lingered on her breasts. To her embarrassment, her nipples hardened as if he had touched them. She crossed her arms over her chest.

It wouldn't be a mistake. Gavin Vincent was not a bondsman or a cop or another agent. He was not one of her peers. She didn't have to convince him that she was all-work-and-no-play because he couldn't have cared less. And no one else would have to know. Well, she knew she'd end up telling Derek, but he could keep a secret.

'I have to get back to work,' she said.

'OK. See ya around.'

Gavin unfolded himself from his chair and stood. He slipped on his sunglasses and walked away from her. Freddie watched him go, her gaze lingering on his bare legs, hairy and thick with muscle. God, he was tempting.

'Hey, Vincent,' she called.

He turned.

'You ever surf?' Freddie asked before she could change her mind.

'Never.'

'Want to learn?'

'Depends on who's teaching.'

'What if it were me?'

Gavin looked at her for a moment. 'You're serious?'

'Yeah. I've got a board and wetsuit you can borrow.'

'OK. When?'

'Next Saturday morning. Six. I'll meet you at the Santa Monica Pier.'

Gavin shook his head, a slow grin spreading over his features. 'You're a piece of work.'

'So I've been told.'

'See you Saturday, then.' Gavin lifted a hand in farewell and began walking in the opposite direction.

Freddie headed back to her apartment, feeling a pleasurable combination of anticipation and nervousness. Getting involved with an informant wasn't a mistake, but it didn't seem exactly ethical, either. Then again, a surf date was hardly 'getting involved'. No matter what happened, Freddie would just have to make damn sure that she retained the upper hand.

The air was humid with testosterone and the smell of alcohol. The Who's *Substitute* blasted from a jukebox in the corner over the rasp of voices. Neon signs advertising beer flashed over the wooden bar. Several customers, mostly men, sat at the barstools or hunched over their drinks in vinyl booths.

Anna bent over the pool table and positioned her cue for a straight shot. She drew the cue back, shot and sank her five-ball into the side pocket. With a rush of satisfaction, she straightened and looked at the man standing on the other side of the table.

'Nice,' he said.

Anna stepped back for another shot, which she missed. She chalked her cue while her opponent assessed the table and readied for his next shot. She watched him with approval. He was the kind of man she appreciated – a brawny worker who loaded cargo down at the Port of Los Angeles. His name was Ben, and he wore torn and faded jeans and a plain navy T-shirt. His face and neck were rough with whiskers. His biceps bulged from the sleeves of his shirt. He smelled of sweat and grease. He wielded a pool cue as if it were a twig.

He sank the eight-ball into the corner pocket. Anna raised an eyebrow.

'Not exactly a shark, are you?' she asked.

Ben gave her a grin that made her suspect he'd intended to sink the eight-ball. 'I guess I owe you, huh?'

'We didn't bet.'

'We should have.'

Anna put her cue back on to the wall rack. Although she liked to win legitimately, she didn't particularly care that Ben had thrown the game.

'What should we have bet?' she asked.

'You won the game. You tell me.'

'It's no fun betting if you already know the outcome,' Anna said.

'Fine, then come up with another bet.'

'I bet you that I can tie a cherry stem into a knot with my tongue.'

'That old bar trick?'

'You've seen it done?' Anna asked.

Ben grinned. 'Never. I'll bet you can't do it.'

'I'll bet I can.'

'If you can do that, I'll kiss you.'

'And if I can't?'

'You'll kiss me.'

'Sounds like you win the bet either way.'

'That's the idea.'

'Well,' Anna said, 'I always did appreciate honesty.'

She went to the bar and requested a maraschino cherry. After returning to the pool table, she bit off the cherry and crunched into it. A small crowd had gathered around the table after word of her alleged talent had spread. Anna held the cherry stem out to Ben.

'Need to inspect it?' she asked.

'I trust you.'

Anna popped the stem into her mouth and chewed just enough to soften it before working it with her tongue. She folded the stem in half, crossed the ends and clamped them gently between her teeth before slipping one end through the loop. She pulled the stem back to tighten the knot, then opened her mouth and slid her tongue out with the knotted stem displayed at the tip.

The crowd chuckled and applauded. One man slapped Ben on the back and declared him a 'lucky guy'. Ben approached Anna, his eyes on her tongue.

'I have to make sure it's really a knot,' he said.

'Go ahead.'

He plucked the stem from her tongue and held it up to the light. 'I'll be damned. Where did you learn to do that?'

'Nowhere. I practised a lot when I was alone.' Anna brushed her thumb over her lower lip. 'Plus, I have a naturally talented tongue.'

'I'll say. I guess you won the bet, then.' He was already moving closer to her.

'I guess so.' Anna backed a few steps away.

She liked his mouth. His lips looked dry, chapped from the sun and wind. His skin was darkly tanned, his eyes blue, his neck thick, his forearms heavy with muscle. Yes, she liked everything about him.

His big hands slipped around her waist. Anna felt her bottom hit the edge of another pool table. Ben's legs and pelvis pressed against her. He ducked his head so swiftly that Anna readied herself for a hard kiss, but his lips descended with surprising gentleness on to hers. Anna nearly groaned with pleasure at the simultaneous feel and taste of him. His stubble abraded her skin. He tasted like salt and dark beer. His hands tightened on her, his fingers digging into her lower back alongside her spine. His tongue pressed into her mouth.

Anna did groan then, her mouth open and hot against his, her eyes drifting closed. She slid her hands along his arms, her fingers tracing the tendons that appeared like ropes underneath his skin. His belt buckle pressed against the bared skin of her belly. Her breasts flattened against his impressively wide chest. His knee pushed between her legs so that she was spread over his thigh. Anna suppressed an intense urge to grind herself against him, to satisfy the growing ache in the centre of her body. She imagined he would fuck the way that he felt – hard and rough. Her blood quickened at the thought.

Ben's mouth slid along her cheek to her ear. His breath rasped against her neck as he took her earlobe between his teeth.

'Where should we go?' he hissed.

Anna shuddered. 'Your place.'

'Follow me.' His fingers gripped her wrist like a hand-cuff as he guided her towards the door.

Uncaring of the looks being tossed in her direction, Anna grabbed her bag and followed him to the parking lot. She got into her car and waited for him to exit the lot in a beat-up Ford pickup truck. They drove to a side street not far from San Pedro Bay and parked in front of a boxy clapboard bungalow.

Anna stepped out of her car, somewhat charmed by the little house that belonged to this big man. She walked across the ragged lawn to the front porch. Ben opened the door and ushered her inside. The interior was unassuming and simple with a tiny kitchen, brown sofa and an open door leading to the bedroom.

Without a word, Ben grasped her waist from behind and tugged her against him. His erection pushed against her bottom, making her fairly quiver with anticipation. His hand slid underneath her T-shirt and flattened against her torso. With a swift movement that both impressed and aroused her, Ben flicked open the front clasp of her bra with one hand. He squeezed her breasts in his meaty hands, rolling the nipples between his fingers. His mouth pressed against the back of her neck.

Anna let out a moan of pleasure. The core of her body felt as if it were melting, warming her from the inside out. Her sex pulsed with increasing heat as a band of urgency tightened around her. Her breath came in quickening pants. Ben's hands moved to unzip her jeans. He pushed them off her legs, then thrust one hand beneath the elastic of her flimsy panties. Anna groaned when he found the centre of her damp pussy, one finger sliding into her as his thumb rotated around her clit.

'Hot.' The word, deep and throaty, scraped against her neck. 'I knew you'd be hot.'

His hands skimmed over her hips as he guided her into the bedroom. The bed was unmade, white sheets tangling over the surface like whipped cream. Anna turned, reaching for his belt buckle. She unfastened it, a strap of soft leather worn to the colour of tarnished copper. Her fingers shook as she removed his jeans and released his imposingly large cock. Ben took off his T-shirt and stood naked in front of her. Anna sat on the bed and stared at his brawny physique, all bulging muscles and tight skin. A mat of dark hair covered his chest, arrowing down to the curly nest of hair between his legs. An elaborate tattoo of snakes entwined with a rose bush curled around his left biceps and shoulder. Anna's heart throbbed with excitement at the thought of exploring every inch of his body with her hands and mouth.

She started by grasping his thick stalk in her fist and drawing him into her mouth. He tasted salty and pungent against her tongue, his balls weighty in her hand. She licked her way down his shaft, enjoying the smooth, veiny sensation of him sliding over her lips. She felt his body tense, his hands tightening in her hair. She pulled away and looked up at him.

'Take your shirt off,' he ordered gruffly.

Anna slipped out of her shirt and bra and let him stroke his calloused hands over her body. She backed up on to the bed and parted her legs in invitation. He lowered himself over her, his frame a delicious weight on top of her leveraged by the strength of his arms. She loved how men like him covered her so completely; it was like being wrapped in endless quilted layers on a cold winter's night.

Ben slid one hand underneath her thigh to spread her wider before positioning himself at the opening of her body. He teased her first, rubbing the tip of his penis over her glistening folds before easing into her. Anna moaned and wrapped her legs around his hips as he began to slowly stretch and fill her. A delectable friction began to stoke the fire within, Ben's increasingly urgent thrusts fuelling her own excitement. She clutched his back, pressing her fingers into his shoulders, her breath catching with every hard plunge. Ben's hands pawed at her breasts, pulling at her nipples almost painfully. Before she knew it, he grabbed her hips and rolled over on to the bed so that he was beneath her.

Anna gasped, her thighs tightening as she straddled

him, bracing her hands against his chest. He filled her so completely in this position that she practically felt his cock throbbing in time with the pulsing of her blood. Sweat rolled down her neck and between her breasts. She lifted her hips and brought them down again, tightening her sheath around him. Her bottom bounced in rhythm with her movements.

Ben seemed to be touching her everywhere – his hands rough against her shoulders, stroking her hips and sweat-slick back, digging into the globes of her ass. A taut spring coiled inside her. Anna increased the pace of her ride, leaning over Ben so that he could take the tips of her breasts into his mouth. He sucked hard, causing an electric sensation to crackle along her nerves down to the tips of her toes. The spring tightened more intensely before Anna lost control and came with a force that felt like an explosion.

With a growl, Ben rolled her over again and pushed her legs wide apart as he drove into her. Anna cried out with pleasure as Ben pulled out and spurted creamy seed over her belly. He drew in a ragged breath and collapsed on the bed beside her. The air thickened with the sound of their heavy breathing and the smell of sweat and semen.

'Ah, good,' Ben groaned. 'Your tongue isn't the only talented thing about you.'

Anna rolled over on to her side and traced the line of his tattoo with her fingers. She stroked her palm over his arms and chest, his muscles like smooth rocks underneath his skin. Before she had halfway finished with her exploration, a light snore indicated that Ben had fallen asleep.

Anna smiled. It was a predictable pattern with her men, one that she didn't mind. She'd never been one for talking after sex, anyway, and sleeping men gave her the opportunity to examine them thoroughly. She liked watching them in their most unguarded moments, the pattern of their breathing, the subtle twitches of their bodies.

They were uncomplicated, these men who worked hard and never played games when it came to sex. They appreciated whatever she was willing to give them and treated her with care. They didn't ask needless questions or even wonder about anything beyond her name. They were a far cry from the kind of man her father and stepmother had hoped she would marry, the slick, white-collar corporate workers who wore designer suits and paid for professional manicures. A man like Ben probably didn't even know what a manicure was.

Anna reached over the side of the bed and grabbed Ben's T-shirt, which lay in a heap on the floor. She slipped it over her head and went out to the kitchen to examine the contents of his refrigerator. She would be gone before he awoke, as she always was, leaving them both to wonder whether they would see each other again.

3

'She likes slumming.' Richard Maxwell had hair the colour of gunmetal and eyes that were just as steely.

Derek's pen halted over the page of his notebook as he assessed the other man.

'Slumming,' Derek repeated.

'Yeah.' Richard waved his hand in a gesture of both disgust and dismissal. 'Hanging out with lower-class people. Blue-collar workers. You find the sleaziest part of town, and you'll find my daughter.'

'How do you know that?' Derek asked.

'She's like her mother,' Richard replied.

'Meaning what?'

'Her mother was a diner waitress. Grew up in a trailer park. She might've made something of herself if she'd finished college, but she dropped out and became a stripper.'

'How did you meet her?'

Richard's eyes grew colder. 'What does that have to do with finding my daughter?'

'She might be where her mother is.'

'If that's the case, Mr Rowland, then you can head straight to the cemetery. Anna's mother is dead.'

'When did she die?'

'Years ago. Anna never liked the fact that I remarried.' Richard rubbed a hand over his forehead and sighed. 'Look, there's not much I can do to help you. Anna has been on her own for quite some time. I have no idea where she might be.'

'Yet she was working at a branch of your company in LA.'

'I was trying to give her one more chance to straighten out. Clearly it didn't work. I broke all contact with her after she was arrested.'

'That's why I'd also like to talk to her sister and stepmother.'

'I'm afraid that won't be possible. Neither of them has been in contact with her either.'

'Still, I'd like to –'

'Not possible, Mr Rowland,' Richard interrupted.

Derek took a business card from his pocket and pushed it across the desk. 'I'd appreciate a call if you hear from Anna. In my experience, most people who skip bail contact a family member at some point.'

'Anna is not most people.'

'Yeah, you've made your opinion on that quite clear.' Derek stood and held out his hand. 'Thanks for your time.'

He went out to his car. The information analyst hadn't turned up any activity on Anna's credit cards or bank accounts. There was also no evidence that she had moved from her apartment, although her landlord claimed not to have seen her in several weeks. Derek figured he'd go back down to LA and start talking to people she knew.

He started the car just as there was a knock on the driver's-side window. A young woman stood outside. Derek rolled down the window. The woman bent to speak to him.

'I'm Erin Maxwell,' she said. 'Anna's sister. I overheard you talking to our father.'

Derek turned off the engine. He got out of the car and introduced himself. 'I'm hoping to find Anna soon,' he said. 'She's already in enough trouble.'

'That's the story of her life,' Erin said. She lifted a hand to shade her eyes from the sun as she assessed him. She was a petite young woman with light-brown hair and elflike features. She didn't much resemble Anna, but it was still clear that they were sisters. 'I can give you the names of a few places Anna frequents.'

'Why would you do that?'

'I co-signed on her bond,' Erin explained. 'Anna doesn't have collateral. If she doesn't show up in court, then I'm liable.'

'Why didn't you just give her the money?'

'I don't have it. I don't have access to my trust fund until I'm twenty-five.'

'How old are you now?'

'Twenty-two.'

'Anna doesn't have a trust fund?' Derek asked.

Erin shook her head. 'Anna has basically been disowned by our father, Mr Rowland. He's always considered her something of a disgrace. It's why he suspected her of stealing from him.'

'You don't think she did?' Derek half expected her to vehemently defend her sister, so he was surprised when she shrugged.

'I don't know,' Erin said. 'It's possible. Anna's no angel, and she's smart. She'd know how to access the company's accounts.'

'So why did you co-sign her bond?'

'She's my sister.'

'Does your father know what you did?' Derek asked.

'No,' Erin admitted. 'That's another reason I'm willing to help you however I can. If my father found out, he'd probably disown me as well. And call me shallow, but I don't want to lose my trust fund.'

'What about your relationship with your father?'

'My father changed after he remarried,' Erin said. 'I love him, but he's a different man. The father I once knew would never have cut Anna off the way that he did.'

'So you've kept in touch with her, obviously.'

'Mostly by email and the occasional phone call. She

called me when she was arrested. I suspect she's probably still down in LA.'

'Why do you think that?'

'She knows her way around there. I visited her a few times over the years. That's how I know where she hangs out.' Erin paused. 'And, believe me, it's not the library.'

'Erin!'

A woman's voice came from the direction of the house. Both Derek and Erin looked towards a tall, elegant blonde who stood in the front doorway.

'It's time to come in, Erin,' the woman reported.

Erin gave Derek a look of resignation. 'My stepmother. Cassandra.'

'You think she'll talk to me?'

'I doubt it. Besides, she and Anna have always locked horns. Cassandra won't know or care where Anna is.'

'Can we meet later? I'd like to know what you know.'

'Sure. There's a coffee shop on Market Street called Brew Job. I can meet you there around nine tonight.'

'Good. Thanks.'

Erin nodded and headed back to the house. She slipped past her stepmother and went inside. Derek got back into his car just as the blonde woman approached him. She walked like someone who had attended finishing school, her posture ramrod straight with a high head and silky stride.

'Mr Rowland, I'm Cassandra Maxwell.' She stopped beside his car, hands on hips. Her voice was slightly throaty and as smooth as good whisky. 'I know you're looking for Anna, but I'd suggest that you leave the rest of my family out of it.'

'It's been my experience, Mrs Maxwell, that most family members are willing to help when someone has broken the law.'

'We have helped,' Cassandra replied. 'My husband told

the police where Anna was so that she could be properly arrested. We've done our duty.'

'You can do more by helping me find her.'

'I don't wish to do more,' Cassandra said. 'Anna is a blackmailer and a thief. She deserves to go to prison.'

'She can't go to prison if I can't find her.'

'Then that's your problem.'

'You don't care what happens to her?' Derek asked.

'Of course, but we've given Anna plenty of chances. She has brought nothing but dishonour to this family.'

'Don't you want her to pay for what she did?'

'She will, Mr Rowland,' Cassandra said. 'In some way, she will.'

Derek gave her the once-over. Her skin was flawlessly concealed with a layer of makeup, her hair scooped into a twist with not a strand out of place. She wore a single strand of pearls and a form-fitting green dress that displayed her ample curves. Derek had known women like her – polished, cool, composed as a marble sculpture. He also had an inkling of what happened to women like her when their façades cracked.

He pulled out his card and held it out to her. 'Nevertheless, if you hear from her, I'd appreciate a call.'

Cassandra didn't move to take the card. Derek reached out the window and took her wrist. She had long fingers, immaculately manicured and adorned with several gold and diamond rings. Derek deliberately slid his fingers over her palm as he pressed the card into her hand.

'Just in case,' he said.

She didn't respond, but her fingers curled around the card. 'Good day, Mr Rowland.'

'Good day, Cassandra.'

He backed out of the driveway, aware that she was watching him leave.

Derek spent the next few days trolling around half a dozen seedy bars and nightclubs. Erin Maxwell had given him the names of several places Anna patronised both in Los Angeles and the semi-industrial port city of San Pedro. They were hardly the upscale, trendy clubs that he'd expect a woman of her upbringing to frequent. He asked questions of a number of people and showed her mugshot to the bartenders and select patrons.

He obtained one lead from an off-duty cop in a San Pedro bar called The Cave. The bar was at the corner of an intersection that included a strip club and a gas station. Neon beer signs flashed in the window, and the inside was shabby and dark with wooden tables and vinyl booths. The patrons were mostly blue-collar working men, which made Derek wonder again about the bar's appeal for Anna.

'Yeah, I've seen her here,' the man said. 'She's blonde now. She can do that trick with her tongue.'

'With her tongue?'

'Yeah. Tying a cherry stem. Never seen anyone that could actually pull it off.'

'She been here recently?'

'Last I saw her was a few nights ago. Tuesday, maybe. She plays pretty good pool.'

'Thanks.'

Armed with solid information at last, Derek returned to Redondo Beach. He wasn't surprised that Anna was still spending time at her favourite bars. Most bail jumpers slipped up by clinging to something familiar.

'Derek, you busy tonight?' Maggie stood at the end of the dock, clad in a pink and orange bathing suit that made her look like a luscious popsicle.

'Yeah, sorry.' Derek tossed his suitcase on to the deck, experiencing a mild regret that he didn't have time to give her a few licks. 'Got a job.'

'You're sure you can't spare me a couple of hours?'

The suggestive tone of her voice was enough to make him want to give in. 'No, I've got work to do. Soon, though.'

He gave her a quick salute and climbed on to his boat before she had a chance to change his mind. He started to enter the cabin when he heard the sound of his name.

Freddie came strolling down the dock towards his boat, her skin reddish from the light of the setting sun. She looked as unaffected as she always did, clad in tan shorts and a snowy Oxford shirt. Her long hair was scraped back into a plait and her worn backpack was slung over one shoulder.

'Hey,' Freddie greeted. 'You're back soon.'

'Got everything I need.'

'Hi, Maggie.' Freddie waved in Maggie's direction. 'Good to see you again.'

'Sure. You too.' Maggie didn't look particularly pleased as Freddie hopped aboard Derek's boat.

'She looks good,' Freddie remarked.

'Doesn't she always?'

'The boat, I meant.' Freddie patted the side of the cockpit. 'Looks like you're almost ready to go.'

Derek gave her a wry smile. 'Almost is a relative term.'

He hadn't told anyone except Freddie about his plans for a sailing journey that would take him around the world. He knew she was the only person who would believe he'd actually do it one day.

Derek was confident enough in his sailing and charting abilities. Although he had a GPS system, he knew how to use a sextant and had studied the patterns of hurricanes, gales and tropical storms along his sailing route. He'd tested various methods of shortening the sails and handling the mainsail and jib. He knew how to navigate restricted waters, use a spinnaker and sail at night. He'd spent the last five years honing his single-handed sailing skills and taking *Jezebel* out on short passages to test both her strength and abilities and his own. He knew they were good partners. He also knew they were nowhere near 'ready to go'.

'You making any headway on your job?' he asked Freddie.

'A little. My skip used her credit card in Palm Springs. Looks like she's heading east.' Freddie followed Derek below and plunked herself down at the chair in front of the chart table. 'So tell me what happened with you.'

Derek took two metal gearboxes from the locker. 'I talked to her father, stepmother and sister. The sister co-signed the bond.'

'Has the skip contacted any of them?'

'They said she hadn't. I think they're telling the truth considering Richard Maxwell disowned Anna.'

'Any leads?'

'I found out she likes a certain bar,' Derek said. 'I'm going there tonight.'

'Want me to go along?' Freddie asked.

'You don't have anything more interesting to do on a Friday night?'

'I have to be up early tomorrow.'

'What for?'

Freddie became very interested in examining the charts spread out on the table. 'I'm teaching this guy to surf.'

The remark didn't bother Derek as much as Freddie's suddenly evasive attitude.

'What guy?' he asked.

'The, uh, the ex-boyfriend of my latest skip.'

Derek frowned. 'Freddie, what the hell? Who is he?'

'His name is Gavin Vincent. He's a decent guy.'

'Is that all you know about him?'

'He's good-looking. Nice biceps. Definitely an attraction there. Mutual, too, judging by the way he was looking at me.'

'Why are you teaching him to surf?'

'He doesn't know how.'

'Freddie!'

She shook her head. 'Derek, relax. I'm pretty sure he's harmless.'

'And I'm pretty sure you're nuts.'

Freddie's lips curved into a frown. 'Hey, do me a favour. Don't treat me like I'm a dim bulb. I know this guy wouldn't mind getting into my pants, but it's not as if I don't know any better.'

Derek sighed. He and Freddie had had a few fights over the years, and they always made him feel like crap. He brushed his hand over her hair even as he made a mental note to run a background check on Gavin Vincent.

'OK,' he said. 'I'm sorry.'

Freddie nodded. She scratched her ankle, then pulled her leg closer to examine her skin. 'So where are you going tonight?'

'Down to San Pedro. A cop said he saw her at a bar called The Cave.'

'Really?' Freddie took a razor from her backpack and began scraping away at a few stray hairs on her leg. 'You think she might show up there?'

'No idea, but I'll give it a try. She hasn't been at her apartment for at least two weeks. No credit-card or bank-account activity either. She withdrew a couple thousand right before she skipped, so that's probably holding her out.'

'You want to eat before you go?'

'No.' Derek's prick stirred slightly as he caught sight of the frilly yellow panties peeking out underneath Freddie's shorts. He grimaced. Over the years, the few accidental glimpses he'd had of Freddie's underwear indicated she liked wearing lacy, silky things beneath her practical clothing. He and Freddie might not have a physical relationship, but Derek was still a man. The yellow panties made him wonder just what other secrets Freddie James was hiding.

'You have to eat, Derek,' Freddie remarked as she worked at another patch of stubble.

Derek glanced at his watch. Another idea formed in his mind. 'I'll grab something on the way. Don't you shave your legs in the shower like every other woman?'

'Yeah, but I was in a hurry. I missed a few spots.' Freddie dropped her razor back into her backpack. She nodded towards the map pinned to the wall. 'You changed the route.'

'What?'

'Your sailing route. You changed it.'

Derek hadn't even noticed her look at the map. 'Your powers of observation are impressive, Miss James.'

She smiled. 'What happened?'

'I don't know if she can handle the weather around Cape Horn,' Derek said. 'I decided not to risk it.'

'So when are you going to go?' Freddie asked.

'When I get her fully outfitted and save up a little money. So far, I've had to sink everything into her.'

'How much do you need for the trip?'

'Not much,' Derek said. 'I figure I can find work if I need the cash, but I still need supplies.'

'How long will you be gone?' Freddie asked.

'A year. Two years. As long as it takes.'

'To do what exactly?'

Derek shrugged. 'See the world.'

'Well, be sure to tell me before you leave,' Freddie said. 'I want one of those didgeridoos from Australia.'

'What're you going to do with that?'

'Blow it.'

'In that case, you'll be the first to know when I go.'

She flashed him an appealing grin. 'Hey, can I hang out here tonight?'

'Sure. I'll be back late. Probably around three.'

'I'll be gone by then. I have to be up by five.'

'Be careful.'

'You too.'

Derek went to put the gearboxes in the trunk of his car. He walked to Maggie's boat, unsurprised to find her stretched out like a cat on the deck.

'What're you doing tonight?' he asked.

'Waiting for you,' she replied.

'Good answer. Want to go on a job with me?'

'A job?' Maggie repeated. 'You want me to work?'

'If you want to call it that. I'm staking out a bar. I could use company.'

Maggie peered over the tops of her sunglasses at him. 'Sounds somewhat intriguing. What do I have to do?'

'Anything you want.'

'Sounds definitely intriguing. Give me a minute to dress.'

It occurred to Derek that he had never seen Maggie in anything but a bathing suit. She emerged from the cabin wearing white shorts and a red shirt that made her look like a candy cane. Derek's penis stirred again. She was very lickable, indeed.

Derek suggested that Maggie follow him in her car since he expected to be out until early morning. They headed south towards San Pedro on the 110. As he drove, Derek phoned his information analyst and asked him to check up on Gavin Vincent. The drive was fairly easy by LA standards, and Derek soon pulled into the parking lot of The Cave. A few pickup trucks and sedans were parked outside.

Maggie pulled up beside him and got out of her car. She peered at the ugly square structure with the broken neon bar sign, then climbed into the passenger seat of Derek's Mustang.

'Well,' she remarked, 'it's not exactly the Ritz.'

'Bail jumpers don't frequent the Ritz.'

Derek looked at his watch. He knew the bar scene wouldn't pick up until later tonight, but there was no telling when, or if, Anna would show up.

'So when do I get to do anything I want?' Maggie asked.

'Whenever you want.'

The sun had disappeared beyond the horizon, leaving the sky a light grey colour. There was just enough light for Derek to see the tempting smile curve over Maggie's face. Although it was hardly the pinnacle of professionalism for him to bring her along, he'd never been averse to mixing business with pleasure. In fact, he considered it to be pretty efficient.

'I haven't done it in a car since high school,' Maggie remarked. 'This could be fun. Bench seats, too. How convenient.'

She slid across the seat towards him and leant over to press her lips against his neck. The smell of tanning oil and shampoo filled his nostrils. Maggie's tits pressed into his arm, her nipples hard. She reached for the fly of his jeans and had his stiffening cock in her hand within a few seconds. Derek pushed the seat back, allowing her room to lower her head and take him easily into her mouth.

With a groan, Derek leant his head against the seat. If there was anything he'd learnt about Maggie over the years, it was that she knew how to suck cock. She took him deep into her mouth, her tongue twirling over his shaft, her lips pressing wetly against the tip. She grasped the base in her fist and stroked him with a firm hand. Derek ran his hand down her back, feeling her skin's heat through the thin cotton of her shirt.

Maggie pulled away for an instant, divesting herself quickly of the shirt and her bra. She rubbed her breasts over his prick before enveloping him with her mouth again. Derek reached underneath her to fondle her tits, already feeling as if he were ready to explode. As if sensing his urgency, Maggie lifted away from him and promptly bumped her head against the steering wheel.

'Ow!' She rubbed her head and chuckled. 'The perils of a car fuck. Want to get into the back seat?'

'Not yet.' Derek watched a blue sedan pull into the

parking lot. A woman got out and went into the bar, but she was both too tall and too heavy to even resemble Anna.

Maggie shifted around to pull off her shorts. Derek had to appreciate her complete lack of inhibition. He clutched her hips and drew her towards him, sliding his hands around to her full ass. His fingers dipped lower into her pussy. He was not surprised to find her damp and ready for him.

Maggie lifted one of her legs over him and positioned herself over his lap. Heat emanated from her. She took hold of his penis and lowered herself on to it with a smooth movement. She moaned, her arms going around his neck as she started to ride him. Her breasts bounced temptingly in front of him.

Derek took one in his hand and kneaded it like a ball of dough. His other hand found her waist, his fingers digging into her hips. The coconut oil mingled with the aroma of sex. Derek's blood continued a slow burn, his cock pistoning. The confines of the car made the heat seem all the more intense. Maggie pressed her fingers against her clit, rubbing the hard knot with increasing moans that erupted into a squeal of pleasure. Her body convulsed around him.

Before he could drive into her for his own release, Maggie manoeuvred off him and lowered her head between his legs again. She squeezed the base of his prick and encased him in her mouth, sliding her wet lips rhythmically until the pressure became too much to withstand. Derek shot into her with a grunt as she sucked and swallowed to drain him of every last drop.

She started to pull away from him just as another car pulled into the parking lot. Derek collected his wits swiftly. He eased Maggie out of his lap and reached into the back seat for a pair of binoculars. He watched as a young woman exited the car. Her face was illuminated by the yellow glow of a street lamp.

Maggie, still breathing heavily, peered through the growing darkness at the woman. 'Who's that?'

Derek lowered the binoculars. 'That's the woman I've been looking for.'

4

'Keep your legs apart slightly,' Freddie said. 'Move back a little on the board. Smooth strokes. Good.'

'Yeah, I'm good at smooth stroking,' Gavin replied.

Freddie grinned as she and Gavin paddled out to the line-up beyond the breaking point of the waves.

The air was crisp with a morning chill, the sun just beginning to peak over the horizon. A few other surfers had come out to brave the Pacific waters, looking strong and graceful as they rode the waves. Freddie had started Gavin on some of the smaller beachbreak waves, but he had soon proved adept enough to tackle the larger breakers. The ocean swelled and rolled underneath their boards. Long strands of seaweed drifted over the water's surface.

Freddie lifted herself up and pulled her shortboard between her legs to straddle it.

'Put a hand on each rail,' she reminded Gavin. 'Don't let go. It'll fly out from underneath you.'

Gavin managed to clamber on to the board, then promptly leant too far to the left. He fell off, the board bobbing to the surface as he went underwater. Freddie reached out to grasp his arm. Gavin came up with an irritated sputter.

'Use your legs for balance,' Freddie said. 'And stay upright. Don't lean too far back or forward. Now remember to point the nose of your board toward the beach. When you catch your next wave, get back into the paddling position. We'll tackle standing later.'

She waited until Gavin spotted a wave that he felt comfortable with. He pointed the board towards the beach, took hold of the rails again and slid back into a lying position.

'Paddle!' Freddie called as the wave started to pick Gavin up.

He used his arms to stroke through the water. The wave surged under him and carried him easily back to the beach. Freddie waited until he was safely back on the sand before she looked towards the rolling waves for her own breaker. She paddled out to catch the wave just before it crashed into white crests.

In one movement, she brought her legs up under her body and planted her feet securely sideways on the board. She picked up speed, dropping down the face of the wave as the water broke into froths of sea foam. A lovely, soaring sensation went through her as she carved the wave and rode it back to the shoreline. It was erotic and breathtaking to catch and ride a good wave, controlling her own movements even as she was being controlled by the power of the water.

Gavin was looking at her with unhidden admiration as she approached him. 'You're really good.'

Freddie smiled. She liked his lack of artifice. 'Thanks. Are you hungry? Maybe we should quit for the day and get some breakfast.'

'Yeah, sure.'

They went back to Freddie's SUV, where they had left their belongings. After stowing the surfboards in the back, Freddie sat on the running board to dust the sand from her feet.

She felt good. Her body ached pleasurably from exertion and every one of her muscles was relaxed. She usually surfed the point break of Surfrider Beach in Malibu for its clean glassy waves, and she thought that maybe someday she'd take Gavin there. Freddie was mildly surprised at how much she had enjoyed teaching him to surf. Although she had friendly acquaintances among other surfers, she usually surfed alone, liking the solitude and the feeling of oneness with the water.

It was also one of the few activities that she didn't do with Derek. They worked together, ran, commiserated, sought advice, ate, rollerbladed, scuba-dived, went to the movies, and just hung out. But Derek didn't surf and Freddie didn't sail, which meant that they each had at least one activity that was solely their own – although Freddie knew that Derek had a few others as well.

She looked at Gavin, who was unzipping his wetsuit. A triangle of deliciously tanned skin appeared. Freddie's fingers itched to touch his chest. She imagined his skin would be hot and smooth.

He glanced up and caught her staring at him. A flush rose to colour her cheeks. Gavin grinned.

'Need some help with yours?' he asked.

'No, thanks.'

Freddie was aware of an odd sense of intimacy flourishing between them. Although they were both wearing bathing suits underneath their wetsuits, they were still engaged in the act of stripping down.

She turned away from Gavin and unzipped her suit, pulling the thick neoprene over her shoulders. She heard him step out of his suit and toss it into the back of the SUV. As Freddie tugged at her suit, she felt Gavin's hands close around her bare upper arms. Her breath caught. His hands were warm.

Freddie didn't move. Her body reacted to the simple touch with a surge, as if awakening suddenly after a long slumber. Gavin's body moved closer to her, so close that she could feel the heat emanating from his skin. She knew exactly what he looked like in navy shorts, all long limbs and brown skin, his blond hair drying in the morning sun, the strands stiff with salt. A shudder rained through her.

'Cold?' Gavin asked.

Freddie shook her head. His hand stroked down her arms, easing underneath the waist of the wetsuit. With deliberate movements, he pulled the suit over her hips and legs, leaving her clad in her modest green bikini. Water evaporated on her skin from the growing heat of her body. Gavin's mouth pressed against the back of her neck. Freddie couldn't move. Warmth spilled from the touch of his lips clear down her spine.

He stepped even closer so that his chest was touching her. She could feel his growing erection pressing against her bottom. One hand stroked down her arm while the other settled flat against her bare torso. Freddie couldn't breathe in that instant as she wondered which direction that hand would go. Gavin kissed her neck, his mouth moving to her shoulder and leaving a trail of heat. His hand moved up to cup one full breast. Freddie tightened her fingers on the edge of the car door. She was aware that they were protected from sight by her SUV and the other vehicles, but there was still a chance of their being seen. She tried to muster up some resistance and failed. Gavin felt too damn good.

Before Freddie could react further, Gavin's other hand slipped into her bikini bottom. His fingers rested against the soft curls of her mons before dipping lower to investigate the folds of her pussy. Freddie was almost embarrassed by how wet she already was, but Gavin's husky murmur of approval elicited another wave of moisture. His hips shifted, grinding his cock against her cheeks as his forefinger began to swirl over her pleats. Arousal tightened the delicate nerves radiating from her sex throughout her lower body. She wanted to rub herself against his hand, to feel him pressing hard against her clit. More than that, she wanted to bend right over the car seat and let him fuck her from behind.

Freddie closed her eyes as an image of that very activity burnt into her brain. Gavin slipped his hand underneath her thigh, easing her leg on to the running board to facilitate the access of his fingers. Freddie moaned, feeling her sex spread open for him. His forefinger slipped into her passage, and she tightened around him as if it were his penis. Gavin's breath was hot, his teeth biting gently into her shoulder. His stubble rubbed against her neck with delicious friction.

Freddie let her head fall against his chest. Abandon, that was what she wanted. She wanted to give herself up to someone with complete abandon, to shed the control she always worked so hard to maintain. She absorbed the pleasure of his hand kneading her breast, rolling the nipple between his thumb and forefinger. The thumb of his other hand pressed against her clit, causing a shock to spread through her. Freddie's hips jerked against his hand. He pressed his palm against her stomach to still her movements as he began to massage her pussy with deliberate strokes.

She knew she would not, could not, last long. Within seconds, her excitement built to breaking point. Freddie gasped, her limbs stiffening as if in warning.

'Let it go,' Gavin whispered, hot against her neck. 'Let it go.'

His throaty encouragement did her in. Freddie let out a cry as a small earthquake swelled through her body. Pleasure flowed from the pressure of his fingers to the very tips of her toes. She clutched the car door as Gavin continued rubbing her to ease every last sensation from her body.

Freddie sighed with sheer contentment. Gavin pulled his hand away from her, his mouth still warm against her neck. Freddie reached behind her to find the ridge of his erection, but Gavin's hand closed around her wrist.

'This one was for you,' he said.

Although she ached to touch him, to see what he looked like completely naked, Freddie had to give him credit for being selfless. She turned in his arms and pressed her mouth against his. He tasted like sand, salt water and sweat, just as she had anticipated.

'I don't suppose we could go to your place,' Gavin suggested.

Freddie shook her head. 'No. Not now. Not yet.'

He teased her lower lip with his tongue and nodded. 'How about I buy you breakfast instead?'

Freddie agreed. She watched as he retrieved his clothes from the back seat and went to change. Nice guy. No pressure, no attempt to coerce her into doing something she wasn't yet ready for. Still, Freddie suspected that it wouldn't be long at all before she invited him back to her apartment.

Derek stood outside Anna's apartment building, his hands in his pockets as he leant against a street lamp. He was primed for the arrest, but the timing hadn't been right. Anna had spent the previous night with a steroid job whom Derek hadn't wanted to involve in the arrest. He'd apprehended fugitives in countless ways, but he preferred to wake them from a sound sleep. They were disoriented, sleepy and far less likely to put up a fight. Derek fought when necessary, but the skip always ended up the worse for wear. It was easier on everyone to arrest them as effortlessly as possible.

He checked his watch. Anna had entered her apartment alone three hours ago. The lights had gone off an hour ago. With a different fugitive, Derek might have waited, but Anna wouldn't pose much of a physical challenge.

He climbed the exterior steps of the building and shook his head at the sight of the flimsy lock on the door. One quick twist with a pick and the door opened. The interior was dim, shafts of yellowish light coming through the slats of the blinds.

Derek crept towards the bedroom, his shoes soundless against the carpet. His body tensed. The weight of his .45 was heavy against the small of his back. The bedroom door was cracked open. He pushed it further, letting his eyes adjust to the darkness.

A mattress rested on the floor alongside an open suitcase. The form of a woman was outlined underneath a thin sheet. Just as he was about to move closer, a moan emerged from Anna's throat.

Derek froze in the doorway. He knew she was alone. He didn't know whether she was asleep or not. His gaze fixed on her face, which was illuminated by the dusty light of the street lamps. Her eyes were closed, her shoulders and arms bare. Derek reached for his gun.

Just as his hand closed around the grip, Anna's eyes opened. She didn't look in his direction, but stretched one arm up to run her fingers through her hair. There was just enough light for Derek to see exactly what his fugitive was doing. The sheet slipped, exposing Anna's breasts. They were small and firm like peaches, the nipples hard.

Derek grimaced as he felt his cock twitch. He told himself to focus. Anna lifted her other hand to cup one breast. Her fingers tweaked and pinched the nipple, causing her to emit another moan. She pushed the sheet away. Her naked body was slender and taut. She lifted her knees and spread her legs apart, revealing an enticing view of her shadowed pussy.

Fuck! Derek was getting harder by the second. With a stiff prick, he'd find it difficult to move, let alone make an arrest. He closed his eyes and tried to think of baseball, but then Anna let out another guttural moan. Derek opened his eyes. Anna was sliding a hand over her belly towards her cunt. She toyed with the springy nest of curls before dipping a finger into the cleft. Her body jerked in reaction. Her knees drew wider apart. She pressed her fingers into the wet folds, spreading herself as if for a lover.

Derek knew he was going to keep watching. Anna rose up on one elbow and leant over the side of the bed, clutching what appeared to be a thick-handled hair-brush. Derek nearly groaned. Anna pressed the brush handle against her pussy folds, moving it up and down with evident ease. She arched her back, her head pushing against the pillow as she began to slide the handle into her. Her eyes closed. Her mouth opened. She bucked her hips against the brush, gasping as the thick handle slid inside her.

Derek's prick was hard as a rock, but he resisted the temptation to jerk off. Anna's breathing grew raspy. She pulled the handle out of her pussy before sliding it back in again. The movement of her hand began to increase in pace. Her hips rotated against the handle. She reached down with her other hand and began to massage her clit. Her ass came off the bed as she plunged the handle deeper and deeper.

'Oh, yes!' The word emerged on a hiss as Anna's body became taut with urgency. She tossed her head from side to side against the pillow, her fingers working rapidly as she urged her body to orgasm. Her tits bounced in time with her escalating frenzy.

Derek wanted to pull that damn brush out of her and drive his prick into her sweet little box. He knew she would prefer a hot, pliable cock to unyielding plastic. His hand tightened on the door handle as Anna continued to thrust the handle into her pussy and work her clit. She came hard and suddenly, crying out in pleasure as her body shook.

With a gasp, Anna dropped the brush on to the floor and fell back against the pillow, her arms over her head. She closed her eyes, drawing in deep breaths. Her body went slack with satisfaction.

Derek rested his forehead against the doorjamb and took a few deep breaths of his own. He wished he could fuck Maggie, but then forced Maggie from his mind after realising that thinking of her wouldn't help matters.

He tried to will his erection into submission. He tried

to think unpleasant thoughts. After a few minutes, he finally felt his prick begin to soften. He waited until he was certain he had himself under control before he turned back towards the bedroom.

Thankfully, Anna had pulled the sheet over her naked body before settling in to sleep. Derek snapped his mind to the task at hand. He grasped his gun and moved into the room.

'Anna.' He didn't point the gun at her, but held it ready at his side. The sound of his deep voice fairly echoed in the quiet. He reached to turn the light on.

Anna bolted upright as light flooded the room. Her hand went to her chest, and her eyes widened with fear. 'What the ...?'

'Anna, you're under arrest.'

'What the ...? Jesus, who the fuck are you?' She scrambled to cover herself, clutching the sheet with both hands. Her eyes clashed with his in the dim light. 'Get out of my house!'

'You're under arrest, Anna,' Derek repeated coolly. He still didn't point the gun at her, but moved it slightly so that the metal caught both the light and Anna's attention. 'You violated the conditions of your bail.'

'What the fuck? Who are you? Get out!'

'You can make this easy or you can make it hard,' Derek said. 'Either way, I'm taking you in.'

Her breath was coming in quick gasps. 'You son of a bitch. You're not taking me anywhere.'

Derek reached for his handcuffs. As he did, Anna hurled herself off the mattress towards him. Her body crashed into his, bringing them both to the ground. His gun fell. His head cracked against the hard floor.

Anna went at him like a hissing cat, her hands striking out at his face, his chest, anywhere she could reach. She managed a particularly good slap against his jaw before Derek caught her wrists. He flipped her over and pinned her to the ground, pressing his body against hers to still her flailing movements.

'Anna,' he said. 'Calm down.'

'The hell I'll calm down!' she spat. Her eyes were wild, her entire body taut with fury. 'How dare you break in here? Who sent you? Was it my father? You have no right to –'

'I have every right,' Derek interrupted. 'I wouldn't be here if you didn't jump bail. It's your own damn fault.'

A slow understanding dawned behind her furious expression. 'Oh, fuck! You're a bounty hunter, aren't you?'

'Bail-enforcement agent.'

'Who hired you?' Anna snapped as she arched her back in an attempt to buck him off. 'Gus or my father? It was my father, wasn't it? That asshole never –'

'Anna! Calm down.' Derek's grip tightened on her wrists. He was uncomfortably aware that she was still naked. Her hard-nippled tits were pressing against his chest, her legs spread beneath him. Under other circumstances, he would have welcomed such a position. She was small, firm, and she felt damn good.

Derek pushed Anna's arms over her head and grasped both of her wrists in one hand. He held them against the floor as he pulled the handcuffs from his hip pocket. He slapped the cuffs on her and lifted himself off her body with a mixture of relief and regret.

He turned away and grabbed the sheet, tossing it in Anna's direction without looking at her. The sound of their heavy breathing filled the room. Derek retrieved his gun and stuck it in the waistband of his jeans.

'OK,' he said. 'I've gotta take you in.'

He glanced at her. She had managed to cover herself with the sheet, but the look in her eyes was one of pure hatred.

'How'd you find me?'

'Asked around,' Derek replied evasively.

'Who'd you ask? My stepmother? That witch would love to see me locked up for ten years.'

'I don't think anyone would love to see you locked up.'

'How would you know, you prick? You don't know anything about me.'

'I know you can tie a cherry stem with your tongue,' Derek said. 'I know you play good pool and that you like dive bars. I know you fuck men who look like Charles Atlas.'

Anna looked stunned. 'You've been stalking me?'

'That's one word for it.' Derek went to the open suitcase and pulled out a pair of jeans and a button-down shirt. 'Get dressed.'

'How am I supposed to dress with handcuffs on?'

'You'd better figure it out because they're not coming off.'

Anna muttered another unflattering insult as she picked up the jeans. She managed to struggle into them, hitching them awkwardly over her thighs and hips.

Derek took the shirt and wrapped it around Anna's shoulders, then worked to fasten the buttons. The scent of her wafted into his nose, an aphrodisiac combination of cinnamon and sex cream. His cock started to stiffen again. He fastened the last button quickly and stepped away from her.

'OK, let's go.'

'Where are you taking me?' Anna snapped.

'Police department.'

'What about my stuff?'

'I'll pack it up and bring it to you later.'

'Oh, gee, lucky me. I've got a bounty hunter with a heart.'

'Bail-enforcement agent,' Derek corrected. He gestured towards the door. Anna didn't move.

'Do you even know why I was arrested?' she asked.

'You stole from your father's company.'

'I was framed for stealing from my father's company,' Anna retorted.

'Framed. Sure. You and every other bail jumper in town.' He grabbed her arm. 'Come on. I don't have all night.'

'Yeah, well, I do,' Anna snapped. 'Especially when I've been arrested for something I didn't do.'

'Tell it to the judge.'

Anna yanked her arm out of his grip. 'Did you talk to Cassandra?'

'Your stepmother didn't have much to say.'

'Did she tell you she wanted nothing to do with me?'

'Yeah. Your father said pretty much the same thing.'

Derek was unprepared for the depth of sheer hurt that flashed in Anna's eyes. He steeled himself against feeling any remorse.

'From what I gathered, you already knew that,' he said.

'Yes, well, that doesn't make it pleasant to hear,' Anna replied curtly. 'Look, I'll make you a deal.'

'I don't make deals with fugitives.'

'Give me half an hour to explain,' Anna said. 'If you don't believe me after you hear me out, then I won't put up a fight.'

'You already put up a fight,' Derek reminded her. 'It didn't work.'

Anna tossed her hair back and looked at him with defiance. 'I can still make it tough for you to bring me in.' She eyed his groin. 'Unless you're wearing a protective cup.'

Derek shook his head with a mixture of admiration and amusement. 'Look, honey, I'm doing a job. You missed your court date. Not my problem. You have some sob story, save it for your lawyer.'

'In case you can't tell, I'm not stupid. I know you have every right to arrest me, but jumping bail was the only chance I had to prove my case.'

'What the hell did I just say? Prove your case in court.'

'I can't because I don't have any evidence yet,' Anna said. 'And I can't get the evidence from a prison cell, can I?'

Derek sighed. 'What kind of evidence is going to prove you were framed?'

Anna bit her lip. The gesture made her seem unexpectedly vulnerable. With her dyed blonde hair and pixie face, her body sheathed in the oversized shirt, she looked like a lost little fairy.

'Well, I don't know yet,' she confessed.

'All right, enough of this. I'm taking you in, and, if you try to knee me in the groin, I'll bring out the leg cuffs.'

He grasped her arm again to hurry her along. Anna dug in her heels, her chin set with determination.

'It's Cassandra,' she said. 'She's always hated me and my sister because we stand to inherit most of my father's money. Or we did. Now most of it is going to Erin.'

'My heart is breaking.'

'Cassandra was no doubt thrilled when my father disowned me,' Anna continued stubbornly. 'But, before that happened, I discovered something about her. Something she doesn't want anyone else, least of all my father, to find out. She knew she had to get me out of the way.'

'So why didn't she call in a shady Sicilian uncle?' Derek asked.

Despite his caustic tone, he was mildly intrigued by the thought that the elegant Cassandra Maxwell harboured a secret she didn't want anyone else to discover.

'What's the secret?' he asked.

Anna gave him a tight smile. 'Well, wouldn't you like to know? Let me go and I might tell you.'

'I said I don't make deals.' Even as he said the words, something Cassandra had told him echoed in his mind. *Anna is a blackmailer.* Gus Walker hadn't told him anything about blackmailing, and, as far as Derek knew, there were no extortion charges against her.

He crossed his arms over his chest and levelled his gaze on Anna. 'So you discovered this so-called secret,' he said. 'How did Cassandra know you found out?'

Anna's eyes darted briefly away from him. 'She just did.'

'Uh huh. And why did she think you'd tell your father?'

'Because I told her that I would,' Anna snapped. 'I threatened to tell him, not to mention a good number of her society friends.'

'What were the terms?' Derek asked.

She gave him a mutinous look. 'I wanted her to leave my father.'

'Which she obviously wouldn't do.'

'No. So she had to get rid of me. She works at my father's company, you know. She's not some dim trophy wife. She's an executive VP. She knows exactly how things work. And she'd know how to frame me.'

'Why can't you still just tell your father?'

'He won't speak to me! I can't even get in touch with him. And even if I tried, that bitch Cassandra would somehow keep me away from him.'

'So you think she has the money stashed away somewhere?'

'Half a mil? Damn straight she does. Deeply hidden and untraceable to her, I'm sure. I don't exactly have the resources to try to find it.'

'So what were you planning to do?' Derek asked. In spite of himself, he was beginning to find an edge of truth to what Anna was telling him.

'I said I don't know,' Anna replied. 'I have to think of something, though, or I'm going right to the pokey.'

Derek grinned. 'The pokey, huh?'

Anna gave him a wan smile. 'I know I broke the law by jumping bail. I didn't want to leave Gus in the lurch, but I can't do anything from prison. I need time.'

'I'm sorry.' He had never before apologised to a skip. 'I can't give you time. I need to take you in.'

'How much are you getting?'

'Twenty per cent of your bond.'

'I'll double it if you give me two weeks. I have some money saved from my last few paycheques. If I can't come up with a plan in two weeks, you can arrest me.'

'How many times do I have to tell you I don't make deals?' Derek said. 'And what makes you think I'd trust you, anyway?'

'I give you my word.'

She said it with such conviction that Derek almost smiled again. He shook his head.

'You really think I'm going to walk out of here and let you go,' he said. 'If I did that, I'd be damn lousy at my job.'

'Look, my father has disowned me,' Anna said. 'I've only been able to talk to my sister secretly. Almost all I have is in these two suitcases. I'm facing I don't know how many years in jail. If I can't do something now, I have everything in the world to lose. But, if you don't arrest me this minute, what do you have to lose? Nothing.'

'I have a reputation in this business. I've never let a skip escape a second time.'

'I'm not going to escape. I have nowhere to go anyway. I just need two weeks of freedom. I need to find a way to prove that Cassandra stole the money.'

Derek scratched his head. He should haul Anna out the door and into his car right this second. He should tell the police he was bringing her in. He should call Gus and tell him he'd arrested his latest bail jumper. He should collect his payment and move on with his life.

He grasped Anna's arm and urged her towards the door. 'Let's go.'

She wrenched herself away from him and tried to kick his kneecap. Anticipating the move, Derek stepped back.

'You son of a bitch.' A sheen of tears shone in Anna's eyes. 'You're making a huge mistake.'

'So they all say. And don't forget I have leg cuffs. If you make a scene, the police will be here in less than a minute.'

He pushed her outside and down the stairs towards his car. Anna didn't put up a struggle as he guided her into the back seat and fastened her seatbelt.

Derek got into the driver's seat and started the car. He glanced in the rear-view mirror at his captive. She was sitting rigidly, her expression stonelike as she stared through the side window. Tears still glistened in her eyes, but they didn't spill over. She sniffed.

Derek pushed the car into gear and headed out to Fairfax. The Hollywood community police department was located on Wilcox to the north, but Derek drove south to reach the I-10. He headed west to merge on to the 405 south. After fifteen minutes of driving, he finally heard Anna's voice.

'Hey,' she said. 'Where are you taking me?'

'You'll see.' He glanced at her in the mirror again, aware of the edge of fear in her voice. 'Don't worry. I won't hurt you.'

'How the hell do I know that?'

'If I'd wanted to hurt you, I would have by now,' Derek said.

'How do I know you're a legit bounty hunter and not some sex-crazed maniac?' Anna asked. 'You people don't carry badges or IDs, do you?'

'Some do, but you can get a badge made anywhere these days. As for my not being a sex-crazed maniac – well, that's debatable.'

'Oh, yeah, be amusing. That makes this situation all the better.'

She fell silent for the remainder of the drive. Derek parked in the marina lot and opened the back door. Before Anna got out, he bent and put his lips close to her ear.

'Remember,' he said. 'If you want the police to show up, make a scene.'

Her eyes flashed with anger. 'I'm beginning to think I might want the police here after all.'

Derek held open the door. 'Your choice.'

Her choice. Anna had made many choices in her life, but never before had someone offered her a choice between the unknown and jail. She climbed out of the car slowly. The bounty hunter's hand closed around her arm like a vice.

Anna looked at him warily. He was tall and well built, but he lacked the overblown, beefy physique that characterised most of her men. The bounty hunter was more athletic and confident, moving with masculine grace rather than machismo. No, he wasn't her type of man, but he did have a rather mouth-watering appeal that caught Anna off guard.

His grip tightened on her arm as he led her to the harbour. The moon was high and full, shedding pale light on to the boats swaying in the harbour. It was so quiet that she could hear the water splashing gently against the hulls.

Anna stopped when they reached a sailboat emblazoned with the name *Jezebel*. 'Is this yours?'

'Yes. You can stay here for now.'

'Why?'

'Against my better judgement,' he said, 'I'm giving you half a chance. I don't trust you not to run, but a couple of weeks won't make much of a difference. I can hold Gus off. So, whatever you want to do, I'd suggest you get started.'

'Wait a minute. You're giving me two weeks, but you're keeping me here?'

'That's the deal.'

'I thought you didn't make deals.'

'I said it was against my better judgement.'

Anna shook her head. 'I don't get it. How am I supposed to do anything if I'm stuck on your boat?'

'Where you go, I go,' he said flatly. 'If I'm not here, you're locked in the cabin. Take the deal or leave it.'

Anna stared at him. 'Why?'

'Temporary loss of sanity,' he muttered half to himself. 'And an apparent weakness for pixies.'

He held open the cabin door. Anna passed him as she stepped inside, so close that she caught a whiff of his scent, an enticing combination of laundry soap and shaving cream. She could almost feel the heat radiating from his body.

The boat's cabin was functional and even somewhat spacious with a dining table and dinette sofa, a door leading to what looked like a stateroom, lockers and an adjoining galley. A shelf lining the wall was filled with books on ocean voyages, meteorology, atlases, sailing directions and cruising guides. Several maps and charts were tacked to the walls and spread over the chart table.

Anna looked at the bounty hunter again. He was still at the door, his shoulder leaning against the jamb as he watched her without expression. He had a hard face composed of angles whose sharpness was mitigated by thick eyebrows, dark eyelashes and a surprisingly sensual mouth.

Anna silently held out her restrained wrists. The bounty hunter didn't move. For an instant, she thought he wouldn't remove the cuffs, but then he stepped forward and took a set of keys from his pocket. He unlocked the cuffs and tossed them aside. His fingers brushed the delicate skin of her wrists.

Anna rubbed the reddened skin. 'What's your name?'

'Derek Rowland.'

'Well, Derek Rowland, I appreciate this.' The words sounded weak and inadequate. 'Really.'

He shrugged. 'You have a limited amount of time. I suggest you use it wisely. You can sleep on the bed. I'll bring your stuff over tomorrow.'

He headed towards the door.

'Wait,' Anna said.

Derek turned back to look at her.

'What do you –' Anna swallowed hard. 'What do you want from me?'

He didn't respond, but, even from a distance, she could see his eyes darken with something akin to arousal. Her breath tangled in her chest as she remembered exactly what she had been doing before he'd woken her up so abruptly. Had he be in her apartment at the time? Had he seen her squirming around on the bed, naked and wanton?

A flush heated Anna's cheeks. Even with her uninhibited nature, she was still embarrassed at the thought of this man witnessing her most private moments. She knew innately that there was something decent about him.

'You're paying me twice my fee,' he replied.

'That's all you want?'

'You think I want more?' he asked.

'I don't know. Do you?'

'I hadn't thought of other forms of compensation,' Derek said. 'But, now that you mention it, I'll keep it in mind.'

As she watched him leave the cabin, Anna imagined with a shiver what would happen if he requested a payment from her that didn't involve money.

5

Cassandra Maxwell shifted her legs together underneath the table. Richard stood at the front of the boardroom, making a presentation about Jump Start Computers' last fiscal year. Cassandra let her gaze wander over him. He looked impressive and controlled in his tailored suit, a charcoal grey that she had selected to match his hair. All of her friends thought that Richard was so handsome, so distinguished.

He was, Cassandra acknowledged. Pity there wasn't enough beneath his polished exterior. Richard could talk endlessly about motherboards, CPUs and gigabytes. He could analyse budget reports and databases. He could spend hours figuring out how to optimise a web browser. What he couldn't do was give his wife what she needed in the bedroom.

Cassandra pressed her thighs together more tightly. With her cream-coloured Chanel suit, her tasteful gold earrings and necklace, she knew she projected an image of cool professionalism. Unlike the employees at so many other Bay Area computer companies, she had categorically rejected the casual dress of jeans and button-down shirts.

Cassandra had been raised with the belief that women had to work twice as hard as men to succeed in the business world. Dressing appropriately and profession-ally was the first step towards garnering success. Throughout the course of earning her MBA and climbing the ranks of Jump Start to her VP promotion, she com-manded initial respect with her appearance. And she sustained respect with her intelligence and acumen.

She turned her attention back to Richard. She had

married him several years after her promotion, which mitigated some of the company gossip about their relationship. All of their employees knew that she had legitimately earned her position within the company, that it wasn't the result of an affair with Richard. A 25 per cent increase in sales due to her aggressive marketing campaign confirmed her status.

Cassandra loved the fact that she and Richard had such a power marriage. They were one of the most sought-after couples on the social circuit. Everyone admired their management of a highly successful company, not to mention their charity work and entertaining. To be invited to a Maxwell fête was an indication that one had truly reached the upper echelons of society.

If only Richard were as capable of discerning her needs as he was at explaining a fiscal report. They had a reasonably good sex life, but it was never enough. Cassandra sketched a doodle of a star on the front of her folder. She wondered what he'd think if he knew she wasn't wearing any panties underneath her very expensive suit. Or that she loved the feeling of air brushing under her skirt, tickling her cunt.

She also wondered what Richard would think of the thin black cord she wore. The cord was tied unobtrusively around her waist with one string going between her bottom cheeks and legs before being reattached to her waist. Every time she moved, the cord rubbed against her inner folds, electrifying her with sensation. She wore the cord twice a week, on Tuesday and Thursday, days she spent in a perpetual state of arousal.

Relieved when Richard brought the meeting to an end, Cassandra collected her papers and stood. She made small talk with a few of the other employees before excusing herself and heading back to her office. With every step, the cord chafed deliciously against her clit. She knew that, if she didn't control herself, she could come at any minute.

She went into her office, a large corner room that overlooked the tidy little park of the building complex. She sat at her desk and pulled up the latest marketing report for a new photo-editing software package they had launched. She focused her attention on the work, looking up only when a knock sounded at the door. Richard entered without waiting for an invitation.

'Interesting meeting,' Cassandra lied.

'No, it wasn't.' Richard closed the door behind him. 'Has Erin told you anything about Anna?'

'No. Why?'

'I think they've been in touch.'

Cassandra's eyes narrowed. 'Why do you think that?'

'I have Erin's cell phone,' Richard said. 'She forgot it this morning and was going to come by to pick it up. She got a call from a payphone in Redondo Beach.'

'So?'

'So, when I answered it, there was a second of silence before the phone went dead. I'd swear it was Anna.'

'Why would Anna call Erin?'

'I have no idea.'

'Did you ask Erin?'

'I will when she stops by,' Richard said. 'If she knows where Anna is, she's going to tell me.'

Cassandra's mind began working. She had been cautiously relieved when Anna jumped bail, hoping that meant Anna would simply disappear to avoid being caught. There was an element of danger to her being a fugitive, however, since there was always the chance that she could reappear and wreak havoc in their lives. The safest place for Anna was in prison, but that meant enforced contact with her. It was a precarious situation – one that Cassandra hadn't fully considered until now.

'I'm sure Erin will be honest with you,' she told Richard in her most soothing voice. 'She's not like Anna.'

'No.' Richard rubbed his forehead and sighed. 'Anna's

not stupid, though. She wouldn't do anything to jeopardise her freedom. At least, I don't think she would.'

'Well, she's not your problem any more.'

'She's still my daughter.'

'You've said countless times that you want nothing more to do with her,' Cassandra said. 'Maybe it's time you put your words into action.'

'Disowning her isn't enough?'

'I just meant you should stop putting so much energy into worrying about her,' Cassandra replied. 'After all, she is an adult. Not to mention a criminal.'

'Maybe I should contact that bounty hunter,' Richard mused.

Cassandra narrowed her gaze. If Richard had a hand in finding Anna, he would probably want to talk to her after she was arrested again. Cassandra did not want that to happen.

She pushed herself away from the desk and approached him. 'Darling, you need to concentrate on other things. We made our decision about Anna. It's time to let her fend for herself.'

'Yeah, but –'

'But nothing.' Cassandra twisted a lock of his hair around her finger. 'Leave her alone, Richard. She'll never make anything of herself.'

She saw his eyes shift to her ample cleavage and almost heard Anna slipping out of his thoughts. Cassandra smiled to herself. Richard was an intelligent man, but he was also easily distracted. She bent to press her lips against his forehead.

'Do you have any plans for the next hour or so?' she whispered.

'Not yet.'

'Good. Hold that thought.'

Cassandra moved away and went into the bathroom that adjoined her office. She looked at herself in the mirror, patting her already perfect hair into place. Her fingers shook as she pulled her skirt up over her thighs and unfastened the cord. An arrow of regret went through her as she slipped it off and placed it in a drawer underneath the sink. She straightened her skirt and returned to Richard.

Her gaze went to his groin. His erection was already pushing against the fly of his trousers. That was one nice thing about Richard. He rarely had trouble getting and staying hard. Cassandra let her fingers drift across the bulge as she bent to kiss him. His mouth opened, his hot tongue thrusting against hers.

A rush of arousal swept over Cassandra. Her pussy was already ripe from the friction of the cord, warmth radiating from her inner core throughout her entire body. Richard's hands went to her hips as he drew her skirt up, his fingers brushing against her bare ass. He paused in surprise.

Cassandra smiled, catching his lower lip between her teeth. 'I just took them off,' she murmured. 'No need for anything to stand in your way.'

'Nice.' His voice deepened an octave. His fingers slipped between the full cheeks of her bottom, exploring the shadowy cleft. Cassandra shuddered as he moved lower into the damp folds of her sex.

'Christ, you're wet already.' He pulled away to look at her, his excitement increasing. 'Doesn't take you long, does it?'

Cassandra didn't bother telling him that she spent most of her days in a perpetual state of arousal. She smiled and shook her head. 'Not with you, my love.'

Richard's fingers moved teasingly over the little valley, his thumb brushing against her clit. Cassandra drew in a sharp breath and spread her legs wider apart. Her pussy was fully shorn, every crease laid bare to a man's touch. Richard had initially balked at the idea of her being shaven, but she had convinced him that it enhanced her own pleasure. He soon learnt to love the smooth sensation for his own pleasure as well. His fingers stroked her sleek mons. Her body grew hot.

Cassandra bent to unfasten his trousers and pull them over his hips. He had a lovely cock, nice and thick if not particularly long. It sprang up towards her as if in invitation. Cassandra lowered herself on to her knees and bent to take his penis in her mouth. Richard groaned, his hips bucking towards her as she enveloped him in her mouth. She worked her tongue with expert precision, sliding it up and down the shaft, twirling it around the tip. She moved lower to gently caress the twin sacs between his thighs as Richard's hand cupped the back of her head.

'Gently, dearest,' Cassandra whispered, not wanting him to snarl her expensive twist.

She stood and went to her desk, moving aside some papers. She looked at Richard over her shoulder and pulled her skirt up around her waist, baring her creamy bottom to his gaze.

'You have one gorgeous ass, Cassandra,' Richard said thickly as he grasped his prick.

Cassandra suppressed an urge to feel his hand slap hard against her behind. Instead, she bent over the desk and parted her legs, giving him a full view of her pussy spread open like a juicy oyster. A rush of cool air kissed her lower body. She shuddered and pressed her hand between her legs. She slipped one tapered finger into her opening, moving it back and forth while Richard watched. Her sheath clenched around her finger.

'Come here and give it to me,' she hissed.

Richard approached her, his cock still in his fist. He rubbed the moist tip between the cleft of her bottom. Cassandra lowered her head on to the desk, her breathing rapid against the polished wood. Richard pressed himself against her clit, one arm going around her waist. Expanding rings of excitement spread through Cassandra's blood like a pebble dropped into a pool of water. Her hands clenched into fists as Richard began circling the tip of his penis around her hole.

'Shove it in,' Cassandra whispered.

His hips pressed forward. His stalk began to fill her with delicious ease. The thick shaft slid easily into her damp passage, stimulating her arousal with every subtle movement. With a groan, Cassandra went pliant against the desk, arching her back so that her bottom pressed towards him. Her legs trembled. Richard's hands grasped her hips as he began to drive forward. Panting, he thrust in and out of her with increasing force, his belly slapping against her ass.

Cassandra rested her forehead on the desk, her body jerking with every plunge. Her breasts rubbed against the silk of her bra, and she wished that she could squeeze the painfully stiff nipples. She slid one hand between her legs and splayed her fingers around her clit. So ready. She had been so ready all day. Sensations twisted lusciously through her body. She closed her eyes and absorbed the feeling of Richard fucking her. His method was good. It was always the same, but at least it was good.

She rubbed the knot harder as her tension began to build. The combination of Richard's shaft thrusting into her and the pressure of her own fingers drove her towards release. She came with a muffled groan, her body shuddering as Richard's strokes began to slow.

'God, Cass, I can't hold it any more,' he gasped.

He pulled out of her and gave a shout as he shot creamy seed over her upturned bottom. His body rested heavily against hers as he struggled to catch his breath. The smell of sex filled the air.

Cassandra shifted underneath him. 'Richard, dear, you're a bit heavy.'

'Sorry.' He pushed away from her.

Cassandra lifted herself up and turned to look at him, reaching for a few tissues from the box on her desk. She smiled.

'Lovely, darling,' she murmured.

He smiled and kissed her. 'Nice break in the day, hmm?'

'Yes, but you'd better go before people start wondering what we're doing in here,' Cassandra advised.

'None of their damn business.'

'Richard!' Her tone was reproving.

'All right, all right.' He kissed her again and stroked his hand over her face. 'I'll see you later.'

'Mmm hmm.'

Cassandra went into the bathroom, certain that she had wiped thoughts of Anna from her husband's mind. Temporarily, at least. She cleansed herself and retrieved the black cord, fastening it back around her waist with fingers that trembled.

Anna paced back and forth in the confines of the cabin. She had been aboard Derek Rowland's boat for two days, and she had yet to accomplish anything. Much as she appreciated his not arresting her, she failed to see what she could do to prove her innocence if she was stuck on the boat 24/7. Then again, she hadn't come up with many ideas when she was on the run, either.

Anna sighed and plucked a crimson cherry from a bowl on the table. Derek had brought the cherries back from a farmers' market that morning before he'd left again. The fruit filled an entire bowl like a pile of rubies.

'Yoo-hoo! Hello?'

Anna turned in surprise at the sound of a female voice. The cabin door opened and a bronzed, attractive woman in her mid-forties entered. Dressed in a bikini top and a pair of shorts, her short hair tousled, she looked as if she didn't have a care in the world. She stopped at the sight of Anna and smiled.

'Oh, hello. Sorry to barge in like this.'

'Who are you?' Anna asked.

'My name is Maggie. Is Derek around?'

'No. He's out.' Anna frowned as she tossed the cherry pit into the trash. 'Do you have a key?'

'A key?' Maggie repeated.

'Yeah. To the door.'

'I don't have a key.'

'Then how did you get in?' Anna asked.

'The door was unlocked.'

Anna stopped in mid-motion. 'Unlocked?'

'Unlocked,' Maggie confirmed.

'There's no padlock on the door?'

'No. Should there be?'

'I guess not.' Understanding dawned in Anna's mind. She shook her head with a combination of admiration and irritation. That bastard. He'd made her think he'd padlocked the door knowing that she wouldn't try to open it.

Maggie leant against the door and eyed Anna speculatively. 'Mind if I ask who you are?'

'Just a friend of Derek's,' Anna replied.

'Mmm hmm. Me too.'

Anna wondered briefly whether Maggie was giving her some sort of warning about Derek, but no: the other woman was looking at her with interest and more than a little curiosity.

'You were at a bar called The Cave, weren't you?' Maggie asked.

Anna gave her a startled look. 'How do you know about The Cave?'

'I was with Derek when he was staking out the place looking for you,' Maggie replied. 'Terribly exciting. I'd never been on a stakeout before.'

'So you – I mean, you know about me?'

'Well, if Derek was looking for you, you must have jumped bail,' Maggie said.

A hint of fear broke open inside Anna. If Maggie knew her circumstances, that could put both Anna and Derek at risk. However, Maggie didn't appear to be the slightest bit concerned about the possibility of Anna's being a criminal.

'Don't you want to know why Derek didn't arrest me?' Anna asked carefully.

'I'm sure he has his reasons,' Maggie said with a shrug.

'Are you also a bounty hunter?'

Maggie laughed. 'Heavens, no. I'm a writer and an artist.'

The tension in Anna's neck eased slightly. Maggie lowered herself into a chair and stretched her legs out in front of her. She stroked one hand over her tanned thigh.

'So you thought there was a padlock on the door, hmm?' she asked. 'Did Derek lock you up in here? How utterly romantic.'

Anna flushed. 'Well, I guess I thought he'd locked the door from the outside.'

'So you couldn't escape?' Maggie considered the idea. 'I suppose there are many worse things in the world than being Derek's prisoner.'

'I suppose. How well do you know him?'

'Oh, Derek and I go back several years.'

'Derek and I go back several days,' Anna said.

Maggie grinned. Anna let her gaze drift over Maggie's body. She had a pleasingly abundant figure with full breasts and muscular legs. She also exuded a complete awareness of her own sexuality. It was a highly attractive quality in a world of insecurities.

An image of Derek and Maggie writhing naked together appeared in Anna's mind. Her breath caught in her throat as a spark of arousal flared inside her. She imagined they would make a lusty and uninhibited pair.

'Do you live around here, Maggie?' Anna asked.

Maggie nodded towards the opposite side of the dock.

'Right over there. You should come and visit me sometime.'

'Maybe I will.'

'I would enjoy that.' Maggie lifted her arms over her head for a long stretch. Her breasts rose appealingly, taut nipples pressing against the fabric of her bikini. 'I get lonely over there all by myself. That's why I encourage Derek's visits.'

'I'm sure you do,' Anna said. She couldn't help liking the other woman and her forthright nature. She held out the cherries. 'Want one?'

Maggie selected a red cherry and crunched into it. 'Mmm. Good season for cherries.'

Anna remembered the last time she'd had a cherry. She had been busy seducing a hunky dock worker named Ben. It seemed as if that night had happened a lifetime ago.

'Want to see a trick?' she asked Maggie.

'Sure.'

Anna plucked a stem from one of the cherries and popped it into her mouth. She worked it with her tongue, then removed the knotted stem and held it out in her palm. Maggie chuckled and picked up the knot to look at it more closely.

'Neat.'

'I've been told I have a talented tongue.' Anna flashed Maggie a smile.

'I'll say.' Maggie was looking at her with frank appreciation. 'So is Derek aware of this talented tongue of yours?'

Not yet, Anna thought. 'I haven't shown him the trick, no,' she replied evasively.

'Then I consider myself lucky,' Maggie said.

Something hot lit between them suddenly. Anna cleared her throat and bit into another cherry.

'You want to know the truth?' she asked, mildly surprised when the words came out of her mouth.

'Only if you want to tell me.'

Anna figured she had little to lose. The worst that could happen would be that Maggie told the police about her, but somehow Anna knew that she wouldn't. Besides, Maggie already knew that she was a fugitive. Anna gave her an abbreviated version of the whole story. Maggie listened intently.

'So Derek is giving me a second chance,' Anna said.

'Isn't that noble.' Maggie gave her a warm smile. 'I always knew he had a heart.'

'Don't tell him that.'

'Derek may act like a tough guy, but he has a soft spot for women,' Maggie said. 'I'm sure he'd help you if you asked him to.'

'Maybe I will. I'm not getting much done here, that's for sure.'

'Well, as I said, you're more than welcome to come over to my boat if you'd like,' Maggie offered. 'I mean, so Derek doesn't have to lock you up and all sorts of dramatic things like that.'

'Derek probably wouldn't think that was a good idea.'

'Why not?' Maggie asked. 'You'd have company. I'd have company. And I won't let you get away.'

She winked. Another ember of arousal flared inside Anna. She'd had a small number of liaisons with other women, but none who had the level of self-assurance that Maggie did.

'I'll ask him,' Anna promised.

'Do that.' Maggie stood and stretched, the muscles of her body lengthening. 'Derek knows he can trust me. It was a pleasure to meet you, Anna.'

'You too.'

Maggie headed back up to the deck. Anna picked another cherry from the bowl and bit into it. A burst of sweetness filled her mouth, tasting like a sunrise.

6

'And you said *I* was nuts for dating Gavin!' Freddie shook her head in disbelief. 'You are out of your freaking mind, my friend.'

'So I keep telling myself.' Hearing the same from Freddie didn't make his decision any easier to live with. Derek thought he'd scraped the bottom of the barrel as far as professionalism was concerned. 'Anyone hears about this, my career is over.'

'Nah, they'll just think you're starting to lose it,' Freddie said cheerfully. 'Which I've pretty much known all along.'

Derek sighed and shoved his hands into the pockets of his shorts as he and Freddie walked along Santa Monica Pier. The pier was crowded with people wandering in and out of souvenir shops and fast-food places or waiting in line to ride the Ferris wheel and roller coaster at Pacific Park. A vintage carousel circled around in time to tinny music, the sculpted horses basking in a multitude of coloured lights. The sand-fringed bay stretched out endlessly around the pier.

Derek paused at one of the food stalls and bought two coffees for him and Freddie before they left the pier and stepped back on to the beach.

'I don't know what I was thinking,' he said as they found a place to settle on the sand. A line of palm trees stretched along the edge of the state beach. Traffic noise rumbled from PCH.

'You weren't thinking, that's the problem.' Freddie spread a towel on the sand and stripped out of her shorts and T-shirt. 'Or, more likely, you were thinking with your other head.'

Derek gave her a mild glower. 'Thanks for the analysis.'

'Come on, Derek. She must be a bombshell.'

'She's no bombshell. She's cute, but that's not why I –'

'Uh huh.' Freddie adjusted the strap on her bathing suit and sat down. She pulled a bottle of sunscreen from her backpack and began smoothing the lotion over her arms and legs.

'She was actually beginning to make some sense,' Derek insisted. He looked in the other direction so that he wouldn't have to watch Freddie stroking her honey-coloured skin. 'I met her stepmother. I wouldn't put it past her to do something like that.'

'Oh, for God's sake!' Freddie said with exasperation. 'Anna has you totally snowed. She sweet-talked her way into buying some time. She's guilty as sin and you know it.'

'I *don't* know it,' Derek said, giving her another glare. 'And thanks for thinking I'm stupid enough to let a woman sweet-talk me out of a job.'

To his irritation, Freddie grinned. 'I don't think you're stupid. Every man eventually falls prey to a woman like Anna Maxwell.'

'I didn't fall prey to her! I'm giving her a lousy two weeks.'

'What's she going to do in that time?'

'I have no idea. She spent most of last night writing in a notebook. I assume that's what she's doing right now.'

'How efficient.' Freddie reached out to pat his arm. 'Look, I know I'm giving you a hard time, but this really isn't your style. I've never heard of you even carrying on much of a conversation with a skip, let alone providing one with room and board while she tries to prove her innocence.'

Derek rested his arms on his knees and stared out at the ocean. A few sailboats glided against the horizon.

Beachgoers meandered along the shoreline, some dipping their toes in the cold Pacific while others braved the deeper waters. Whitecaps shifted in the wind. The sand was dotted with people baking in the sun.

'Well, I'm not reneging on the deal,' he finally said. 'I doubt she would, either.'

'What exactly did she promise you?' Freddie asked. She took a thick folder from her backpack and opened it.

'Twice the percentage Gus offered.' Derek took a swallow of coffee. 'I could use the money.'

Anna's money wouldn't close the gap between his dream of a sailing voyage and making it a reality, but it would help.

He looked at Freddie. She was stretched out on the towel, her long limbs glistening with sunscreen. Even in a modest, one-piece bathing suit, she couldn't hide her natural appeal. The suit hugged her full cleavage and moulded against every curve. A pair of sunglasses and a ponytail held Freddie's long hair away from her face as she perused the contents of the folder.

'What're you reading?' Derek asked.

Freddie held up the papers for him to inspect. 'Background file on my attempted murderer. Last known address is his mother's house. I'll bet he's paid her a visit.'

Derek knew Freddie was incapable of just sitting on the beach. If she wasn't working, she had to be doing something active. Idleness wasn't a word in Freddie's vocabulary.

'You shouldn't take that case alone,' he said.

'I can handle it.'

'You shouldn't,' Derek repeated. 'I'll go with you.'

Freddie didn't respond, but he could tell she was irritated.

'How was the surf date?' he asked to prevent her from protesting. To his surprise, Freddie flushed.

'Really nice,' she said, not meeting his gaze.

'Just nice?'

'Yeah. Gavin's fun to be with. He picked up surfing basics pretty quickly, too.'

Based on her reaction, Derek suspected that more than surfing had been involved. He wasn't at all sure he liked that idea. 'What does he do for a living?'

Freddie shot him a glare. 'What difference does it make?'

'I'm only asking.'

'You are not. You're trying to find some reason I shouldn't see him.' Freddie turned one of the pages. 'Too late. I'm seeing him again tomorrow.'

Derek suppressed the urge to tell her to be careful. 'Don't do anything stupid,' he said instead.

'Like lock him up in my boat's cabin, you mean?'

'Yeah,' Derek said, tilting his head back to drain the last of the coffee. 'Like that.'

'Don't worry.' Freddie flipped over on to her stomach. Her breasts squeezed together into a tempting deep valley. 'So do I get to meet her?'

'Anna? Yeah, if you want to. As long as you don't tell anyone about her.'

'My lips are sealed.'

'Pity.'

Freddie chuckled and gave him a half-heartedly reproving kick. Derek hauled himself up and dusted sand off his legs.

'Speaking of my fugitive, I should go check on her.'

'OK. Maybe I'll come by later.'

'I'll be there.'

'How are you going to take another job if you have to keep an eye on her?' Freddie asked.

Derek grimaced. 'I guess I'm not going to.'

Freddie shook her head and turned her attention back to the papers. 'She's gotta be a bombshell.'

As he returned to the Queen Marina, Derek wondered what it was about Anna Maxwell that had persuaded him agree to this. He figured it had to be the fact that she had actually made some sense.

He went below *Jezebel*'s deck and found Anna seated at the table, studying a thick book entitled *Ocean Passages for the World*. She looked up when he entered. Dressed in torn jeans and a black T-shirt with her half-toned hair, she looked like a misplaced sprite.

'That going to help you with your stepmother?' Derek asked.

Anna shrugged. 'I'm still thinking.'

'Starting tomorrow, you have twelve days left,' Derek said.

'I'm well aware.' Anna closed the book. 'You planning an ocean voyage?'

'Why do you ask?'

She nodded towards the books lined against one wall. 'All those books, not to mention the maps and charts. Seems like you're planning something.'

'I might be.' For some reason, he was unwilling to let her in on his plans. He rested his hands on his hips and levelled his gaze on her. 'Find anything to prove your innocence?'

'Sorry. I wasn't snooping. I was just bored.'

Derek shook his head. 'Twelve days, Anna. You'd better use your time wisely.'

'I'm trying to, but even you have to admit I can't do much cooped up here. You don't even have an Internet connection.'

'OK.' Derek sat down across from her. 'What kind of evidence do you need?'

'Evidence that Cassandra stole the money.'

'What *kind* of evidence?'

'A bank account with the money,' Anna suggested. 'She used a fake vendor account, so maybe something in the paper trail leads back to her. I don't know. A confession.'

'You think anything would make her confess?'

'Doubtful. She's too smart for that.' Anna glanced at him. 'You should know something about her. She's having an affair.'

'That's her big secret?' Derek was hardly impressed.

'Well, it's kind of a kinky affair,' Anna explained.

'Kinky how?'

'She's with this man who controls her,' Anna said. 'Ties her up, spanks her, that kind of thing.'

'How do you know this?' Derek asked.

'I walked in on them once. My father was out of town, and Erin was away at college. I was supposed to be in custody, but I was out on bail at the time. Again.'

'Where were they?'

'At my father's house. In one of the bedrooms. I heard them first and walked in. He had her lashed over the footboard and was giving her a sound thrashing. Needless to say, they were quite surprised to see me.'

'What happened?'

'Cassandra came after me and tried to convince me not to tell my father,' Anna explained. 'Once I realised how desperate she was to keep it a secret, I knew I had something I could use against her. I told her if she left my father, I'd keep her secret.'

'Which she didn't do,' Derek said.

'No. That's why she framed me. To get me out of the way. She knew my father would cut off communication with me, which he did. I haven't been able to contact him at all, otherwise I'd have told him exactly what was going on with his wife.'

'What about email or a letter?' Derek asked.

Anna shook her head. 'I tried. Cassandra has access to his emails. I'm sure she's been monitoring them. He won't take my phone calls, and a letter would never get past Cassandra.'

She shrugged. 'She doesn't want anyone to know about the affair. She knows my father would divorce her and that it would ruin her socially and professionally.'

'You think people would care that much?'

'I don't know about people,' Anna replied. 'But Cassandra certainly would. She'd never be able to stand it if her friends and colleagues found out about her kinky side.'

'What's the guy's name?' Derek asked. 'Her lover.'

'Victor. Victor Thane. Why?'

Derek stood up, a preoccupied look on his face. 'Never mind. Leave it to me.'

'But –'

'You want help proving your innocence, then leave this to me,' Derek repeated. 'An affair like that shouldn't be hard to trace.'

'Maggie was pretty certain you'd help if I asked,' Anna said.

Derek frowned. 'Maggie?'

'Your neighbour. She stopped by yesterday when you weren't here.'

'Why didn't you tell me that?'

'I'm telling you now. She seemed harmless enough.'

'What did you tell her?' Derek knew he could trust Maggie, but the fewer people who knew about Anna, the better.

'I told her the truth,' Anna said. 'Sounds like she has a bit of a weakness for you.'

Derek was slightly embarrassed. 'She's just a friend.'

Anna grinned. 'That's what Cassandra tried to tell me about Victor, if you can believe that. But then she has a weakness for men in general.'

'All men?'

'Well, certain kinds of men.' Anna flushed. It was rather becoming. 'Men like you, I'm sure.'

'What does that mean?'

'Are you fishing for a compliment?'

'Maybe.' He eyed her speculatively. 'What about you?'

'What about me?'

'What's your weakness?' Derek asked, although he suspected he already knew.

Anna shook her head and stood, turning away from him. 'Not men like you, if that's what you mean.'

'I'm sorry to hear that.' He half expected a caustic retort, so he was surprised when she looked at him with something akin to sadness.

'Yeah, me too,' Anna said softly. 'You're one of the good guys, aren't you?'

'That's debatable.'

He went to move past her into the galley, then stopped when she stepped in front of him. Her expression was a combination of curiosity and apprehension. Against his will, Derek tugged on a lock of her blonde hair.

'Your roots are showing,' he said.

'Tell me something I don't know.'

Derek met her gaze. 'I was in your apartment for about half an hour before I woke you up.'

Anna looked at him as understanding dawned. Her flush deepened even as a spark of arousal flashed in her eyes.

'I, uh, I kind of thought you might . . .'

'You', Derek murmured, 'are something to see.'

Anna's slender throat worked as she swallowed. Her lips parted to draw in a breath. A responding arousal flared in Derek's blood. He stared at her mouth. Her lips were full, smudged with bright red, and shaped like a bow. Without thinking, he lowered his head.

Anna met him halfway as their mouths came together in a tentative kiss. She tasted warm and sweet. Derek's lips opened. His hands closed around her shoulders. A sigh of pleasure escaped Anna. She spread her fingers over his chest. Her body relaxed. Their tongues touched. A vivid image of her stretched out on the bed appeared in Derek's mind. He wanted to see her naked again, to stroke his hands over her firm, slender body, to feel her underneath him. He drew her closer. Her breasts pressed against his chest. The kiss deepened.

Derek's hands touched the small of Anna's back, his fingers resting against the swell of her small bottom. He pulled her hips against his. She gasped softly at the sensation of his growing erection. Hot breath escaped her and entered him.

Desire began to heat Derek's veins. With no other woman had he experienced an intense want combined with the urge to help her. She was like a little lost soul who had worked hard to build a thick wall around herself. He wanted to break that wall down.

Her hands moved under his shirt to explore his chest. She touched him with a confidence that belied her apparent defenceless position. She stroked her palms over his chest, her fingers rubbing the flat nipples. Her mouth opened fully to let him drive his tongue inside. He could almost feel the surge of lust that went through her body.

He took off his shirt. Anna pressed her mouth over his chest, her tongue stroking around one nipple. With a mutter, she unzipped his shorts and thrust her hand down to his groin. Her small hand wrapped around his prick. Derek nearly groaned. He started to remove her shirt, wanting to feel her skin naked against his.

'Hello? Derek?' The voice was accompanied by a knock against the side of the cabin. 'Are you here?'

Derek broke away from Anna. She stepped back, drawing a hand over her mouth, her eyes wide.

'Who – who's that?' she asked.

'That's Freddie,' Derek said. Regret twisted through him. 'She's one of the good guys. No debate necessary.'

He turned to go back on deck. Freddie was standing near the cockpit, her arms crossed over her chest.

'Took you long enough,' she remarked, eyeing his bare chest.

'Yeah. Not a good time.'

Freddie raised an eyebrow. 'For me, maybe. I wouldn't say the same for you.'

'What's that supposed to mean?'

Freddie reached out and swiped her finger over the side of Derek's mouth. She held up her finger for him to inspect. 'Red lipstick. Not your colour.'

Derek scowled and wiped his mouth with the back of his hand. He was aware of Freddie's growing disapproval.

'Don't say it,' he muttered.

'I won't.' She turned to climb back on to the dock. 'You already know you're in trouble.'

7

Derek polished off the last of his Apple Pan hamburger and set the paper wrapping and plate aside. The old-style burger joint with its plaid wallpaper, open kitchen and gruff waiters was one of his and Freddie's favourite haunts. She was sitting next to him at the U-shaped counter, her concentration focused on her own burger. They hadn't spoken for the last fifteen minutes as they ate, although Derek sensed that Freddie had plenty to say to him.

'I offered to help her,' he finally said.

She chewed a fry and glanced at him. 'Aren't you already helping her by not arresting her?'

'I mean, I offered to help her with her stepmother.' Derek picked up a napkin and reached out to wipe a spot of ketchup off Freddie's chin. 'The one she thinks framed her.'

Freddie rolled her eyes. 'She really has you snowed, doesn't she?'

'She does not.' Derek was still irritated that Freddie thought he was that gullible. 'She makes a lot of sense.'

'A lot of sense to your prick,' Freddie muttered.

'I haven't slept with her.'

'Not yet.'

Derek scowled. 'And how is this different than dating an informant?'

'Gavin is not a wanted fugitive,' Freddie replied curtly. She reached for her soda and took a long swallow. 'That's how it's different.'

'You sound jealous of Anna.'

'Why in the world would I be jealous of her?'

'It's kind of romantic, don't you think?' Derek asked. 'The bounty hunter aiding a fugitive. You've never had that chance with a skip.'

'Yeah, well, my skips have mostly been sleazy men with either bad comb-overs or outbreaks of acne.'

'That's why you're jealous. Anna is really cute.'

Freddie glowered at him. 'That doesn't make it OK, Derek. But, hey, you don't like what I'm doing with Gavin, I don't like what you're doing with Anna. Must mean we're even.'

'I'm not doing anything with Anna.'

'Not yet,' Freddie repeated.

'I guess you can't say the same about Gavin.'

'Never mind what I'm doing with Gavin.'

'That about answers my question.'

'You didn't have a question.'

'OK, then, what are you doing with Gavin?'

'None of your damn business.'

Derek couldn't help grinning as he reached for his wallet. Even when Freddie was irritated with him, he liked hanging out with her. Maybe because he knew that her irritation always stemmed from their basic and mutual attachment.

Plus, he had to admit that he kind of liked pushing her buttons. When she was annoyed, her brown eyes flared up, her skin flushed a becoming red, and she acted as if he were lower than a cockroach on the bottom of her shoe. He rather enjoyed that spirited side of her.

'OK, Fredericka,' he said after paying the bill. 'Let's go.'

'Don't call me that.' She slung her backpack over her shoulder and marched towards the door.

'Sure thing, Fredericka.'

When Derek caught up with her outside, he could tell that she was trying to suppress a glimmer of amusement.

They crossed West Pico Boulevard to the Westside Pavilion mall and went inside. A blast of artificial cold air greeted them. Fluorescent lamps mixed with sun rays from the arched glass skylight that ran the length of the mall. Glass-fronted shops lined the main walkway like soldiers standing at attention. Benches and glossy potted plants were stationed at strategic points throughout the mall.

As they walked past the stores, Derek noticed several men eyeing Freddie. She was certainly appealing in faded jeans that hugged her long legs and a pink, V-necked T-shirt that couldn't conceal the fullness of her breasts. Her hair was pulled back in its ever-present ponytail, the long length swaying with every step she took. She appeared entirely unaware of the attention she generated.

Derek thought that Freddie's lack of perception only added to her appeal. And while he could certainly understand why men would stare at Freddie, that didn't mean he had to like it. Even though it happened often when they were out together, he still wasn't used to it and he still didn't like it.

'You know, it's only because I don't want you to get hurt,' Freddie eventually said.

He brushed a hand over her hair and nodded. 'I know.'

'And if anyone finds out, Derek, you could be charged for aiding a fugitive.'

'I know that too.' He'd thought of that more than once, but somehow it didn't seem that serious when considering what Anna was up against. 'You're the only one I've told.'

'What about Maggie?'

'She's met Anna.'

Freddie threw him a look. 'How much does she know?'

'Anna said she told Maggie the truth.'

'Derek.'

'Maggie doesn't care, Freddie. She's all about living and letting live.'

'But, if you want to talk about jealousy, she might be jealous that Anna's taking up your time.'

Derek shrugged. 'I'm not worried.'

'Maybe you should be.' Freddie stopped and faced him, her hands on her hips. 'I'm serious, Derek. This could end badly for you.'

'Look, I can handle it,' Derek said. 'I'm not a damn rookie.'

She held up her hands as if in surrender. 'All right, then. How do you plan to help her?'

'Anna claims her stepmother is having an affair,' Derek said. 'I called my information analyst and asked him to look into both the stepmother's and her lover's finances.'

'What if you find something incriminating?' Freddie asked. 'Then what?'

'Then it's up to Anna to figure out what to do.'

'Are you planning to arrest her at all?'

'Not if it's proven that she didn't commit a crime, but she won't be off the hook until the charges are dropped.'

'*If* they're dropped,' Freddie said.

'Yeah.'

'Well, just be careful, all right?' Freddie glanced at her watch. 'Why don't you go get what you need and I'll meet you back here in about an hour?'

'I don't need anything.'

'Don't you have any shopping to do?'

'No, I'm only keeping you company.'

'There must be something you need,' Freddie insisted.

'There really isn't.' Derek sensed her sudden discomfort before glancing up and noticing that they had stopped close to a lingerie store. He almost grinned at Freddie's embarrassment.

'I'll just go with you while you shop,' he offered as he headed for the lingerie store. 'Come on.'

'Derek, this really isn't necessary,' Freddie hissed as she came up beside him.

'I'll help you pick something out.'

Derek went into the store and was greeted with the heavy scents of perfume and lotion. The place had a lush, sensual feel with thick carpeting and floral wallpaper. There were dozens of racks holding pyjamas, bras, panties and other sexy underthings. Classical music filtered from hidden speakers.

'Sir, can I help you?' An attractive young woman hurried up to greet him.

'Yes, we're looking for something for my friend here.' Derek tilted his head in Freddie's direction.

'Your, ah, friend, hmm?' the woman asked.

Freddie's skin was flushed, but a glint of amusement twinkled in her eyes again as she shook her head in reprimand at Derek.

'Something silky and lacy,' Derek continued. He lifted a bra from a rack and held it up. 'Lots of that around here, I see.'

'Well, yes, we obviously have plenty of options,' the saleswoman said. 'If you would care to –'

'I'll just look around,' Freddie interrupted. 'Thanks for your help.'

'Certainly. Let me know if you'd like to try something on.'

'Oh, she will,' Derek said. 'Of course, I'll have to approve it.'

Freddie gave him a hard pinch on the arm after the saleswoman left.

'Ow! What was that for?'

'I'd like to buy my own clothes, thank you,' Freddie said.

'These are clothes?' Derek eyed a little scrap of lace that didn't look as if it would conceal much of anything.

'Would you please go wait outside?'

'No way.' Derek plucked an orange corset-type thing from another rack. 'What about this?'

'I don't like orange.' Freddie turned away from him

and began checking out the merchandise on her own, apparently deciding that ignoring him would be her best course of action.

Derek continued perusing the store before it finally occurred to him that Freddie was probably buying something to wear for her little surf buddy. He looked at her as she examined a price tag on a black lace bra.

A wave of possessiveness gripped him suddenly. The entertaining nature of the situation dissolved, only to be replaced by an image of Freddie wearing that bra, her breasts lifted and cupped by black lace. His prick twitched. He couldn't help wondering what kind of lingerie she was wearing now.

'Well, hell,' he muttered, not at all happy about the sudden turn of events. 'Hey, Freddie, I'm going to wait outside.'

'Good. Go.'

Derek left the lingerie store and went to sit on a bench in the middle of the mall. He tried to shed the sexy image of Freddie from his mind, but it was firmly entrenched.

It certainly wasn't the first time Derek had had a hot thought or two about Freddie. And although he'd have to be a eunuch not to notice Freddie's natural charms, he still felt sort of guilty about it. He knew how hard she worked to be taken seriously as a professional, and he couldn't help feeling as if he were somehow betraying her by actually noticing that she was an attractive woman.

He spent the next half-hour looking surreptitiously at other women and trying to replace the image of Freddie with the image of a stranger. Freddie eventually emerged from the store with a paper bag looped over her arm.

'Are you finally done?' Derek asked, still a little annoyed by his reaction.

'I didn't take that long.'

'Well, at least show me what you bought.'

Freddie handed him the bag. Knowing well that he was making a mistake, Derek peered inside at several lace bras with matching panties and a silky camisole top. A filmstrip of images crossed his mind, all of them with Freddie's delectable body clad in the lingerie and looking entirely tantalising.

'Nice. I'm sure your surf boy will like them.' He closed the bag.

'What makes you think I bought them to wear for Gavin?' Freddie asked.

'Didn't you?'

'Not necessarily.'

Derek frowned. 'Who, then?'

Freddie frowned back. 'Why is that your business?'

'You can lecture me about Anna, but I can't ask you about who you're dating?'

'I'm not even entirely sure I'm dating Gavin,' Freddie admitted. 'We've only been out a couple of times.'

'Looks like you're planning to do a hell of a lot more with him,' Derek remarked.

'So?' Her voice was edged with cold.

'Do you know anything about him?'

'We've been through this before, Derek,' Freddie replied shortly. 'I can handle it.'

'Hey, you were just lecturing me about Anna,' Derek said. 'At least I know what she's about. You're messing around with an informant who, for all you know, is also a criminal.'

'Gavin is not a criminal.'

'You don't know that.'

'Would you please stop questioning my judgement?' Freddie grabbed the bag. 'I've had enough of that.'

'Your judgement was lacking with your last boyfriend,' Derek reminded her, knowing very well that he was being entirely unfair. He couldn't figure out why he was annoyed with her for his own licentious thoughts.

'Yeah, well, he was a loser,' Freddie muttered.

'And Gavin isn't?'

'Hey, cut it out,' Freddie snapped. 'I said I've had enough of your mistrust.'

'It's not you I don't trust,' Derek said. 'It's them.'

'I get it. And I'm tired of you thinking that I can't choose a decent man just because I made one mistake.'

She turned, her ponytail swinging as she strode away, her back tense. Derek silently cursed himself, even as he tried to believe that he was doing the right thing.

Freddie's last boyfriend had not only cheated on her, but he'd managed to steal from her as well. Even after she'd found that out and broken up with him, she slept with him again. Derek had been furious when Freddie admitted that to him. He'd wanted to go and smash the guy's head in, hating the idea of anyone taking advantage of Freddie either mentally or physically.

As it turned out, the guy had left town before Derek could get his hands on him. Good thing, too, Derek thought as he followed Freddie with the intention of making peace. He'd probably have ended up killing the bastard.

Her wrists chafed against the leather cord binding them together. Her body felt constrained in the merry widow that was a size too small. Cassandra closed her eyes as her blood pulsed hot and excited through her veins. She gasped softly as a male hand twined through her loose hair, pulling her head back. A hard mouth came down on hers in a kiss that was as punishing as it was arousing.

'How many times did you take it off?' Victor asked.

'Um, just last – last week. Only that one time.' Cassandra opened her eyes to look at him beseechingly. 'I had to. Richard was –'

'Your husband is no excuse.' Victor's hand tightened in her hair.

'I know. I'm sorry.'

Her heart quickened at the thought of what he might do to her. Older than she was by about twenty years, Victor Thane was like a jagged piece of rock, all hard angles and corners. He was a big man, solidly build, his features sharp and pointed. His hair was black and streaked with grey, his eyes a brilliant green that could spear through her with the intensity of a laser. Cassandra both adored and feared him.

She shifted, trying to ease the tightness in her arms. She was standing beneath a wooden frame, her arms fastened over her head, her body taut.

Victor's hand spread over her plump ass, easing beneath the fabric of the merry widow and between her cheeks. The black cord was fastened securely between her legs. Victor unfastened the hooks of the merry widow and dropped it on to the floor. Cassandra let out a sigh of relief as her body relaxed from the constraint.

'When did you put it back?' Victor asked.

'Right after.'

'After what?'

'After Richard and I...' Her voice faltered on the words.

'After he fucked you?'

'Yes,' Cassandra whispered. 'After that.'

'Such a bad girl,' Victor said. 'You know you are not to remove this cord without asking me first.'

'I know, but there wasn't time. I'm sorry.'

She knew the plea in her voice would do no good. She pulled futilely against the restraints, catching sight of herself in a mirror on the opposite wall. Her body was naked except for the black cord around her waist. It stood out with the starkness of a brand against her pale skin. Her breasts were lifted, hard nipples dangling like berries, her leg muscles long and strained. Her blonde hair flowed around her shoulders.

Before she could ask Victor what he was going to do to her, he slid his hand over her belly and between her legs. He rubbed his fingers over her shaven mons.

'Hmm. Some grooming to be done, I believe.'

Cassandra forced herself not to protest. She tried to keep herself as smooth as possible, but sometimes she forgot or didn't have time. Victor then took it upon himself to whisk away stubborn hairs, an act that never failed to make Cassandra nervous.

Victor reached up to unfasten her wrists. Relieved, Cassandra lowered her arms. Without needing to be told, she went to the bed. She lay down and parted her legs, blushing when Victor chuckled.

'Nice and wet already, aren't you?' He dipped his finger teasingly into her pleats. 'That's my girl.'

Cassandra looked at him with embarrassment and pride. He was naked beneath a loosely tied black bathrobe, his big chest hairy, his penis half stiff. Cassandra hoped that he would order her to suck him off as she loved the subservient position of getting down on her knees.

Victor untied the cord from her waist and set it aside before going into the adjoining bathroom. Cassandra heard the sound of water running. Her hand clenched into a fist as she tried to keep herself from touching her aching pussy. Victor returned with a bowl of hot water, shaving cream and a razor.

Cassandra's heart beat with anxiety. Although she trusted Victor implicitly, she didn't like the feeling of the sharp razor between her legs. Moreover, she detested having to restrain herself from an inevitable orgasm.

She leant her head back and closed her eyes as Victor dabbed at her with a towel. He lathered up the cream and smoothed it over her mons. Cassandra bit her lip as his fingers stroked her. He was the only man who could make her come with the slightest touch. The cream was cool and frothy against her skin. Victor positioned the razor at the top of her thigh, drawing it over her skin and leaving a trail of smooth skin. He worked with expert efficiency as he dipped the razor in water before stroking it over her mound again.

Cassandra's clit pulsed. She could feel Victor's breath on her inner thighs. His fingers spread her lips apart as he worked to remove all traces of offending stubble. After what seemed like an eternity, he wiped her clean with a towel and stood back to admire his handiwork.

'There. Smooth and silky.' He picked up a small bottle of oil and poured a few drops on to his fingers.

Cassandra's hips jerked upward as Victor began to stroke the oil into her skin. He smiled and slipped his hand into her pussy, his forefinger dipping into her opening. Her cunt clenched around his finger. Cassandra thought she might burst from the effort of controlling her arousal.

'Please,' she gasped. 'Please don't.'

'Poor thing,' Victor murmured. 'Just like a cat in heat.'

He put the shaving accoutrements aside and snapped his fingers. 'Turn over.'

Cassandra didn't have to ask what he meant. She turned over and positioned herself on her knees, lowering her head against her arms as her bottom turned up temptingly towards Victor. This was Anna's fault, Cassandra thought resentfully. If that little bitch hadn't started this whole thing, there would be no need for Victor to punish her.

She gave a small cry when Victor's hand slapped against her globes. His hand was hard, his slaps definitive. He gave her a few more spanks until she felt her skin grow rosy and warm. Her fingers dug into her arms as she waited. A seed of fear broke open inside her. A wooden paddle stroked against her chafed behind. Cassandra gritted her teeth as Victor spanked her hard with the paddle. Again. And again.

'Ow! Victor, please.' Cassandra's hips squirmed to

avoid the blows as they began to increase in pace. Pain flared into her skin. She buried her head against her arms. Tears filled her eyes.

'Cassandra.' His voice was stern.

With effort, Cassandra pushed her ass up towards him and was rewarded by a gruff, 'Good girl.'

The paddle continued to rain spanks over her cheeks, heating them with a spectrum of red ranging from pink to crimson. Cassandra struggled to absorb the pain, even as she felt juices dripping between her thighs. The heat between her legs seemed to increase on the same level as that of her bottom. Her body lurched forward involuntarily as Victor punished her to his satisfaction. A delicious combination of pain and heat spread through her blood. The tears spilled over, her pleas muffled against the bedspread.

Finally, Cassandra heard the paddle clatter on to the nightstand. She drew in a breath of relief, somehow remembering to keep her buttocks jutting upward. Victor's fingers stroked over her inflamed cheeks, stimulating her pain again. This time, however, Cassandra didn't mind. She pushed herself towards him as if in invitation. Her body burnt with the need for satisfaction.

Victor chuckled again before she felt his cock pressing against her spread pussy. His belly pressed hard against her bottom.

'Ah, good,' he groaned. 'Nice and hot.'

He dug his fingers into her hips and pulled her back against him. His penis pushed into her channel with sudden force. Cassandra gasped, arching her back as he began to thrust inside her. He reached underneath her to grasp her breasts, tweaking the nipples hard.

Cassandra closed her eyes, soaking up the multiple sensations pouring through her body. She was suffused with layers of heat, pain and pleasure – Victor's belly slamming against her reddened ass, his prick plunging repeatedly into her, his fingers rubbing her breasts, his balls slapping against her cunt. She pressed her head against her arms as the painful ache expanded in the centre of her loins. She flinched when she felt Victor's hand slip between her legs to her clit.

'Oh, Victor,' she moaned. 'Please. Please don't.'

'Control yourself, Cassandra,' he ordered, his voice raspy.

Cassandra reined in her excitement with everything she had. She knew that, if she came without permission, Victor would punish her even more severely. His fingers splayed over either side of her clit, massaging her in the way he knew she liked. Cassandra's whole body throbbed. Victor's thrusts grew longer and slower. She could feel his excitement beginning to peak. He pulled out of her with a shout and sprayed over her bruised behind. Even though she still ached for physical release, happiness spilled through Cassandra at the knowledge that Victor had found satisfaction with her. She wriggled her bottom against him.

'Please.' Her voice was tight.

'Yes.'

He rubbed her throbbing clit. Three strokes was all it took for Cassandra to come violently, her ass arching up as she shook with vibrations. Ecstasy flowed from the pressure of Victor's fingers through her body. Cassandra's eyes filled with renewed tears of relief and gratitude. She collapsed on to the bed in a cloud of satiation and lingering pain.

'Now.' Victor stretched out beside her, his chest heaving. 'You take your punishment well, my darling. But I will not have you doing things without my permission.'

'I know. I'm so sorry.' Cassandra hated the notion that she had displeased him in any way. 'I had to keep Richard from talking about Anna.'

He frowned. 'Does he know where she is?'

'No. I don't think that bounty hunter has found her, either. Otherwise I'm sure we'd know about it.'

Victor pushed himself off the bed. His satiation seemed to slip away from him like a discarded coat. 'I don't like this. I don't like the fact that she's on the loose.'

Cassandra rested her head on her hand. 'She hasn't caused trouble yet.'

'But she could.' Victor's features hardened as he looked at her. It was an expression that pierced Cassandra like an icicle.

'You find out what that bounty hunter is doing,' Victor said. 'She needs to be behind bars. I don't want her showing up on your doorstep. Or mine, for that matter.'

'What do you want me to do?'

'Find out how close the bounty hunter is to arresting Anna,' Victor replied, a thread of irritation in his voice. 'The sooner she's arrested, the better.'

Cassandra lay back and stared at the ceiling. All she cared about was keeping her affair with Victor a secret. If Richard found out, she knew he would divorce her. And she would get hardly anything based on the terms of their prenuptial agreement. More than that, her reputation would be destroyed. She would have to give up everything she had worked so hard for. An affair was one thing, but Cassandra knew that Anna wouldn't hesitate to divulge the wicked nature of her relationship with Victor. The girl had backed her into a corner.

Leave my father or you'll regret it. It hadn't been difficult for Cassandra to make it look as though Anna had stolen the money. It was, however, difficult for her to determine whether or not Anna was truly out of the picture.

8

The tree was covered with little fairies buoyed by gossamer wings and perfect round breasts. Their expressions were sly and secretive, their long-fingered hands hovering close to one another's hourglass figure. Their bodies were concealed by their long flowing hair, which allowed glimpses of white skin, pink nipples, shadowy crevices. No doubt they were sexy little things.

Derek turned away from the picture. Small paintings and sketches hung like jewels on the walls of the Armand Hammer Museum. A few visitors were wandering around the gallery, leaning forward to get a closer look at the precise work of Hanson Jangliz.

Freddie was standing nearby, her expression concentrated as she looked intently at an oil painting. Clad in her usual attire of jeans and a V-necked purple T-shirt with her hair pulled into a sloppy knot, she looked both wholesome and appealing.

Derek approached her with the unwelcome thought that Freddie's body could easily rival those of the fairies. He wondered briefly what kind of lingerie she was wearing underneath her practical clothing. And he wondered if she'd worn it for Gavin Vincent. Somewhat to his disappointment, his information analyst hadn't produced any kind of record on the guy. Not even a speeding ticket. Although Derek was glad Freddie wasn't dating a guy with a record, the thought of her dating anyone still made him uneasy.

He stopped beside her and looked at the painting. A satyr had one of the buxom fairies in his clawlike grip, pressing one hand between her legs as he grabbed at her breast with the other. The fairy seemed torn between excitement and resistance.

'Exotic and perverse,' Derek said, remembering Freddie's comment about the artist's work. 'I guess that's an accurate description if you like fucking fairies.'

'Or fairies who fuck,' Freddie replied dryly. She slanted him a glance. 'I suspect you wouldn't mind either one.'

'Not if they look like that.' Derek followed her to the next painting. 'So what makes this art and not fairy porn?'

'Why can't it be both?'

'Put these fairies in a skin magazine and no one's going to call it art,' Derek remarked.

'There's nothing imaginative about a skin magazine,' Freddie said. She paused in front of a glossy painting that depicted a weird birdlike creature fluttering his wings around a voluptuous fairy skimpily dressed in rags. 'You have to admit this is creative.'

'Sure. Kind of a turn-on, too.'

'Derek!' Freddie chuckled, even as she looked around quickly to make sure no one had overheard his comment.

'Well, it is.' Derek nodded towards another painting of a centaur and a fairy engaged in a lusty encounter. 'Come on. Even *you* have to admit that's pretty sexy.'

'What do you mean, even *I* have to admit it?'

'Just that you're not exactly one for exotic perversion.'

'That doesn't mean I'm a prude.'

'I never said you were,' Derek countered. 'No one who wears the kind of lingerie that you do is a prude.'

Freddie flushed, her skin glowing a charming crimson. Yeah, she could rival any one of the fairies all right. Derek was beginning to wonder if he was more turned on by the art or by Freddie herself. He cleared his throat and focused on another painting.

'I think this artist is actually trying to say something about society,' Freddie said. 'These images represent the secret desires and dreams that everyone keeps hidden.' .

'I had dreams like these when I was a teenager,' Derek said.

'Derek, would you be serious?'

'I am serious. Believe me.'

'Read the brochure,' Freddie said. 'Hanson Jangliz has created a whole world around a series of characters that symbolise various psychological and physical urges. The satyrs, for example, represent selfish lust while the centaurs represent love.'

'What do the fairies represent?'

Freddie consulted her brochure. 'Uh, female desire.'

'Sounds about right.'

'Female desire is not best symbolised by an erotic fairy,' Freddie muttered.

'What's it best symbolised by, then?' Derek was rather intensely curious about her answer.

Freddie shrugged. 'I don't know.'

'Come on. Flowers? Nature?'

'Good Lord! What are you, a bad poet?'

'Then what?'

Freddie looked at a painting for a moment. 'Fibre,' she finally said.

'Fibre? You mean like oat bran?' Derek could not have been more disappointed.

'Well, if you think about it, fibre has several definitions,' Freddie explained as she and Derek walked out of the gallery and into the light, airy courtyard of the museum. 'It's a filament, something that can be made of different materials. Cotton, nylon, wool. You can spin it into yarn, which can be used to make an infinite number of materials. You can weave anything out of a single natural strand. You can dye it thousands of different colours. Fibre can even be made of glass and can carry coloured light. It also means strength and integrity. Fibre is what gives substance to something.'

'And that symbolises female desire?'

'Sure. A woman's desire is exactly like that. It can be

spun into countless forms, absorb hundreds of colours, transmit light. It helps give texture to a woman's character. It can be as fragile as glass or as strong as a thick rope. Weave together all the various threads of female desire and you have everything from simple, handmade rugs to elaborate, multicoloured tapestries. All because of fibre.'

'Damn.' Derek shook his head. Freddie would never cease to amaze him.

'So what symbolises male desire?' she asked.

'Uh, let me think.' Derek racked his brains. 'Seeds, maybe. Little grains that you sprinkle all over and then they grow into these lush plants and flowers.'

'With the help of a lot of fertiliser,' Freddie muttered.

Derek laughed. He gave Freddie a quick squeeze against his side and was rewarded with one of her easy grins. Even as he let her go, the warmth of her body lingered. In that instant, Derek was struck by an urge to touch her again, to pull her towards him and feel her body fully against his.

He almost reached out. Freddie stopped, as if sensing his tension. Their gazes met. Her brown eyes sparked with a hint of confusion and something else, something deeper and hotter.

Derek stared at her. She had never looked at him like that before. He wanted to say something, but then Freddie turned away, ducking her gaze as she headed into the lobby.

'Are you hungry?' she asked, her voice unnaturally light. 'We can grab some lunch, if you have time.'

'Yeah, sure.' Derek was almost ashamed at the direction of his thoughts.

It was the damn lingerie, he reasoned. If he hadn't known about Freddie's penchant for silk and lace, he wouldn't be thinking about her in that way. Ignoring the fact that it was far from the first time he'd noticed her charms, he was uncomfortable with the growing intensity of his response to her.

He shook his head again as if to clear his thoughts. Maybe it was because of Anna. After all, having a woman like her living on his boat made for a certain degree of sexual tension.

That was it. Derek almost breathed a sigh of relief as he held open the door of a café for Freddie. Between Anna and Maggie, he was wound up to breaking point. He was reacting to Freddie simply because she was there. Once he got things out of his system, his relationship with Freddie would return to normal. Fibre or no fibre.

As he sat across from Freddie at the table, he couldn't help wondering what kind of tapestries her own desire would weave.

'Why haven't you left?' Maggie looked at Anna with curiosity. 'You could go on the run again, couldn't you?'

Anna shrugged. It was true, she could walk out the door right now if she wanted to. Derek hadn't padlocked the door at all, nor did he have any intentions of doing so.

She gave Maggie a faint smile. 'I don't know where I'd run to. Besides, Derek just said yesterday that he would help me. I could use all the help I can get.'

'Anything I can do?' Maggie stretched her long legs out in front of her and rested them against the side of a chair. She was wearing a purple bikini top with a flowered sarong wrapped loosely around her waist. With a tall, frosty glass of lemonade in one hand, she looked as if she should be swinging in a hammock on an exotic Pacific island. 'I'm quite resourceful myself, you know.'

'I need evidence against my stepmother,' Anna said. 'I don't know how to get it. Derek said that he would help me, although he hasn't yet told me what he plans to do.'

'Well, Derek does know a lot of people,' Maggie told

her. 'Law-enforcement officers, informants, criminals, bondsmen. Other bounty hunters. I'm sure he could call in a favour or two on your behalf.'

'Why do you think he'd do that for me?' Anna remembered their kiss with a shiver. She knew that she would be attracted to him whether he helped her or not, but his offer had certainly intensified his appeal.

Maggie gave her a slow smile. 'I suspect he has something of a fairy-tale complex. He wants to be the prince rescuing the lovely damsel.'

Anna flushed. 'Well, he's got the wrong damsel.'

'No, he doesn't.' Maggie continued looking at her as if Anna were a painting to be studied. 'Where did you come from, Anna?'

'What do you mean?'

'You're very unusual,' Maggie said. 'You're sort of this combination of tough and ethereal. How did you get that way?'

'Circumstances, I guess. You'd be tough, too, if you had the stepmother that I do.'

'What happened to your mother?'

'She died when I was young.' A familiar, old rush of sadness went through Anna. 'It's strange. Cassandra is nothing like my mother was. I still can't really figure out why my father married her.'

'Maybe exactly because she's nothing like your mother,' Maggie suggested.

'I don't know. She's never liked me. She tolerates my sister, but only because Erin toes the line. I never have. I guess that's why I'm in the situation I'm in.'

'Being your own person is nothing to be ashamed of,' Maggie said. 'Hell, look at me and Derek. You think either of us ever toed the line?'

'You don't have Cassandra to deal with.'

'Oh, we all have our own version of a wicked stepmother.'

'Who's yours?'

'It was my ex-husband,' Maggie said. She closed her lips around the straw in her glass and sucked. 'You'd never met a man who was more uptight. Even had to iron his undershirts. He couldn't fuck me worth a damn. Anything outside of the missionary position was taboo. I was with him for ten years.'

'Why so long?'

'It took me that long to figure out that I had other options.'

'So what brought you here?' Anna asked.

'To live on the boat, you mean? When I was with John, we lived in the suburbs. Classic little house with a picket fence at the end of a tree-lined cul-de-sac. I drove a four-door sedan. When I finally left him, I wanted a life that was the exact opposite of the life I'd had with him. Living on a boat seemed like a good first step.'

'And did you find that opposite life?'

'I'm happier now than I've ever been,' Maggie said. 'I make a living independently. I set my own schedule. I do what I want when I want.' She grinned. 'And with whom I want. So, yes, I found that life.'

'Good for you.' Anna wished she could say the same. She didn't even know if she had the courage to seek out a life different than the one she had been leading. Nor did she know what that life might contain.

'One day, you will,' Maggie said.

'What?'

'One day, you'll find your opposite life, too,' Maggie said. 'Believe me, you'll know it when you do.'

'I hope so.'

'I'll talk to Derek about letting you come over,' Maggie said. 'As I said, he knows he can trust me.'

'But can I?' Anna murmured.

Maggie laughed. 'Only if you want to. And if Derek said he would help you, then he will. He's nothing if not reliable. Well, he's many things in addition to being reliable.'

'I'm beginning to discover that.'

'Are you sleeping with him?' Maggie asked bluntly.

Anna blinked in surprise. She still didn't have a sense of how proprietary the other woman was about Derek.

'Um, no. I'm not.'

Maggie smiled. 'Not yet.'

'Does that – uh, does that bother you?' Anna asked.

'The idea of you with Derek? I find it quite exciting.'

Maggie had a way of looking at her with such frank admiration that Anna didn't know how to respond. She had always been confident of herself when men were involved, but her experience with women was somewhat lacking.

She allowed her eyes to slide over Maggie's abundant breasts, the delicious cleavage, the tanned expanse of her curvy waist. She imagined her own body pressed against the other woman's, feeling all that warmth and softness.

Arousal pooled in Anna's blood. She swallowed hard and gave Maggie a shaky smile. 'I find it exciting too, if you want to know the truth.'

'Well, of course,' Maggie replied. 'I mean, just look at Derek. What woman in her right mind wouldn't want to fuck him?'

She rose with one movement and approached Anna. Anna's breath caught in her throat. She stared at Maggie, into her eyes, which were the deep green of an oak leaf. Maggie lifted her hand and placed her fingers gently against Anna's cheekbone.

'May I draw you?' she asked.

'What?'

'I'd like to draw you,' Maggie said. 'You know, several pencil sketches. Portraits. I'd like to see if I can capture your uniqueness on paper.'

Anna didn't think there was the slightest thing unique about her, but she was nevertheless flattered by the request. 'Um, sure. I guess so.'

'Excellent.' Maggie's mouth curved into a smile.

She was close enough so that Anna could smell the scent of fresh air clinging to her skin. She stared at Maggie's mouth, lips that curved like a full ocean wave. She had a sudden desire to lean in and kiss the other woman.

Before she could surrender to the urge, the sound of footsteps echoed above. Maggie pulled away from her as the door opened and Derek entered.

He looked quite tasty in jeans that hugged his long legs and a T-shirt emblazoned with the UCLA logo. He looked from Anna to Maggie and frowned.

'Hello,' Maggie said cheerfully. 'I was just getting to know your new tenant.'

'You weren't invited.'

'Since when do I need an invitation?' Maggie picked up her glass and took a sip. 'You're the one that's abandoned poor Anna. What is she supposed to do here all alone?'

'You shouldn't even know about her,' Derek said.

'Hey, you're the one that brought her with you when you were looking for me,' Anna reminded him. 'That's how she recognised me in the first place. I just filled in a few of the details for her.'

'Yeah,' Maggie chimed in.

Anna was unprepared for the self-disgust that appeared in Derek's expression.

'Freddie's right,' he muttered.

'About what?'

'I must be insane. I could get us all arrested. I've never been so fucking unprofessional.'

'Then why are you doing this?' Anna asked.

'Doing what?'

'Helping me.'

'I have no idea.'

'Maybe it's because you believe me,' Anna suggested. 'And there's nothing unprofessional about helping someone you believe has been wronged. In fact, I can't think of anything more admirable.' She eyed him somewhat cautiously. 'By the way, who, exactly, is Freddie?'

'Just a friend. She's also a bail-enforcement agent.'

'Not your girlfriend?'

'No.' He nearly glowered at her. 'Not my girlfriend.'

'She's pretty hot, though,' Maggie remarked.

Anna looked at Derek for a moment. She knew a thing or two about men, and she suspected that his look of discomfort sprang from more than just irritation with Maggie.

'Just friends, huh?' she asked.

'So he says,' Maggie replied.

'Enough.' Derek's voice was short.

Apparently knowing when to take a hint, Maggie rose in a lithe movement and headed for the door.

'I'll see you both later. Behave yourselves.' She tossed Anna a smile as she went out.

Derek went to the refrigerator and took out a beer. His expression was somewhat brooding as he looked at Anna.

'So where did you go?' she asked.

'An art exhibition at the Armand Hammer,' Derek said. He took a swallow of the beer and continued gazing at her. 'Let me ask you something. If you had to come up with a symbol for female desire, what would it be?'

'A symbol?'

'Yeah. Like a rose or a river or something. What symbolises female desire?'

'Where did you come up with that kind of an intellectual question?' Anna asked.

'This artist used fairies as a symbol.'

'I guess that makes sense,' Anna said. 'But I'd have to say a peach. Round and ripe, dripping with sweet juices, soft, yet firm to the touch.'

Derek looked almost relieved. 'Nice.'

'What do you think about female desire?' Anna asked.

'I think I like it.'

Anna smiled, even as a nagging thought plagued her.

'So, um, you've never slept with Freddie?' she asked.

'What kind of question is that?'

'Hey, you're the one who brought up female desire.'

'No. I've never slept with Freddie, for God's sake.'

'What about Maggie?' Anna asked.

'What about her?'

'She seems to know you intimately,' Anna suggested.

'Why are you so interested in my sex life?'

'Is that what I'm asking about?' Anna said, although she thought she hadn't been so curious about something in a long time.

She let her eyes slide over Derek's lean, muscular body. Even though he wasn't quite her type of man, she still wanted him badly. A memory of their kiss dominated her thoughts. Derek had had such an exquisite combination of strength and tenderness that she couldn't help but wonder if his kiss reflected his sexual approach. She suspected that it did indeed.

'I like her,' Anna said. 'Maggie.'

'Evidently she likes you too,' Derek said. He rested his hands loosely on his hips and looked down at her.

'Is that a bad thing?' Anna asked.

'Not if you don't think so.'

'I don't.' Anna's blood was still warm from Maggie's sensual appeal. She reached out a tentative hand and placed it on Derek's chest. 'It's true that you've taken a risk for me. I really do appreciate it.'

'You'd better.'

'I do.' Her hand slipped down the front of his T-shirt. He didn't move when she slipped her hand underneath the cotton and spread it over his hard abdomen. His skin was warm and taut.

'What have you done with Maggie?' Anna asked boldly.

'What do you think?' Derek curled a lock of her hair around his forefinger.

'Was it good?'

'She's always good.'

'I thought so.' Anna moved her hand down to the fly of his jeans. Although she knew he was a physical man, she was mildly surprised to discover that a hard bulge was already forming beneath the denim. She paused.

She was nervous. It was a foreign emotion to her. Men rarely intimidated her, but Derek was different. She wasn't afraid of him, but she suspected that she could become more attached to him than she had any right to be. And attachments were the last thing she needed.

Anna let out her breath slowly. Maybe it was just physical attraction. Maybe once she satisfied that urge, she would get rid of this nagging fear of her own emotions. Based on his reaction to their kiss, Anna knew he was just as aware of their attraction as she was.

She tilted her head back to look at him.

'Remember when I said you weren't my type of man?' she asked.

Derek nodded.

'I was wrong,' Anna said. 'You are.'

'Prove it.'

The husky challenge went straight to her blood. Her heart began to thud with a heavy beat. She could feel his gaze on her as if it were a touch.

'How?' she whispered.

'You figure that out.'

Anna's hands trembled slightly as she worked the buttons of his fly and dug her hand underneath the elastic of his shorts. His growing erection was smooth and warm against her fingers. Anna gave a little murmur of excitement as her own body began to respond to his arousal.

She glanced up at Derek again, thrilling in the growing heat of his grey eyes. She had always loved this moment when anticipation thickened between her and a man, the instant when everything had yet to be discovered.

Derek's hand moved around to the back of her neck. He drew her towards him while simultaneously lowering his head. Their mouths met with clumsy but urgent pressure. Anna closed her eyes as her lips parted, as his tongue swept into the moist cavern of her mouth. His penis swelled against her hand. She stroked her thumb over the tip, rubbing a drop of moisture back into his skin. A shudder rained through his body.

Derek moved his mouth more insistently over hers. His hands grasped her waist, pulling her hard against him. Anna remembered clearly what the weight of his clothed body had felt like over hers. Naked, she knew it would be exquisite.

Her nipples pebbled against his chest. Anna started to try to remove his jeans, but Derek eased her hands away.

'I want you naked first,' he murmured against her lips.

'You've already seen me naked.'

'This time I want you to know it.'

A bolt of excitement spiralled through Anna. She stepped away from Derek, allowing him the ability to unzip her jeans and pull them over her legs. She rested her hand on his shoulder as she stepped out of them. Derek's fingers brushed over the tattoo of a sunflower that decorated her outer thigh.

'How many of these do you have?' he asked.

'Six. You'll see them all.'

'I can't wait.'

Derek pulled her shirt over her head, leaving her standing before him in her black bra and panties. Even though he had already seen her wearing even less than that, an unexpected glimmer of modesty rose in Anna. It had been some time since she was with a man for reasons that extended beyond pure sex. Derek already knew more about her than any man had in a long time.

Anna stripped slowly out of her underclothes, her gaze on his. Derek's eyes raked over her pale body as if he were assessing everything about her. His eyes shifted from her face to her small-boned shoulders, the slender curve of her waist and flat belly, her short legs and neatly trimmed mound. His hands cupped her breasts, his fingers lightly pinching her nipples before he grasped her waist again and lifted her on to the table. Anna's gasp was lost in the renewed pressure of his mouth. Her pussy dampened with a swell of arousal.

'How do you want to fuck me?' she whispered.

'Hard.'

Anna shivered. She reached into his jeans again and closed her fist around his cock. The shaft pulsed heavily against her palm, throbbing into her blood. Derek eased away from her to strip out of his clothes. Anna drank in the sight of his athletic body – the smooth, tanned planes of muscle, the dark hair covering his chest, the thick erection projecting from a nest of curls, the hard sinews of his arms and legs.

'Do it now,' Derek said.

She looked up at him. 'Do what?'

'Touch yourself,' Derek said. 'Get yourself hot.'

Anna's skin grew crimson. She had never been an uncertain woman, but Derek was so different from the men she was usually with that she couldn't help feeling somewhat shy. She watched him watch her.

'Go on,' he urged, his voice husky.

Anna moved back on the table, spread her legs apart and slipped her hand between her thighs. She dipped her fingers into her inner folds as if testing the waters. She was hot and slick. Derek's eyes moved down her body and settled between her legs. Anna's awareness of Derek's gaze was like the most potent of aphrodisiacs. Her breathing was rapid.

She drew a forefinger over the damp crevices, brushing her thumb against the increasingly taut button of her clit. Her hips bucked upward involuntarily, as if seeking the penetration of her own hand. Her thighs quivered. She stared at Derek's groin with growing hunger for the pleasure of his thick cock. She rubbed the slippery folds of her sex, already feeling a familiar and luscious tightening of her nerves.

Derek's gaze grew smoky as he watched her. He grasped the base of his erection, sliding his fist up and down the shaft in a rhythm that matched the movement of Anna's hand. The sight of him pleasuring himself stimulated Anna's excitement all the more powerfully. She cupped her breast with her other hand, rubbing her fingers over the hard point. A light perspiration broke over her skin. Her pussy was beginning to ache with the need to be filled. She pressed her forefinger into her channel, her flesh tightening.

Derek moved closer. Somewhat to Anna's surprise, he spread his body over hers and bent to place his lips against her throat. His teeth bit gently over the pulse throbbing at the side of her neck. Anna drew in a sharp breath, her hand going slack between her legs. Derek's body was heavy over hers, his naked skin both rough and smooth. She closed her eyes as he began to slide his mouth over her, his tongue tracing the various tattoos that adorned her arm, her hip, the swell of her breast. His hand slipped over her mound, covering her hand and pressing her fingers into her pussy again. Anna opened her eyes to stare at him as their hands began to move simultaneously against her pleats.

'Don't make me wait,' Anna whispered.

'I won't.'

He eased away from her. Anna spread her legs wider, allowing Derek a full view of her splayed sex. He took hold of her right calf and hooked her leg over his forearm. Anna's heart thudded hard against her chest, filling her with a mixture of anticipation and desire. She watched Derek with heavily lidded eyes as he positioned the head of his cock against her. She almost expected him to drive into her with sudden force, but instead he began to ease into her with deliberate slowness. His hard flesh felt sensational against her sleek interior, pulsing hot against her. Anna moaned, stretching her arms over her head in a posture of utter submission.

Derek's body tightened with the effort of retaining control as he placed his hands on the table and began to thrust into her. Anna lifted her legs, drawing them up towards her chest to allow him to penetrate her to the fullest extent. Her mind fogged with pure sensation. His groin began to slap against hers with the wet, rhythmic sound of sex. Her bottom lifted off the table.

'Oh, fuck,' Anna hissed, her hands grabbing at his forearms to steady herself. 'Do it. Fuck me raw.'

His cock drove into her with increasing power. Anna's body jounced. Derek lowered his head to capture one of her nipples between his teeth. Sparks of sheer pleasure spilled through her body. Before Anna could ask him, Derek slipped his hand between their sweaty bodies and found the aching bud in which her pressure was centred. He circled it with his thumb, spreading his fingers along the sides until the tension became too much to withstand. Anna came with a shriek, clutching Derek as if he were a life raft in a storm-drenched sea. Her fingernails dug into him as rapture exploded through her body. Her hips bucked upwards as Derek drove into her with a shout and the release of his own pleasure.

She wanted him to collapse on top of her. She wanted to feel the full weight of his body covering her, but instead Derek lifted himself away from her.

His mouth lingered briefly against hers, his breath hot, his hand skimming over her belly.

'A peach,' he muttered. 'Could not be more accurate.'

9

Freddie got out of her car, tugging her baseball cap lower over her forehead. The hot night air was layered with the typical smog of the Inland Empire – the collection of Riverside and San Bernardino County cities that stretched east of Los Angeles into the heart of California. Freddie put her hand on her lower back and stretched, easing the tightness after the seventy-mile drive from Santa Monica.

She glanced both ways on University Avenue, one of the main thoroughfares of the small city. Riverside was known primarily for one of the University of California campuses, but this part of town was lined with cheap motels and apartment buildings that often served as rooms for prostitutes. Street lamps burnt yellow pools into the cracked pavement. Brown palm trees seemed to sag in the heat. Stoplights flashed red and green. Aside from passing cars and some skimpily dressed women loitering at the corner, the street was relatively quiet.

Freddie checked her Glock 9mm semi-automatic, which she carried in an Archangel holster underneath a lightweight jacket. She also had easy access to a canister of mace.

She glanced at her watch. Raymond Thompson's mother had promised that she would be out of the apartment for the weekend visiting her sister in Palm Springs. She had told Freddie that her son might very well be at the apartment that weekend.

Freddie crossed the street and checked the cars in the building's parking lot. She didn't see a pickup truck that resembled Raymond's, but she went up to the apartment anyway to see if he was there. No one answered the door. Freddie returned to the parking lot to wait.

She sat down on the low concrete wall that bordered the lot. She had started making arrests on her own only for about the past year. Before that, Derek had always insisted on accompanying her. Even now, he still often told her that he wanted to go with her on a job. Freddie had quickly learnt that the only way to prevent him from insisting was not to tell him when she was planning an arrest. Of course, he was never happy when he learnt about it after the fact, but at least the tactic gave Freddie a degree of independence.

Derek. He drove her crazy sometimes, but she knew he always had her best interests at heart. That was more than she could say for most of the previous men in her life. Derek's overprotectiveness might very well prevent her from making a mistake, but Freddie also wanted to learn from her mistakes rather than go through life with extreme caution. If Derek had his way, she wouldn't date anyone, let alone have sex. That was no way to live. It certainly wasn't the way Derek lived.

Freddie couldn't help being amused as she recalled his behaviour in the lingerie store. She'd known that he was aware of her penchant for silk and lace. Several times over the years, she had caught him glancing at the open neckline of her shirt if she happened to be leaning over. And there was the time that she'd worn a dark-green bra underneath a pale-yellow T-shirt because most of her other clothes had been in the laundry. Derek had noticed that, all right. She'd noticed him notice. His gaze had caused something hot and pleasurable to swirl in her blood.

Freddie stopped her line of thought when a beat-up Ford truck pulled into the parking lot. A big man wearing overalls emerged and went up the outside stairs. Freddie checked the licence plate to confirm this was Raymond's car.

She wasn't surprised that he'd shown up at his mother's house. Skips often found it difficult to stay away from their mothers and girlfriends. Mothers like Edith Thompson were willing to help bring their sons in out of fear of what might happen to them or what they might do to others.

Considering Raymond Thompson was wanted for stabbing a man, Freddie understood why Edith was anxious to see her son pay his dues.

She climbed the steps to Edith's apartment. A light burnt in the window. Freddie peered through the window into the living room. It was quaint and grandmotherly with dried-flower arrangements, a crocheted quilt over the tattered sofa and family pictures on the walls. No sign of Raymond.

Freddie tried the door handle. It turned. She opened the door slowly. Country music drifted out from one of the back rooms. Freddie stepped into the foyer. For some reason, she paused to wipe her feet on the floral welcome mat.

She pulled out her Glock and took a few cautious steps. Her heart rate sped up. The sound of running water and a man singing emerged from the bathroom. Freddie crossed the living room and peered down a darkened hallway. Light glowed from the half-opened bathroom door.

Freddie eased into position against the door. Raymond continued to sing off-key about losing both his woman and his pickup truck. Freddie waited.

After what seemed like aeons, the shower finally turned off. Freddie began pushing the door open.

'My woman left me heart-broke and sad,' Raymond sang as he pushed open the shower door. 'Man, but I was feeling so bad.'

Freddie stepped into the bathroom just as he reached blindly for a towel. She whipped the towel out of his reach and pointed her gun at him.

'Hands up, Raymond,' she ordered. 'You're under arrest.'

Raymond's eyes flew open. He was a burly bearded man with a substantial potbelly and thick arms and legs. Freddie assessed him quickly in case she had to use physical force.

'What the fuck?' he snapped.

'Get 'em up,' Freddie repeated. She stepped into the steamy bathroom, her gun trained on him. 'You jumped bail. You're a wanted man.'

Raymond stared at her for a second before he threw back his head and started to laugh. 'Oh, you're good, honey. You're going to take me in, are you? Since when did women become bounty hunters?'

'Bail-enforcement agents,' Freddie said. She grabbed a towel from the rack and tossed it to him. 'I'm taking you in, Raymond.'

He grinned, making no move to cover himself. 'You just try it, honey.'

A bolt of anger shot through Freddie. She was accustomed to being patronised, both by people in the business who didn't know her and by male skips, but their attitudes only fired her determination.

'One of us is at a serious disadvantage here,' she said. 'I'll give you a hint. It's not me.'

'Oh, a tough talker, huh? Do you talk dirty as well as you talk tough?'

Freddie reached for her handcuffs. 'Turn around, Raymond. Put your hands behind your back.'

'Yeah, OK. Sure.' He reached for his clothes, which were piled on the toilet seat.

Freddie lunged for the clothes and swept them out of his reach. His shorts hit the floor with a clanking noise. Freddie rooted in the pockets with one hand until she came up with his gun, a .38 Derringer. She stuck the gun in her pocket and kicked the shorts back in his direction.

'Get dressed, or I'll parade you down to jail in all your glory,' she ordered.

'Bitch, put that gun down before you hurt yourself.' Raymond stepped out of the shower and reached for his shorts. 'You ain't taking me anywhere.'

He made a move as if he were going to put his jeans on, but then swerved and launched his big body towards Freddie. His fist slammed into her jaw with a cracking noise. Pain radiated up the side of Freddie's head. Raymond hurled into her, taking them both to the floor. Freddie grunted. Before his weight landed fully on her, she brought her knee up and drove it into his groin. Raymond yelped and doubled over.

Freddie pushed him off her and grabbed her can of mace. Before he'd recovered, she gave him a punishing spray in the face.

'Ow! Son of a bitch!' He clawed at his eyes with one hand while clutching at his groin with the other.

Freddie stood up, breathing hard. Her head throbbed. 'Your mother wants you brought in, Raymond. Get dressed.'

'You bitch.' He scrambled to pull on his shorts. 'You ain't –'

Before he could zip the fly, Freddie pushed him forcefully on to his stomach and yanked his arms behind his back. She slapped the cuffs on his wrists, then fastened a pair of leg shackles on to his ankles.

'Stand up.' Freddie grabbed his arm and pulled him up. 'Stop whimpering, Raymond.'

'You're a bitch. What the fuck was that stuff?'

'Mace. Let's go. You cause any more trouble and your neighbours will have quite a scene.'

She saw his shoulders slump in defeat, even though his expression remained defiant. She'd brought in enough men to know that they considered it humiliating to be arrested by a woman.

Freddie let him slip his feet into a pair of moccasins, but didn't risk allowing him to dress in anything other than his shorts. She nodded towards the door.

'Let's go. You'll be spending the night in the Riverside detention centre.'

She ignored the pain in her jaw as she herded him downstairs to her car. She drove him to the jailhouse and left him with the officers in charge. As soon as the paperwork was filled out, she called the bondsman and told him that she'd completed the Thompson case.

Freddie snapped her phone closed and sat in her car for a minute. Her entire head still ached from Raymond's blow, but satisfaction overrode the pain. There was no feeling in the world like successfully bringing in a skip. Well, almost no feeling like that.

Freddie rolled down the windows, thrust the car into gear and headed back towards Los Angeles.

'Nice.' Freddie watched Gavin approach her from the ocean. Water sluiced off his wetsuit. He looked like a sea creature, all sleek and wet. 'You're improving.'

His white teeth flashed at her. 'I've been practising.'

'Have you?'

'Yeah. Don't want to disappoint my teacher.' He stopped in front of her, still grinning. 'With my luck, she'll make me stay after school.'

The rate of Freddie's breathing increased slightly, as it always seemed to do when she was just a few feet away from Gavin.

'Would that be such a bad thing?' she asked.

'Nope.' He leant closer to her and lowered his voice as if in confidence. 'In fact, I'm counting on it.'

He winked and headed off to grab a towel. Freddie shook her head as she watched him stripping out of the wetsuit. She liked being with him. He was all charm and little substance, but so wonderfully uncomplicated. She didn't have to keep a tight rein on herself when she was with Gavin. Nor did she want to.

Freddie followed him to where they had left their belongings. She gathered up her stuff and slung her backpack over her shoulder. She hadn't been in the mood to surf today, but she had certainly enjoyed watching Gavin. Her gaze wandered over his bronze chest.

'You want to borrow my shower?' she asked. 'I live just down the street.'

Gavin rubbed a towel over his wet hair. His muscles moved smoothly underneath his tight skin. 'I thought you'd never ask.'

Freddie told herself to make it clear that things would remain platonic, but the words refused to emerge. Her blood quickened. Derek would go ballistic if he knew what she was letting herself in for.

She frowned. What did she care what Derek would do? It was none of his damn business if she invited Gavin to her apartment. And it was really none of his business what she chose to do with Gavin once he was there. Besides, she wasn't the one making out with a skip she should have arrested days ago. And probably doing other things as well.

'Hey, what's up?'

'What?' Freddie turned her attention back to Gavin.

'You were frowning.'

'Nothing. Sorry. I was just thinking of something else.' Freddie resolutely pushed Derek from her mind. 'You ready to go?'

'Yeah. How's your jaw?'

'OK.' Freddie had told Gavin that the impressive bruise she sported was the result of an unpleasant encounter with a surfboard. Thankfully, he appeared to believe her.

As she and Gavin walked to her apartment, Freddie became increasingly nervous. She tried to shake off the feeling. She tried telling herself that this was a bad idea, but she couldn't make herself believe it. Derek never seemed to have a problem taking pleasure when and with whom he wanted, so Freddie didn't see why she should be any different. She sighed and reminded herself that she wasn't supposed to be thinking abut Derek.

She unlocked her apartment door and ushered Gavin inside.

'Nice place,' he said, looking around at the light, breezy furnishings. 'Doesn't seem like you, though.'

'Why not?'

He shrugged. 'I don't know. You seem more practical. This is kind of girly.'

Freddie grinned. 'I can't be practical and girly at the same time?'

'You can be anything you want.'

Freddie went to get him a clean towel and pointed towards the hallway. 'Bathroom's at the end of the hall. Take your time.'

Gavin went into the bathroom and closed the door behind him. The shower started. Freddie went to pour herself a glass of lemonade. She'd been dealing with showering men a lot lately, although she knew that Gavin would look far better naked and wet than Raymond Thompson had.

A warm shudder ran down her spine. An image of Gavin appeared in her mind – water raining down on his strong body, his hands soaping his tanned skin, wet hair plastered to his head, rivulets running over every muscle.

Freddie pressed the cold glass to her forehead. Her whole body was hot just thinking about Gavin in the shower. She thought this must be what a cat in heat felt like.

After a few minutes, the shower turned off. Freddie watched the bathroom door open. Gavin emerged naked except for a towel wrapped around his waist. His chest was shorn of all hair and looked temptingly smooth. He lifted his hands to rub his hair dry, causing the towel to slip lower.

'Um, do you want some lemonade?' Freddie asked.

'Is it spiked?'

'No.'

'Then yes.'

She poured him a glass and pushed it across the kitchen counter. 'Why don't you want it spiked?'

'Because I want to have a totally clear head when I fuck you.'

Freddie's head snapped up at the rawness of his words. A lightning bolt of arousal was followed by a hint of annoyance.

'What makes you so sure you're going to fuck me?' she asked, making an effort to keep her voice cool.

'You don't want me to?' Gavin asked.

'That's not the point.'

He moved closer to her. The clean smell of soap drifted from him. Freddie's blood heated.

'OK, then,' Gavin said. 'Maybe you could fuck me instead.'

Freddie's hand tightened around the glass. 'Pretty confident, aren't you?'

Gavin stopped in front of her. He was about as tall as she was, so their eyes were level. His were a clear dark blue ringed with gold.

In all her years as a bail-enforcement agent, Freddie had learnt to trust her instincts. From the beginning, she believed that Gavin Vincent was at heart a decent man who would not intentionally hurt her. He was well aware of his own appeal, but she could relax around him. She could have fun. Maybe she could even be a little dirty for once without worrying about her professional reputation.

Gavin's blue eyes softened slightly as they looked at each other.

'It's been a while for you, hasn't it, Freddie?' he asked.

Freddie swallowed hard. She stared at the tanned column of his throat. He smelled so good. She leant in with hesitation and pressed her mouth gently against the hollow of his throat. His skin was smooth and warm. She let her fingers drift over his hard abdomen. She heard his sharp intake of breath.

'Maybe,' she whispered. 'We could fuck each other.'

Gavin's hands smoothed up over her shoulders to her neck. He tilted her head back and angled his mouth over hers. Heat burst through Freddie's blood when their lips came together. Gavin pressed his tongue into her, sweeping the inside of her mouth. Her whole body yielded.

Gavin wrapped the length of her ponytail in his hand as he deepened the kiss. Freddie let her fingers slide lower until they were at the edge of his towel. His muscles were smooth and hard. His lower body pressed against hers. She felt his penis begin to stiffen under the towel.

He slid his mouth gently over her jaw. His tongue traced the shell of her ear, swirling around the little whorls and causing shivers to rain down her back. Freddie closed her eyes. She moved her hand tentatively lower and cupped his growing erection through the towel. He muttered encouragement, shifting his hips to position himself more securely in her hand. His cock felt delicious, heavy and firm.

'Are you wet?' The question rasped against her ear. His breath was hot.

'What do you think?'

He responded by sliding his hands underneath her T-shirt. He unfastened her shorts and slipped his fingers into her panties and between her legs. His touch alone sent a shock of pleasure through her, and Freddie let out a moan when he began to fondle the damp folds of her pussy.

'I want to see you naked,' Gavin whispered.

'You first.'

He smiled against her neck. 'Easy enough.'

With one movement, he loosened the towel and let it fall to the floor. Freddie drew in her breath at the sight of his thick, jutting penis. Her sex throbbed. She grasped him in her hand and rubbed her fingers against the taut sacs below.

'Your turn,' Gavin said.

Freddie stepped back. Her fingers trembled slightly as she stripped off her T-shirt and shorts. She had always been self-conscious about the size of her breasts, which, while they weren't enormous, always seemed to attract attention from the men in her line of work. She was wearing pink lace panties and a matching bra through which her stiff nipples were clearly visible.

Gavin's eyes swept approvingly over her body. 'I guess you can be practical and girly at the same time. You are one sexy lady, Freddie James.'

He cupped the weight of her breasts in his hands, rubbing his thumbs over her nipples. The combination of his touch and the coarse feel of the lace caused sensation to coil through Freddie's loins. She pressed her thighs together as her clit pulsed in rhythm with her heartbeat. Her grip tightened on Gavin's cock, her thumb smoothing over the moist tip.

He reached behind her to unfasten the clasp of the bra. Her breasts fell unfettered into his hands. His breathing increased as he plucked at the nipples with his fingers, then stroked his hands over her curved waist. Freddie grasped the edge of the countertop for support. She watched Gavin as he hooked his fingers into the elastic of her panties and pulled them slowly over her hips. He pressed his lips between her breasts, his tongue teasing her skin as he moved to capture one of her nipples in his mouth.

Freddie's grip tightened on the counter as arousal radiated over her nerves. Gavin's tongue swirled lusciously around her areola. Then, to Freddie's surprise, he went down on his knees in front of her. He took off her panties and slid his mouth in a line down her belly, dipping his tongue into her navel before reaching the curly nest of her mons. Freddie's lips parted on a groan as Gavin's fingers spread her open, his thumb brushing lightly against her clit. Her hips bucked against him. His tongue twisted around her inner pleats, stoking her heightened arousal. Sweet juices coated his mouth.

Freddie delved one hand into Gavin's hair, trying to press him even closer to her. He gripped her bottom. His tongue dipped into the humid channel of her sex. Freddie gasped. Her legs trembled. Gavin moved to press his mouth gently against her clit while he eased his forefinger into her. The tension grew more intense. Her skin dampened with perspiration. Before she could control herself, Freddie came against Gavin's mouth with a volatile force. She let out a cry of pleasure as her body shook violently.

'Good,' Gavin murmured. 'Good.'

His hands tightened on her bottom, his tongue easing as the shudders continued to vibrate through Freddie's body. She went slack against the counter as she tried to catch her breath.

Gavin smiled up at her. 'Only the beginning, Freddie.'

The look in his eyes sparked her arousal all over again. He lifted himself up and pressed his mouth against hers. Freddie moaned at the taste of her own salty flavour on his lips.

'Where's the bedroom?' Gavin whispered.

'Just down the hall.'

He pushed his hands under her thighs and lifted them around his waist. Freddie wrapped her long legs around him and let him carry her to the bedroom.

'Don't trip.'

'Don't worry.'

His belly felt taut against her spread pussy. She wanted to grind herself against him until she came over and over again. He lowered her on to the bed, his tongue driving into her mouth again as his own urgency began to peak. Freddie parted her legs wider and hooked them around his hips. His penis pushed against her before easing into the tight opening. Freddie gasped, stretching her arms over her head and shifting her lower body to facilitate his access.

'Ah, Freddie. You're so damn tight.' Gavin held himself up on his arms as he continued pressing into her.

His cock felt like hot wax. She could feel him pulsating against her inner walls. She had almost forgotten what a good cock felt like inside her body. She gripped Gavin's hips and thrust herself up towards him.

'Go on and fuck me,' she whispered.

He thrust into her, causing her breasts to bounce with the movement. Freddie cried out with pleasure. Gavin slipped his hands underneath her thighs and pushed her legs out wider so that she was fully spread. He plunged into her with increasingly wet noises, his chest damp with sweat, his muscles tight. He leant over her and massaged her breasts, tweaking the nipples between his fingers and raining pleasure through her once again.

'What do you want?' Gavin whispered.

'I ... I want ... I want to come again.'

'Touch yourself for me.'

Unable to help herself, Freddie reached down to rub her hard clit, wanting to come again as she had never wanted to before. She couldn't take her eyes off Gavin's body, his muscles moving smoothly under his damp skin like a well-oiled machine. His thrusts were hard and rhythmic, stoking her excitement all over again, driving into her blood.

'Come,' Gavin said as he lowered his head to press his mouth against hers. 'Come all over my cock.'

He captured her tongue between his lips just as Freddie's stimulation erupted for the second time. Her body stiffened and bucked against him as she fairly squealed with pleasure. Gavin increased the pace of his thrusts until his own gratification peaked. He grabbed her hips and drove into her pussy, giving a shout as he exploded inside her.

Gavin collapsed on top of Freddie, his chest heaving. Freddie gathered her arms around him and stroked her hand through his thick hair. She closed her eyes and absorbed the delicious sensations still twining through her blood.

'You were right,' she murmured.

'About what?' His voice was muffled against the junction of her neck and shoulder.

'It's been a while.'

Gavin lifted his head to look at her. 'But it was OK?'

For the first time, Freddie saw through his overconfidence to the vulnerable core. She smiled and continued stroking his hair. 'Oh, yes. More than OK. I could get used to this.'

Gavin returned her smile. 'I plan to help you do that.'

He rolled over and took her with him so that she was nestled against his side. Freddie rested her head against his arm and closed her eyes. Good. Finally. This was good. She could enjoy Gavin and not be worried about anything or anyone. Not even Derek could – dammit!

Freddie stopped that persistent line of thought, irritated that she couldn't even make love to a man without wondering what Derek would think. She hated hinging even her personal life on his approval or disapproval. Freddie lifted her head to kiss Gavin, determined once again to banish all thoughts of Derek from her mind.

10

Anna stared at the stapled papers Derek had given her. The documents were blurry but legible photocopies of Victor Thane's bank-account activity over the past few months. The most prominent activities were deposits made at regular intervals that – Anna suspected – would match the amounts stolen from Jump Start's accounts.

She looked at Derek. 'Where did you get this?'

'I know a good information analyst.'

'This is it, isn't it?' Anna asked with a growing sense of excitement. 'This is exactly what I need. Now we just need to tie Cassandra to Victor.'

'Which shouldn't be difficult if they're still having an affair.'

For the first time since this entire mess started, Anna began to feel as if she might actually have a way out.

'Thank you,' she said.

Derek shrugged. 'Just took a phone call. You want to give that to your father?'

'After we prove that Cassandra is really having an affair with Victor,' Anna said.

'I've found out where they usually meet,' Derek said. 'Seedy motel in south San Francisco. I'm going to take a flight up there this weekend.'

Anna looked at him with a mild sense of wonder. 'Why are you doing this for me?'

'Like I said. Weakness for pixies, I guess.' He turned and headed out on deck. 'Come on.'

Anna followed him. She hadn't been out of the cabin since Derek brought her here. She sat down in a deck chair. The horizon had swallowed up the last bit of sun, leaving the sky streaked with red and gold. As she breathed in the scent of salty air and listened to the water lapping against the hull, Anna could easily understand why Derek would choose to live on his boat.

'Why *Jezebel*?' she asked.

'She was the queen of Israel who turned Ahab against his god and towards the worship of her own god. She was also accused of sexual immorality.'

'You have a thing for her?' Anna asked.

'Just a general thing for scheming, sexually immoral women.'

He winked at her. Anna smiled faintly.

'You'd have a thing for Cassandra, then,' she remarked.

'No. Only for her stepdaughter.'

A seed of warmth broke open inside Anna along with an emotion that was bittersweet. Much as she liked Derek, much as she desired him, she couldn't help but think that their time together was limited. She couldn't foresee any kind of a future with him – at least, not if she were to reconcile with her father. Richard Maxwell would appreciate Derek's sense of honour, but the two men couldn't have been more opposite. As far as Richard would be concerned, a bounty hunter who lived on a boat was no match for either of his daughters.

Anna herself wasn't even certain that Derek was anything beyond a sexual equal and a friend for her. She had to straighten her own life out before there would be room for anyone else.

She turned her gaze towards the sky and stared at the sprinkle of stars.

'I can't imagine talking to my father again,' she eventually admitted.

'You think he'll even see you?' Derek asked.

'I don't know.'

Anna bit her lip. She hadn't spoken to her father in months. He had made it clear that, if she screwed up one more time, he'd not only fire her but cut her off completely. As it turned out, he'd had her arrested and disowned her. Anna guessed she was probably fired as well.

'I haven't been easy on him,' she admitted. She stood and went to the side of the boat, resting her hands on the railing. 'I used to run around with the wrong kind of man a lot.'

'Used to?' Derek asked.

Anna smiled wryly. 'Haven't run into the wrong kind of man for a while. I was in jail a few times for disorderly conduct. Once for petty theft. Had a stint in juvenile hall when I was seventeen. Ran up my father's credit cards. Generally I was a pain in the ass. I guess it shouldn't be a surprise that my father thinks I'm capable of stealing that amount of money from him.'

'Why were you such a pain?'

Anna was surprised at the question. No one had ever asked her that before. 'I don't know. Maybe I was trying to get back at him for marrying Cassandra. Or maybe I just haven't known what else to do with myself.'

'Sounds like you had a pretty good job with Jump Start.'

'Only because my father gave it to me. I would never have gotten the job on my own. Or any other job, for that matter.'

'Why not?'

Anna shrugged. 'Not much I'm good at, I guess.'

'I find that hard to believe,' Derek said.

'Believe it.'

'Everyone's good at something. Just a matter of finding out what it is.'

'I wish I knew how to do that,' Anna said. 'How did you find out you were good at bounty hunting?'

'I went to UCLA with a guy whose brother was a bounty hunter,' Derek said. 'I thought it sounded like the coolest job. I ended up working for him until I graduated, then started my own business. It was more interesting than anything I'd learnt in college.'

'I never went to college,' Anna confessed. 'Well, I started to go to San Francisco State, but I dropped out after only one semester.' She gazed at him for a minute. 'What about your parents?'

Derek stared out at the harbour, his elbows resting on his knees, his hands loosely clasped. 'My father left town when I was five. Never saw him again.'

'What about your mother?'

'She died about ten years ago.'

'Did she approve of your job?'

'She approved of anything that would make me happy,' Derek said. 'She was a great lady.'

'She'd have to be to raise a son like you.' Anna shook her head as soon as the words were out of her mouth. 'I didn't mean that to kiss up.'

'I don't mind you kissing up,' Derek said. 'In fact, I encourage it.'

They both smiled, even as something flared between them. Anna's hands tightened on the railing. Her pulse increased a few beats as her gaze slid over Derek's tanned, hairy legs, his strong hands, the breadth of his shoulders. She remembered his hands on her, pressing her legs apart.

'Come here,' Derek said.

A little thrill rose in Anna at the order. She approached him cautiously and stood in front of him. He didn't move. Anna slipped her hand around the back of his neck. His skin was warm, even hot, his thick hair brushing against her wrist. Anna brought her mouth down to his, her tongue flickering out to stroke his lower lip. She felt the shudder that went through him. Encouraged, she eased her legs over his so that she was straddling his thighs. His lips parted. Her hand drifted down to his groin. Ah, yes. His reaction to their mere kiss was bold and immediate.

Anna's hips stirred as she rubbed herself against his leg. His breathing grew more rapid. His hands settled on her waist. Anna wanted to strip down completely, to feel the cool night air on her naked skin, but she was dimly aware of the possible presence of others. Although discretion had never been her forte, this was hardly the time to draw unnecessary attention to herself.

She pushed her hands into Derek's hair, enjoying the sensation of the coarse strands against her palms. She knew that his hair would feel delicious sliding across her body. Her sex contracted, blood pulsing into her increasingly sensitive clit. She moved her hands to Derek's groin and fumbled to unfasten his shorts. Within seconds, she had him in her hand. Her breath caught. He really did have a gorgeous cock, long and thick with veins. Anna traced the veins with her fingers, then grasped the base and began to stroke him.

Derek shifted and groaned. His eyes drifted half closed as Anna continued to stimulate him. Her own arousal was augmenting like a pressure cooker.

'When you were watching me,' she whispered against his lips, 'did you touch yourself?'

Derek shook his head. His hips pushed upward, driving his prick into the vice of her fist. Male fluids lubricated her movements so that his erection moved easily against her fingers.

'Did you want to?' Anna asked.

'God, yes.' His hands tightened on her waist as he guided her to writhe against his leg.

Anna did, grinding her pussy with heightened intensity. His thigh was rock hard underneath her. The air seemed to compress around them. Anna began to increase the pace of her strokes. She cupped his balls with her other hand, squeezing them with light pressure.

'Next time, I want you to touch yourself when you're watching me,' she said, her voice hoarse with excitement. 'I want to watch you.'

'Oh, you will,' Derek grunted as his lower body bucked towards her. 'You definitely will.'

Anna felt his body tighten. She continued to stroke his cock from base to tip as his augmenting pleasure fuelled her own. She pushed her sex hard against him, loving how the friction of her panties and jeans rubbed her in all the right places. Fire pooled in her lower body, even as her sex felt achingly empty. She remembered what Derek's cock had felt like inside her, how he stretched and filled her beyond capacity. The thought burst a rocket of arousal through her, pouring sensations into her blood. Anna gave a squeal of delight, her head falling back as she continued to masturbate Derek.

His pleasure peaked before hers ended. With a groan, he pushed his cock into her fist as a spray of semen covered her hand. His body jerked, his muscles tightening. Still writhing slowly against his thigh, Anna continued to stroke him as the final sensations ebbed.

'So nice,' she murmured, lowering her lips to his again. Their kiss was long and hard.

Anna eased herself off him as he straightened his clothes. Pressing her thighs together, Anna sank back into a chair. The sound of their breathing filled the air.

'Did you know this would happen?' Anna asked. 'Between you and me?'

'No. I'm not sorry it has, though.'

'Me neither,' Anna said. After a moment, she asked, 'Does Freddie know about me?'

Derek opened his eyes. 'Why are you always asking me about Freddie?'

'Curiosity.'

'Yeah, she knows about you. She also thinks I'm an idiot.'

'What's she like?'

'She's tough, but sweet. A good girl who's a black belt and can take down a man twice her size.'

'Wow. Sounds impressive.'

'She is.'

Anna wondered about the undercurrent of his voice, something both proud and almost wistful. She didn't think Derek Rowland would be wistful of anything or anyone. This Freddie must really be something else.

'You think I'll meet her one day?' Anna asked.

'Maybe.'

He sounded slightly reluctant, as if he were unwilling to share Freddie.

Anna turned to look at the water. Beyond the boats surrounding the harbour and the tall masts silhouetted against the sky, the ocean stretched out like a vast, blue-grey carpet. Anna thought she should probably be a little jealous, but she wasn't. She would never have any possessive feelings towards Derek, maybe because she knew he'd never have any towards her.

She turned her head to look at him. He was sprawled with lazy satisfaction in his chair.

'When are you going?' Anna asked.

'Where?'

'On your sailing trip.'

'Someday.'

'Just you?'

'Just me.'

'Sounds nice,' Anna said. 'Lonely, but nice. Sometimes dealing with other people is a pain in the ass.'

'Don't I know it,' Derek muttered.

'I'll be out of your way soon enough,' Anna said.

'I didn't mean you.'

'Who did you mean?'

'No one in particular.'

'Not me either, I hope,' said a female voice.

Derek and Anna turned to find Maggie strolling across the deck towards them. Anna wondered for an instant whether Maggie had witnessed her and Derek's little display, but, if she had, then she gave no indication of it. She lowered herself into a chair and favoured them both with her provocative smile.

'Did you tell Derek about my request?' she asked Anna.

'Not yet.'

'What request?' Derek said.

'I asked Anna if I could draw her,' Maggie said. 'Just a few sketches. We wanted to make sure you'd let her come to my place.'

Derek shrugged. 'Anna's call.'

'Good. I'll be there on Friday afternoon, Anna. Are you available?'

Anna had to smile. 'More than I've ever been.'

The sun glowed over the horizon and burnished the tops of the Santa Monica mountains. The Venice Boardwalk was just beginning to come to life with the usual array of tourists, bikers, in-line skaters and street performers. Artists were setting up their booths and stalls. The Pacific waters rolled on to the beach, where a few early-morning sunbathers had come to stake their claim. Palm trees sprouted from grassy banks separating the boardwalk from the beach.

Derek watched Freddie as she leant against a park bench to stretch her flexible body before their run.

'A surfboard.' He was not at all convinced.

'Yeah.' Freddie looked away from him towards the beach. She bent her leg to stretch her calf muscle. 'Don't worry. I'm fine.'

'Don't lie to me, Freddie.'

'I'm not lying. I'm fine.' Freddie looked at her watch and started jogging in place. 'Come on. Three miles, and then I want to meet your bombshell skip.'

'Who hit you?' Derek stood there with his arms crossed and a hard expression on his face, as immovable as a massive rock. He never discounted the degree of danger Freddie was in when she apprehended a fugitive, but she didn't often show up with a bruise on her face the size of a large fist.

Irritation flashed in Freddie's eyes. 'I said I was fine.'

'It wasn't that bastard Gavin, was it?' Derek asked, his blood simmering at the very idea.

'No!' Freddie stopped and shook her head vehemently. 'God, no.'

She sighed, reaching up to refasten her ponytail. 'I got into a tussle with the skip I arrested for David. The guy wanted for attempted murder.'

'What the fuck, Freddie! I told you I'd go with you.'

'And I told you I could handle it,' she reminded him.

'What happened?'

Freddie didn't respond. A homeless woman dressed in a tattered coat and pushing a junk-filled shopping cart stopped beside her.

'Got any change?' the woman asked in voice made raspy by too many cigarettes.

Freddie dug into her pocket and found a couple of dollar bills. She handed them to the woman, who thanked her and shuffled off.

'What happened?' Derek repeated.

'He hit me before I could cuff him,' Freddie said. 'But it ended quickly, and I brought him in without further incident, OK? It's over, and I'm fine.'

Derek frowned. 'How did he manage to hit you?'

'He was reaching for his clothes and he –'

'He was doing what?'

'Reaching for his clothes,' Freddie repeated patiently. 'He was in the shower and –'

'You apprehended an attempted murderer in the shower?'

'Yes. And stop looking at me like I'm the biggest damn fool on earth. I knew what I was doing. He couldn't have been more vulnerable.'

'Neither could you have!' Derek snapped. 'What if he'd

overpowered you? What if he'd done worse than hit you?'

'He didn't.'

'He damn well could have,' Derek retorted. 'What did you have on you?'

'A Glock and a can of mace.'

'That's it?'

'It was all I needed,' Freddie replied coldly.

'What about a taser? An ASP baton?'

'I don't own a taser or a baton.'

'You should have borrowed mine.

'I didn't need them.' Her voice was tense.

'You should still have them,' Derek said. 'Better you're overprotected than not protected enough. You shouldn't have been alone. What if he'd knocked you out? Then what? Do you think you could've arrested him then?'

'Enough!' Freddie held up her hand to stop his tirade. Her brown eyes hardened with annoyance and resentment. 'Jesus, Derek. You know better than anyone what I can do. Are you forgetting the time I wrestled a two-hundred-and-fifty-pound biker off you? I believe he was busy pounding your head into the ground.'

She looked away. To Derek's shock, he could have sworn he caught a glimpse of tears in her eyes.

'Hey, Freddie –'

'Look, I have enough bullshit to contend with from other men in this business,' Freddie snapped. 'I don't need it from you, OK? I thought you knew me better than that.' She paused. 'I thought you knew me better than anyone.'

Silence descended between them. Derek walked a few paces away to rein in his anger. He knew she was right. He knew she could handle herself better than most male bounty hunters. He also knew he would never be able to stand it if anything really bad happened to Freddie.

He took a deep breath and approached her again. 'OK. You're right. I'm sorry.'

He expected that she would accept his apology and they'd start their run. Instead Freddie shook her head. She stared out at the beach, her profile set hard.

'What?' Derek asked.

'I'm tired of this, Derek. I'm tired of you not believing in my own judgement.'

'What are you talking about? I believe in your judgement.'

'You do not.' She threw him a resentful look. 'Every time I take a job or make a decision, you find it necessary to tell me to be careful as if I'm totally reckless. I want to go out with Gavin, and you treat me like I'm a nutcase. I bring in a fugitive successfully, and you criticise my methods. You act like everything I do, every decision I make, is wrong.'

Derek lifted his hands in surrender. 'I don't think that. You know I don't.'

'No, Derek, I really don't know what you think.'

'I said I was sorry.'

'Yeah, until you start giving me crap again.' Freddie bent to retie her tennis shoe, even though the laces were already tied.

Derek was annoyed by her effort to avoid eye contact with him. 'So what do you want me to do?' he asked.

'Maybe we need some time apart.'

'What the hell does *that* mean?'

Freddie straightened and put her hands on her hips. 'Look, we spend a lot of time together. Maybe we just need to live our own lives for a while. You're busy with Anna, I'm seeing Gavin, we both have plenty of work to do. I think we should focus on that.'

Derek frowned. 'You're serious.'

'Yes.'

'You don't want to see me any more.' He couldn't believe what he was hearing any more than he could imagine not seeing Freddie at least every other day.

'Just for a while,' Freddie said.

'How long is a while?'

She shrugged. 'A month or so.'

'A month?'

'I don't know, Derek,' Freddie said irritably. 'I need some time alone, OK?'

'Alone or with your surf boy?'

'You see?' Freddie snapped. 'This is what I'm talking about. I need to be away from you, Derek. You're driving me fucking crazy.'

'Fine.' He held up his hands and stepped away from her. 'Forget it. Go be alone or whatever.'

'Don't you get it?' Freddie asked. 'Don't you get why I need to be by myself?'

'Yeah, I get it. I get that you've got something going with what's-his-name . . .'

'His name is Gavin Vincent,' Freddie said coldly. 'And this has nothing to do with him. You obviously don't understand anything I've been saying to you. Maybe not seeing each other will give you time to figure it out.'

'I don't need to figure anything out.'

'The hell you don't,' Freddie said. 'And, by the way, you have no right hassling me about Gavin when you've got a little chippy locked up on your boat. If that's not inappropriate, then I don't know what is. So, if you're going to give me a bad time, at least don't be a hypocrite about it.'

With that, she turned on her heel and started jogging down the boardwalk. Derek suppressed the urge to follow her. He watched her go, then turned and went back to the parking lot.

'Fuck!' He stalked towards his Mustang. His blood was hot with anger. He could cut Freddie out of his life. If that was what she wanted, that was what she would get.

11

Cold air wafted underneath the hem of Cassandra's calf-length, camel-hair coat. Her legs were bare, her feet encased in high-heeled shoes the colour of butter. Gold earrings dangled from her ears, the curvilinear design matching the necklace that encircled her white throat.

The doorman gave her a respectful nod of greeting and held open the door of San Francisco's Bellevue Hotel. Cassandra's heels clicked against the marble floor as she passed the reception desk. Several well-dressed patrons sat in the lobby, their understated clothing and coiffed hair indicative of their upper-class status.

Cassandra crossed the lobby and entered the lounge. Chandeliers hung from the ceiling, and low music drifted through the air. The chairs and booths were swathed in a rich, velvety material, and a curved bar rested along one side of the room. Bartenders with bow ties and crisp white shirts stood before a mirrored wall of shimmering bottles and glasses.

Cassandra let her gaze sweep over the room. Three couples, two women seated together, a small group of businessmen. Not ideal, but certainly better than nothing. She walked to the bar and eased herself on to a barstool.

'May I take your coat, ma'am?' one of the bartenders asked.

'No, thank you. I'd like a Scotch and soda, please.'

She shifted on the stool as the bartender went to mix her drink. She turned slightly to scan the room again, allowing one shapely leg to slip between the folds of the coat. A businessman glanced at her, his gaze lowering to her leg. He was middle-aged and paunchy, but he had a nice face and was wearing a well-tailored suit. His eyes met hers again, and he lifted his glass in an appreciative salute.

Cassandra smiled slightly. She looked towards the door as another man entered. Her heart skipped a beat. This one looked more promising. Perhaps a little younger than she, he had thick blond hair and blunt, arresting features partly concealed by wire-rimmed glasses. He wasn't particularly handsome, but he had an air of command about him that was rather appealing.

Cassandra's heart rate increased when he started towards the bar. He was halfway across the room before he looked at her. Unlike the other man, he didn't assess her with bold appreciation. He sat a few barstools away from her and ordered a drink.

'And another for the lady,' he told the bartender.

Cassandra slanted her eyes in his direction. She was accustomed to men offering to buy her drinks, but they usually asked her first before turning to the bartender. In that instant, she knew she had him right where she wanted him.

'Scotch and soda from the gentleman,' the bartender informed her unnecessarily as he placed another glass on the bar.

'Thank you.' Cassandra nodded towards the man and turned her attention back to the drink.

As she knew he would, he moved closer to her. Their gazes met. Behind his glasses, his eyes were a nice blue, the colour of cornflowers. A glimmer of excitement sparked to life in Cassandra. She shifted, allowing the folds of her coat to part slightly and expose the pale triangle of her neck and chest.

'I'm Harry,' the man said, holding out his hand.

'Cassandra.' She slipped her hand into his. His grip was firm and certain. Yet another plus, she thought. Men with limp grips always proved to be weak in other ways as well. 'Thanks for the drink.'

'My pleasure.'

'You're in town on business?' Cassandra asked.

'Yes. I work for a law firm in Boston.'

'You don't have an accent.'

'I'm from Boston by way of Iowa,' Harry replied. 'I'm a corn-fed Midwesterner to the core.'

'Nothing wrong with that,' Cassandra murmured.

'What about you?'

'I'm from the South Bay.'

'What are you doing in the city?'

'Hoping to stay out of trouble.' Cassandra flashed him a smile.

Harry blinked and gave her a smile in return. 'Maybe I can help you.'

'Stay out of trouble, you mean?'

'Or dash your hopes.'

Cassandra chuckled and sipped her drink. The spark of excitement caught flame and began to grow. Her thighs were pressing together, a pulse starting to beat between her legs. She shifted again and let her bare leg slip from her coat.

'So what are you doing tonight?' she asked Harry.

'I don't have any plans,' he replied. 'But things are starting to look promising.'

'Good. Why don't we get some fresh air?' Cassandra picked up her pocketbook, which she had rested on the bar. She put the strap over her shoulder and began walking towards the door.

Harry followed. Men could be so easy, Cassandra thought. She stepped out the door and took a breath of foggy air. Traffic clogged the street amid lights and noise from Union Square. Cassandra turned and walked away from the square up Grant Street. She didn't turn to see if Harry was following her, but she knew that he was. They always followed her.

'Cold out here for a walk, isn't it?' Harry asked as he fell into step beside her.

'Who said anything about walking?' Cassandra replied.

They passed several upscale clothing shops, an art gallery and a restaurant. Street lights cast burnt yellow circles on the pavement. Cassandra's heels clicked. Her legs prickled with goose flesh. She caught sight of a black car parked in front of a French restaurant. Nervous excitement spiralled upwards into her chest.

She turned and ducked into an alley that separated the restaurant from a bookstore. The concrete was littered with bits of trash and grease. Several trash cans rested alongside the brick wall of the restaurant, overflowing with garbage.

'Where are you going?' Harry stopped at the alley entrance, his expression bemused in the dim light.

'Follow me and find out.'

Harry followed her into the alley. Cassandra stopped and turned towards him. Her heartbeat accelerated again. She waited. She always liked to wait and see if these men knew what she wanted them to do. If they didn't, they often weren't worth the trouble. Thankfully, Harry approached her with a purposefulness to his stride.

'You like this kind of thing, huh?' he asked.

'I'm not the only one, I'm sure.' She felt the brick wall against her back, cold and hard.

Harry stopped in front of her. His hands went to her waist as his head lowered to hers. Their mouths connected, hot and tasting of bitter alcohol. Harry's kiss was clumsy and not particularly arousing, but his tongue was adept at swirling over the crevices of her mouth. Cassandra eased her head away from him and pressed her mouth against his ear. He smelled like spicy aftershave.

As she bit gently at his earlobe, Cassandra glanced towards the entrance of the alley. A little thrill raced through her when she saw the tall figure standing there watching them. She stroked her hands over Harry's shoulders, feeling the stockiness of his body underneath his suit. His mouth slid over her cheek to her neck, his lips warm and wet. His breathing became heavier.

Cassandra unfastened the top few buttons of her coat. Harry let out a murmur of surprise as he discovered that she was nearly naked underneath her coat. The cold brushed against her bare skin, a delicious contrast to the heat of his mouth. Her breasts swelled, her nipples hardening in reaction to both the air and her growing arousal. Harry slid his hand down into her coat, over the expanse of skin between her breasts and down to her belly. He paused when he encountered the lacy edge of the ice-blue panties she wore.

'Is this all you've got on?' he asked huskily.

'Yes. And they stay on.'

Cassandra smoothed her hands over his somewhat pliable chest. He was big, but his body was soft. She didn't bother unbuttoning his shirt, reaching instead for his belt buckle and the zipper of his trousers. She dug her hand into his fly and the opening of his shorts. Her hand closed around his half-hard cock. It was thin, but long and straight. She lowered her gaze to look at it, the smooth rod of flesh dusky in the light. Cassandra's manicured hand moved up and down the shaft, working him to a full erection.

Harry drew in a gasp. He clasped one of her large breasts, rubbing his thumb over the nipple as he pressed himself into her grip. His body tensed with increasing urgency. Cassandra's pussy grew damp. She was seized by a desire to feel Harry's prick inside her, even as she knew that would never happen. He fumbled to unfasten the remaining buttons of her coat, exposing her pale body clad only in the skimpy pair of lace and silk panties.

'Good God!' Harry whispered, a sheen of sweat breaking out over his forehead. 'You're fucking amazing.'

Cassandra smiled. Her skin prickled with cold, but her

increasingly hot blood warmed her from the inside out. She braced herself on her heels and grasped Harry's trousers, pulling them over his hips so that they dangled around his knees. Cassandra glanced towards the alley entrance again, her lips curving. She knew she was pleasing him. She knew she was pleasing them both.

Harry's hand began to move underneath the elastic of her panties. Cassandra grasped his wrist.

'I like it on the outside,' she whispered. 'The silk feels unbelievable against my cunt.'

A hard shudder passed through his body. He slipped his hand between the warm flesh of her thighs, pressing his forefinger into the pleats of her sex. Cassandra let out a little moan of encouragement, lifting her leg to wrap it around his and facilitate his access. The silk dampened instantly with her juices, moulding against her inner folds. She moved her mouth over Harry's cheek.

'Rub my clit,' she invited.

He did, splaying his fingers on either side of the sexual bud that protruded against the wet silk. Arousal wound around Cassandra's lower body. She continued stroking Harry's shaft, her fingers slipping down to caress the balls pulled up tightly between his legs. Her body and mind became awash in multiple sensations – the heat of Harry's body against hers, his fingers working at her cunt, the hard brick wall against her back, the softness of her coat, the cold night air. The knowledge that her lover was watching her.

A groan spilled from her throat. Cassandra leant her head against the wall and closed her eyes, her lips parting as Harry's mouth came down on hers again. His tongue drove into her as if he were fucking her. His fingers worked with increasing fervour at her pussy, but, when he slipped one finger underneath her panties to try to push into her, Cassandra had the presence of mind to reach down and stop him.

'On the outside,' she reminded him, stroking her

thumb over the damp tip of his erection. 'Yes, that's perfect. Oh, that feels good.'

It did, too. Harry's touch was clumsy, but what he lacked in refinement, he made up for in enthusiasm. His fingers rubbed her in all the right places, firing her blood and urging her towards the peak of pleasure. Cassandra's body surged. She continued to fondle his cock as his own arousal began to augment. His fingers began to slow. Cassandra worked harder, pressing her mouth against his ear again.

'Are you going to come?' she whispered. 'Are you going to shoot all over my pussy? Are you going to make me even wetter?'

'Fuck, yeah.'

Harry grunted and pushed his hips forward to drive his cock into the tight enclosure of her fist. Cassandra allowed him to fuck her hand, his urgency fuelling her own fire. She reached down with her other hand to cup his testicles, squeezing them lightly as he drove himself towards release. His breath came in hot intermittent puffs, stirring the tendrils of hair at her neck. She felt his muscles stiffening, the familiar pressure just before firing. Then Harry let out a low groan, his hips still pumping as he sprayed over the triangle of blue silk.

Cassandra smiled as she drained him of every last sensation, feeling his fluids dampening her pussy hair and flowing between her legs. The pungent scent of his seed wafted towards her nose. She glanced towards the alley entrance. Victor hadn't moved, but Cassandra knew that he knew that she had brought the stranger to satisfaction. Victor turned and disappeared.

Cassandra released Harry's cock and pressed her mouth hard against his.

'Thank you,' she whispered. 'Take care.'

'What?' Harry frowned, confused. 'I want to make you come.'

Cassandra pulled away from him and closed her coat.

A black car stopped just outside the alley. She gave Harry a pat on the cheek before hurrying towards the car.

'Wait!' Harry called.

She ignored him and climbed into the passenger seat. Warmth enveloped her along with the scent of leather and the familiarity of Victor's cologne. Without a word, he eased the car forward.

Neither of them spoke as Victor manoeuvred the car on to 4th Street towards the entrance to the 80 freeway. Cassandra pressed her thighs together, her arousal still resonating hotly, her legs damp with the seed of a stranger. She waited in the car as Victor pulled into the parking lot of a rundown motel and went to retrieve the key to their usual room.

Traffic noise from the freeway rumbled outside the windows as they entered the room. The furnishings were spare and ugly – a queen-sized bed with a drab cover, a bedside table and clock radio, a scratched wooden table and chair. At this point, however, Cassandra didn't care if they were in the Taj Mahal.

'Take off your coat,' Victor ordered.

Cassandra slipped the coat off her shoulders and stood there in her heels and wet panties. Air shivered over her naked skin. She watched with a hint of concern as Victor's gaze raked over her body.

'Did he make you come?' he asked.

'No! No, Victor, of course not. I would never let one of them do that.'

'Good.'

He stripped out of his clothes, revealing the well-built, bulky physique that she adored. His cock projected outward from between his hairy thighs as if it had a life of its own. He sat down in the chair and grasped his erection, working it to full tumescence. Cassandra's mouth fairly watered as she watched him, her arousal beginning to reach breaking point.

'Come here,' Victor ordered. 'Fuck me.'

Cassandra's heart thudded. She slipped the panties over her legs and left them discarded on the floor. She went to him and straddled his thighs, grasping his thick cock as she guided him into her damp opening. He stretched and filled her, his belly against her buttocks, his hands grasping her waist. Cassandra drew in a sharp breath, closing her eyes as she absorbed the feeling of him buried so deeply inside her.

'Do it,' Victor said.

Cassandra braced one hand on the table as she started to ride him, her body growing slick and hot, her excitement expanding to boundless levels. His hard flesh inflamed her nerves, intensifying her already unbearable arousal. He reached one hand around to find the creamy knot of her clit. One touch from him sent Cassandra into a tailspin.

'Oh, Victor,' she cried. 'My love. Please let me come.'

'Now,' he ordered gruffly, his voice entangled with his own need.

An explosion rocketed through Cassandra's body, so intense that it brought tears to her eyes and caused her body to shudder violently. She continued to work herself on his cock until he lifted her away and positioned her on the bed with her bottom towards him. He drove into her hard and filled her with a flood of his own seed.

Cassandra let out another groan of sheer rapture as Victor's body fell heavily atop hers. She buried her head in the bedcover and thought that no one, that nothing, in the world fulfilled her so completely as he did. Along with that knowledge was the increasing fear, almost a dark premonition, that it was not meant to last.

The motel owner was short, skinny man with a pock-marked face and glasses. He sat picking at his fingernails with a pocket knife while hovering over a newspaper spread out on the counter. Derek reached into his pocket and handed the man a small wad of cash. The owner flipped through the bills briefly to assess the amount before he reached behind him to retrieve a key to Room 106. Without a word, he handed the key to Derek and returned his attention to the paper.

Derek left the office and walked across the parking lot to the stretch of rooms that bordered the highway. The one-level motel was dingy and commonplace, the building covered with peeling paint, the swimming pool lined with leaves and muck. It was the kind of place people stayed when they wanted to be assured of their anonymity.

Derek let himself into Room 106. The bed sheets were a tangled mess, the air still redolent of the smell of sex. He went to the bedside table and picked up the small clock radio that contained a built-in, high-resolution camera and video transmitter. He put the radio into his backpack and went to return the key.

12

There was a knock on the cabin door as a key turned in the lock. Anna looked up with a hint of alarm. Derek never bothered knocking before letting himself in. The door opened and a woman entered. Tall and slender, she wore jeans and a blue T-shirt with a scooped neckline. Her hair was fastened into a knot, her eyes hidden behind a pair of sunglasses. A fading bruise marred her jaw.

'Who are you?' Anna asked.

The woman removed the sunglasses and pushed them back into her hair. 'I'm Freddie. Freddie James. You must be Anna.'

'Yes.' Anna looked the other woman up and down with interest. 'You're one of Derek's friends.'

Freddie looked uncomfortable for an instant before nodding. 'Yeah. I just . . . He's not here, is he?'

'No.' Anna's gaze narrowed. 'Seems like you knew that already.'

'He usually goes for a run this time of morning,' Freddie said. 'I wanted to borrow something.'

'You'll have to wait for him to get back, then.'

'I'll leave him a note.' Freddie walked to the lockers that lined one side of the cabin. She removed a metal box and opened it.

Anna didn't know whether to stop the other woman or not. She obviously had a key to the cabin and knew her way around. Anna figured it was Freddie's problem if Derek didn't want her borrowing something.

'What're you borrowing?' she asked.

Freddie held up a small rectangular object with a

button on the top. 'It's called a Dazer. It's an ultrasonic device that can incapacitate a dog without hurting it.'

'What do you need that for?'

'A guy I'm trying to arrest is staying in a trailer guarded by two German shepherds,' Freddie explained. 'I don't want to hurt the dogs, but I also don't want to get anywhere near them. This will keep them out of the way so I can get inside.'

Anna looked at her curiously. She was a naturally attractive woman with clear, tanned skin and thickly lashed brown eyes. Anna wondered whether Derek really had been telling the truth about his lack of a physical relationship with Freddie.

'Derek will be sorry he missed you,' she said.

Freddie smiled wanly. 'No, actually he won't.'

'Why not?'

Freddie began going through the remaining contents of the box. 'We're sort of . . . not speaking.'

'You had a fight?'

'Sort of. Not really.' Freddie shook her head. 'It's not important.'

'Were you two, you know, involved?' Anna asked.

Freddie raised an eyebrow. 'You get down to business, don't you?'

'I like answers,' Anna said.

'No,' Freddie said. 'We weren't involved. Never have been. We were just friends.'

'Were?'

Freddie shrugged. 'Are. I don't know. Look, if he needs this back before next week, tell him to leave me a message.'

'Sure.' Anna watched as Freddie put the Dazer into a backpack. 'Do you, um, know about me?'

'Yes. Don't worry. I won't –'

Freddie's words died when the door opened again. Derek entered dressed in shorts and a sweaty T-shirt, a bottle of water in his hand and a folder tucked under his arm. He saw Freddie and stopped. His expression hardened.

'What're you doing here?' he asked.

It was almost a snarl. Anna was fascinated.

'I need to borrow your Dazer,' Freddie explained. 'I hope that's OK.'

'Yeah. Whatever.' He tossed the folder on to the table.

An awkward and cold silence plunged between them.

'Would anyone like a cup of coffee?' Anna asked brightly.

'No, thanks.' Freddie turned her attention to zipping her backpack. 'I need to go.'

'It was nice to finally meet you,' Anna said. 'Derek's told me a lot about you.'

'I have not,' Derek countered.

Freddie threw him an exasperated look. 'Thanks for the Dazer. I'll return it next week.'

'What do you need it for?' Derek asked.

'A job.'

'Who's the skip?'

'Just your garden-variety bail jumper,' Freddie said.

'What did he do?'

'Sold drugs.'

'Yo, Freddie!' A man's voice sounded from the deck. 'You down there? I'm getting hungry.'

'I'll be right up,' Freddie called. She avoided Derek's eyes as she slung the pack over her shoulder. 'Thanks. See you later.'

She went to the door. Derek was blocking her path. Freddie stopped. She was tall, but she had to look up to meet his gaze. For a moment, they stared coldly at each other as if ready to engage in a showdown. Then Derek stepped aside. Freddie headed up the stairs.

'Well, she's very –' Anna began.

Derek didn't even seem to hear her. He turned and went after Freddie. Out of sheer curiosity, Anna followed.

A young beefcake on deck was peering into the cockpit. A muscle shirt and shorts revealed his impressive biceps and legs. With his blond hair and tanned skin, he looked as if he belonged in a California surfer calendar. Anna was even more fascinated.

'Let's go.' Freddie took the young man's arm to turn his attention away from the cockpit.

'This is cool,' he said. 'What kind of boat is this?'

'A sailboat,' Derek replied dryly.

'Oh, hey.' The other man stuck his hand out in greeting. 'I'm Gavin. You must be Derek.'

'Correct.'

Derek didn't extend his hand. An instant of tension filled the air. Gavin's smile wavered.

'I'm Anna.' Anna stepped in to grasp Gavin's hand, admiring his tight grip. 'Friend of Derek's. Pleasure to meet you.'

'You too.' Gavin nodded his head towards Freddie. 'Freddie and I are going out to get some breakfast, if you want to come.'

'I thought you had a case,' Derek said to Freddie.

She frowned. 'I do. That means I can't eat?'

'You taking him with you?'

'To eat, yes. On the case, no.' Freddie tugged on Gavin's arm. 'Let's go.'

'Do you think I could see the cabin?' Gavin asked, apparently unaware of Derek's animosity. 'This is really cool.'

'Do you have a job?' Derek asked.

'Derek!' Freddie looked nonplussed.

'It's almost nine,' Derek said to Gavin. 'Shouldn't you be at work?'

'I work nights at a burger joint in Westwood,' the younger man explained.

'Of course you do,' Derek muttered.

Gavin's expression darkened slightly. 'Hey, dude, what's your problem?'

'Forget it.' Freddie stepped between them as if they

might need to be physically separated any minute. 'Come on, Gavin. Ignore him.'

'No, wait.' Gavin put out his arm to push Freddie gently out of the way. 'I want to know what this guy's problem is.'

'He doesn't have a problem,' Freddie said with a sigh. 'He's mad at me.'

'What for?'

'Did she tell you who hit her?' Derek asked.

Gavin looked at Freddie. 'Who hit . . . ? She got hit by a surfboard.'

'She did not,' Derek said. 'A man wanted for attempted murder hit her. So she says.'

'Derek, stop it,' Freddie ordered.

Anna's fascination was boundless. She looked from Derek to Freddie as if she were watching a tennis match.

'You don't know anything about it, do you?' Derek asked Gavin.

'What the fuck?' Gavin's eyes flared with outrage. 'Are you implying it was me? Where do you get off thinking that?'

'Stop it!' Freddie stepped forward suddenly and gave Derek a hard shove. The action barely moved him, but it caught him off guard for an instant.

'God, Derek, you can be such a bastard,' Freddie snapped. 'I told you the truth about what happened.'

'Yeah, after you lied.'

'I didn't lie.'

'The surfboard story wasn't a lie?'

'What the hell happened?' Gavin asked.

'I'll explain later,' Freddie replied curtly. 'We're leaving. And Derek, don't you dare think you'll ever make up for this.'

She pulled Gavin towards the dock, then stopped and looked at Derek again.

'All this time,' Freddie said, her voice low, her words clearly meant for no one except him, 'I thought we were friends. I thought you were different. Turns out you're just like all the rest of them.'

She turned and climbed on to the dock. Gavin followed. Anna gave Derek a wary glance. His features were set like a rock, his eyes frozen-tundra cold.

He stalked across the deck and went below. Anna hesitated for an instant before she followed. Derek sat down on the bed to remove his shoes.

'You OK?' Anna asked cautiously.

'Some reason I shouldn't be?'

'I don't know.'

Derek glowered at her as he stripped off his T-shirt. His chest and abdomen were hard with muscle and matted with dark hair.

'Thanks for your concern, but it's none of your business,' he said coldly.

'Seems Freddie's relationship is none of your business, either,' Anna suggested.

Derek's mouth tightened. 'You don't know anything about it.'

'I know you're jealous that she's seeing someone else,' Anna said.

'Why the fuck would I be jealous?'

'Maybe you like having her all to yourself.'

'Yeah?' He approached her. Anger continued to emanate from him in waves. 'Why would I need her when I have you?'

Anna's heart skipped. She tried not to step away from him. He was the only man aside from her father who could intimidate her.

'Well?' Derek demanded. 'Why would I need her?'

'Maybe you don't,' Anna amended, a little thrill racing through her at the idea of taking advantage of his potent anger.

'Damn right. Take off your clothes.'

A tiny part of Anna wanted to rebel at the harsh order, but that part was quickly subsumed by a dark thrill. She had always liked brawny men because she knew they could overpower her and take control. The problem was that they rarely did. She knew the same could not be said of Derek.

Her hands trembled as she started to unbutton her shirt. Her breathing grew shallow. She could feel Derek's anger as if it were tangible. A hint of fear broke open inside her. She was beginning to regret her forthrightness.

'Everything,' Derek ordered.

Anna let her shirt slip to the floor. She unzipped her jeans and pulled them off her legs. Her blood quickened. Derek's gaze raked over her body. Anna unfastened her bra and removed it, embarrassed by how hard her nipples already were. She didn't meet his eyes as she stepped out of her panties. Then she was naked before him and there was nowhere to hide.

'You like to fuck, don't you?' His voice was husky.

Anna shivered. She brought her arms up to cover her breasts, stunned by how nervous she suddenly was. She felt incredibly exposed.

'Well?' Derek asked. 'Answer me.'

Anna's gaze clashed with his. 'What?'

'Tell me you like to fuck.'

'I – I like to fuck.' The words elicited a bolt of excitement. Anna drew in a deep breath.

'I know about your men,' Derek said. 'What do you like them to do to you?'

'Everything.'

'Tell me.' There was a hardness to the words, like the edge of a knife. 'How do you pick them up?'

'At bars, usually. Nightclubs.'

'Not where. How?'

'Um, I ... well, sometimes they buy me a drink. Sometimes I ask them for one.'

'Do you take them home?'

'Sometimes.'

'What do they do to you?' Arousal was beginning to darken his eyes.

Anna's tongue darted out to lick her lips. She hugged her arms around herself. 'I like it when they undress me.'

'Why?'

'They're – they're big. I like men who make me feel – I don't know. Protected. But there's something dangerous about it, too. Like they could overpower me any second.'

'And you like that.'

Anna nodded. She backed away when he came closer. The ridge of his erection pushed against his shorts. His breathing was growing rapid, but his eyes were still cold.

'Get on the bed,' he ordered.

Anna went to the bed and stretched out on her back. She didn't think she had ever felt more vulnerable. She wished he would join her, but he stopped at the foot of the bed.

'What do you want?' Derek asked.

'I want you,' Anna whispered.

'What do you want me to do?'

'Fuck me.' The words slipped from her mouth on a plea. She closed her eyes, stunned by the mixture of shame and desire that rose inside her. 'Please.'

The clink of metal made her open her eyes. A pair of handcuffs dangled from Derek's fingers. Anna gasped, even as her whole being tightened with excitement.

'You ever been cuffed?'

'Only by you.'

Without asking if she wanted to be restrained again, Derek moved to clamp the cuffs around her wrists, looping the chain around a bedside wall sconce so that her arms were trapped above her head. The metal was cold and hard. Fear rose again, even though Anna knew that he wouldn't hurt her. Still, there was something frightening about being restrained and knowing that there was no way out.

Derek smiled grimly. 'You like that, don't you?'

Anna couldn't reply. It was true, she wanted to be controlled, she wanted to be taken. She didn't want to imagine what Derek thought of her. She pulled at the cuffs and winced as the metal chafed the delicate skin of her wrists.

Derek watched her for a moment before he put his hands between her legs and pushed her thighs apart. Her body shuddered. He spread her open and then, to Anna's shock, he lowered his head. She cried out at the first touch of his tongue on her sensitive folds. Derek slipped his tongue over all the crevices of her sex, eliciting wave after wave of pleasure. His lips gently captured her clit as he eased his forefinger into her tight hole.

Anna gasped and squirmed, her hips wrenching from side to side as she tried to push herself closer to him. She wanted to feel his tongue penetrate her, to come hard against his mouth. Just as she felt the spring of tension begin to tighten, Derek lifted his head. His eyes were dark with satisfaction.

'You want to come, don't you?'

'Oh, yes,' Anna gasped. Shame slipped away from her like water. She suddenly no longer cared what Derek thought as long as he let her ride the crest of pleasure. She twisted and groaned. 'Please.'

Derek removed his shorts. Anna stared at him with fathomless hunger. She spread her legs even further apart in invitation. Derek positioned himself at the juncture of her thighs. The head of his cock pushed deliciously against her. Anna muttered with frustration when he didn't immediately thrust into her. She strained her hips towards him.

'Do it,' she whispered. 'Please fuck me.'

She expected a firm thrust. Instead, Derek eased into her with slow deliberation. His cock moved smoothly against her inner walls, his path effortless due to the combined silkiness of their fluids. Anna lifted her legs and wrapped them around his hips. She gave a groan of pleasure when he lowered his body over hers. He was all solid weight and muscle, his chest hairs tickling her nipples, his hard abdomen pressing her into the bed. His mouth descended on to hers.

Anna parted her lips, her excitement stimulated by the taste of her own juices on his lips. She thrust her tongue into his mouth as he began fucking her with hard strokes. Anna's body bounced with every thrust. Sweat dampened their skin. She tightened her legs around him, loving the sensation of his filling her so completely. The veined stalk of his penis stimulated her very nerve endings, rubbing with tactile friction against her channel.

She let him ride her, her hands trapped over her head, her body in surrender. She had never felt like this, never given herself up so completely to a man. Derek positioned his hands on either side of her head, his expression set and eyes burning as he continued pistoning inside her. Then there was a subtle shift, a slowing of his penetration. His eyes closed. He thrust with one long stroke, a deep groan emerging from his throat as he spilled into her.

'Please,' Anna gasped, thrusting her body up to him. 'Please, Derek.'

He moved his hand between their bodies to massage her clit. His head lowered to rest on her shoulder. Anna's body slackened as release hovered just beyond her grasp. She moaned at the sensation of Derek's fingers spreading over her delicate centre, and then one final stroke propelled her into a shower of ecstasy. Anna cried out, her mouth open against his neck. She pressed her legs together as if trying to trap his hand between them.

'Oh, yes.' The word emerged from her throat on a hiss. She closed her eyes and absorbed the feeling of him on top of her. 'Oh, thank you.'

Derek lifted his head. His mouth touched her warm temple before he moved away from her. Anna watched as he pulled on his shorts. Her chest heaved as she tried to catch her breath.

'Derek?'

He unlocked the handcuffs and dropped them on to the table. Then he took the folder he had brought in and tossed it into the bed.

Anna picked up the folder and opened it. She removed several grainy photographs. For a minute, she looked at the photos in shock before returning her gaze to Derek.

'They're captured from a video I have of Cassandra with Victor,' Derek said.

A bubble of excitement rose in Anna. 'This is it, isn't it?'

'Cassandra is coming to LA on business next week,' Derek said. 'She called me the other day wanting to meet. I assume she wants to talk about you.'

'I want to go with you.'

Derek shook his head. 'No. You're still considered a fugitive. And I don't want Cassandra knowing you're with me.'

'So what happens next?'

'We find out what your stepmother has to say for herself.'

Anna looked at the photos again. She remembered how arousing it had been to have Derek restrain her. Maybe she had more in common with Cassandra than either one of them realised.

13

Derek pulled over to the side of the dirt road. Freddie's SUV was parked in front of a decrepit trailer surrounded by a chain-link fence. Dried grass and weeds covered the yard. Several broken-down cars sat next to the trailer, their bodies rusty and pimpled with dents. There was a wire dog run and a doghouse near the fence, but no sign of the dogs. Beer bottles, old tyres, used cardboard boxes and oil cans littered the grass. The place looked deserted.

Freddie climbed out of the SUV. She was wearing a black T-shirt and jeans, her handcuffs tucked into the waistband.

A wave of hot desert air gusted through the open window of the Mustang. Derek put one hand on the key, which was still in the ignition. He told himself to leave. Freddie could handle it. She'd been handling her job for two years. The trouble was that he'd always known where she was and what she was doing during those years. If he wasn't with her, he at least knew who she was hunting and when she was making an arrest.

For the past two weeks, he hadn't known a damn thing except that she was probably with Gavin. His hand tightened on the steering wheel. Of course, that didn't mean he had any right to follow Freddie.

She reached back to tighten the clasp that held her hair in a long ponytail. After a final check of her equipment, she headed towards the trailer. She looked cautiously for the dogs before opening the metal gate. She went to the front door and knocked firmly.

'Rick, you in there? Rick Peters?'

No answer. Derek could practically hear Freddie curse

under her breath as she went around to the back of the trailer and knocked again. Nothing. She walked around the trailer again and peered into the windows. Then she kicked the side of the trailer in frustration as she headed back to her car.

She stopped just as she reached the SUV. Her gaze narrowed on his Mustang. Derek swore at himself for not parking somewhere less obvious. Freddie started towards him. He got out of the car.

'Freddie –'

'What is it? Why are you here?'

'You said this skip is a drug dealer.'

Freddie stared at him. 'You bastard. You fucking bastard. How *dare* you follow me? What, you think I can't handle an arrest on my own?'

'Not this kind,' Derek said. 'You need a partner. Look at what happened when you arrested Raymond Thompson.'

'Stop thinking you need to protect me!' Freddie stalked towards him with a deadly expression on her face. 'What do I need to do to prove I can handle it?'

'Freddie, you're still a novice.'

'That doesn't make me incompetent, you ass!'

Before he could react, Freddie launched herself at him. Her body crashed into his as they both hit the ground. Unlike Anna, Freddie knew how to fight. She wrestled his arms above his head and tried to pin them down. Derek recovered quickly and flipped them both over. Freddie fought back. Her knee came up towards his groin. Derek moved just in time. He struggled to get her arms behind her back.

'Freddie, stop!'

'You prick. Leave me alone!' She got one arm free and fisted him hard in the gut.

The blow knocked the wind out of him for an instant, long enough for Freddie to twist their bodies around. Derek grabbed her waist, pushing her off as she went for his groin again. They rolled over the dirt road and into a patch of dried grass on the other side. Freddie bucked him off and tried to grasp his neck. Derek tackled her again. Their legs tangled. Dust rose to choke their throats. Freddie started coughing. Derek took the opportunity to pin her down, covering her body with his. His hands tightened around her wrists.

'Freddie –'

'I hate you, Derek,' Freddie spat. Her eyes were hot with fury, her expression mutinous. 'I really fucking hate you.'

'I'm beginning to realise that.'

He was breathing hard. He was also beginning to realise that he was reacting to the sensation of her curvaceous body under his. They'd never been this physically close before. With every breath she took, her breasts heaved against his chest. Freddie grunted with frustration and made one last effort to struggle out from underneath him. Derek tightened his grip and pushed his lower body against hers. Freddie went slack.

She glared at him. Her face was dirty. A long scratch marred her forehead. Her breathing began to quiet, but she still looked furious.

'Happy now?' she snapped. 'Did you prove you're stronger than me?'

'I wasn't trying to prove anything.'

'Yeah, right. You've been trying to prove something since the day we met.'

'And what's that?'

'That I can't get by without you.' She struggled under him again, but he could tell that the fight was going out of her. 'You think because you showed me the ropes, you're responsible for everything I do. Well, guess what. I've spent the last two years earning my way in this job. I've made dozens of arrests by myself. I don't need you any more.'

Derek was stunned by how hard her words hit him.

He hadn't realised until that instant how much he counted on Freddie. Hell, she was practically the only person he'd gotten close to in the past fifteen years. She was the only person he fully trusted, the only person he could talk to about almost anything. If she didn't need him any more, where did that leave him?

He looked down at her. Their faces were inches apart. Her eyes were the colour of chocolate, the irises ringed with gold. Her clean breath puffed against his cheek. Her lips were full and bare. Without thinking, Derek brought his mouth down on hers.

A gasp of shock stopped in Freddie's throat. Her body stiffened underneath him. Derek hardened the kiss. He pried her lips open, pushing his tongue into the warm, wet cavern of her mouth. His cock hardened. He shoved his knee between her legs. He released one of her wrists and brought his hand between them to grasp her full breast.

Freddie made a muffled noise of protest. Derek put his other hand at the back of her head and pulled her hard against him. The spicy sweet smell of her filled his nostrils. Her body was soft and yielding under his. His hand tightened on her breast. Her nipple pressed against his palm. Her thighs parted. Derek's blood grew hot. He wanted to strip her naked, to fuck her right here in the dirt and grass.

'Stop!'

The urgent word broke through his haze of want. He lifted his head and stared down at Freddie. She was looking at him with shock and not a little fear. That expression was like a bucket of cold water. Derek released her and moved away, silently cursing himself.

They both stood. Freddie's skin was pale. She brushed the dirt off her jeans. Her hands were shaking.

'Freddie.' Derek didn't know what to say.

She shook her head and hurried to her SUV without looking at him. Derek watched as she climbed into the driver's seat and started the ignition as if she couldn't get away from him fast enough.

Freddie sped off in a cloud of dust. Derek swore, knowing he had just ripped the final thread of their friendship.

'Nice place.'

Anna looked around with appreciation. The cabin of Maggie's yacht was smaller than Derek's, but more thoroughly outfitted. It also had Maggie's personal touch. Everywhere Anna looked, there were signs of Maggie's libidinous nature. Wall prints of full, throaty flowers, bookshelves lined with erotic fiction, small sculptures of entwined couples, silky bed sheets and pillows. It was like a homage to sensuality.

'Go ahead and sit there,' she told Anna, gesturing towards the sofa seat on the other side of the narrow cabin. 'I like the idea of you in a totally neutral setting.'

Anna went self-consciously to sit on the sofa. No one had ever asked to draw her before. Maggie had told her to wear her usual attire of jeans and a black T-shirt.

'Just relax,' Maggie said. 'I'm just going to do a few quick sketches.'

She flipped open a large sketchpad and began to draw. Anna tucked her hair behind her ears and tried not to be nervous.

'Good. Perfect. Look at me. No, don't smile. You have such a great face, Anna. Belongs on a movie poster. Your eyes alone could tell a thousand stories.'

The sound of the words began to ease away some of Anna's nervousness. She started to relax. Maggie's pencil scratched over the paper. At the other woman's direction, Anna stood, knelt, leant against the table and sat cross-legged on the sofa. She smiled, frowned, kept her face neutral, and tried a couple of times to project an aura of mystery. After a while, she started to rather enjoy the experience. It was almost like being someone else.

Maggie stopped and looked up. 'Anna, would you take your clothes off?'

The request didn't surprise Anna. Knowing what she did of Maggie's sensual nature, she had suspected that nudity would somehow be involved in a drawing session. Still, she hesitated.

'You know,' Maggie said with a grin. 'For the sake of art and all that.'

Anna's apprehension abated. Heaven knew she had never been uncomfortable about her nakedness before. She stood and stripped off her clothes, aware of Maggie's gaze on her. The heat of a nearby lamp warmed her skin. Her fingers paused as she reached for the clasp on her bra.

'Everything?' she asked.

'If you don't mind.'

Anna dispensed with her bra and slipped her panties over her legs. Another rush of nervousness went through her, but then she looked up and saw Maggie looking at her with candid appreciation.

'What a perfect little figure you have,' Maggie said. 'What does your tattoo mean?'

Anna rubbed her hand over the two Japanese characters on her arm. '*Meiyo*. It means honour.'

'How lovely. Turn to the side. Cross your arms over your breasts. I want to see the tattoo. Don't look at me. Yes. Perfect.'

Maggie continued drawing as she directed Anna's poses, most of which were quite modest. She paused only to adjust the lighting. After about an hour, Maggie lifted her head from the sketchpad. 'Good, Anna. I think we're done. That was excellent. Do you want to see what I've done?'

'Sure.'

Anna slipped her T-shirt over her head and pulled on her jeans. She went to stand behind Maggie. Maggie flipped the sketchpad back to the first page and pushed it towards Anna.

'Wow.' The word escaped Anna on a breath. 'Those are amazing.'

She hardly recognised herself. The black-and-white drawings were fine and detailed, the lighting casting just the right amount of shadow. Instead of looking short and small, as she had always thought of herself, her body looked slender and well proportioned. Maggie had highlighted the delicate bone structure of her face, the narrowness of her waist and curve of her hips.

'See?' Maggie gave her a warm smile. 'Didn't know you looked like that, did you?'

Anna shook her head. She felt Maggie's eyes sweep over her with a glance as gentle and warm as a velvet touch. Her skin warmed from the outside in. She was standing just behind Maggie, leaning slightly to look at the sketchpad. The scent of the other woman rose, a smell of sand and fresh air. There was nothing artificial about Maggie, no layered aromas of perfumed soap and shampoo. She smelled like the wind and sun and clouds.

She sensed heat emanating from the other woman. She turned her head to meet Maggie's gaze. She knew what would happen. She had known it since the minute Maggie asked to draw her, but it was still with a nervous sense of anticipation that she watched the arousal kindle behind Maggie's eyes.

Anna's lips parted on a breath. 'I ... I'm not ...'

'You don't want to?' Maggie asked frankly.

'No, I ... I mean, yes, but ...' Anna faltered. She had always been so sure of herself, so confident in her sexual encounters. But lately, between Derek and Maggie, she was beginning to feel like a novice.

'I haven't been with a woman in a long time,' she finally said.

Maggie laughed, a rich and throaty sound. 'I assure you, my dear, that nothing has changed.'

She reached up to cup the back of Anna's head, bringing her mouth closer. Their lips touched with gentle pressure. Warmth flooded Anna's blood. She had forgotten this, forgotten how lovely it felt to kiss another woman, to press her mouth against lips that were full and soft and tasted like berries. She lifted her hand and placed it on Maggie's shoulder. Her skin was already hot, as if the sun had soaked deep into her body. Maggie's lips parted, her tongue darting out to caress the crevice of Anna's mouth.

Anna took her in. She let Maggie remove her T-shirt and jeans again, but this time there was no anxiety. She welcomed the other woman's touch just as she had grown to welcome her appreciative gaze. Maggie was a woman who gave wholly of herself. Her hands skimmed over Anna's arms, trailed down her back to her hips and bottom. Her touch was feather light, eliciting little shivers of arousal over Anna's skin. Maggie dipped her fingers gently into the shadowed crease of Anna's bottom. Anna shuddered. She wanted to see the other woman naked.

She pulled away. A furrow of concern darkened Maggie's forehead.

'What's wrong?' Maggie asked.

'Nothing. I just – would you undress for me? Over there?' Anna gestured to the other end of the headroom.

Maggie smiled. She rose with a languid movement and walked the short distance. The lamp was still glowing hot. Without taking her eyes off Anna, Maggie stripped slowly out of her shorts and bikini top. Her breasts were weighty and full, topped with cinnamon-coloured nipples, her hips pleasantly broad, her legs long and muscular. She was a woman in her prime. She reminded Anna of some sort of exotic animal, like a panther or a wild horse, all strength and sleek muscles.

Maggie stood without a hint of self-consciousness, her hands on her hips as she let Anna drink in the sight of her.

'How did you get that way?' Anna asked. She had always thought of herself as confident, but she realised now that it was false bravado. She had none of the self-assurance that Maggie did.

'What way?' Maggie asked.

'I don't know. So confident.'

Maggie's tanned shoulders lifted. 'Once I left John, I realised I could do anything. Whatever is holding you back, Anna, that's what you need to get rid of.'

Anna thought she'd been trying to do that with Cassandra for years now. 'Some things are easier to get rid of than others.'

'What about your inhibitions?'

Anna smiled. She approached Maggie almost cautiously. Maggie didn't move. Anna knew she was waiting for her to take the initiative. She lifted her hands and cupped Maggie's breasts. The nipples pressed against her palms. She began stroking the other woman slowly, running her fingers underneath the juicy crevice of her breasts, over her wide hips, the arch of her spine, the juncture of her thighs. Maggie's mons was neatly trimmed, her inner thighs warm.

Their mouths met again. Anna's head filled with the scent of Maggie. She pressed her body against her as they went slowly down to the floor. Maggie's body enfolded hers, legs entwined, arms wrapping her in a haven of warmth. Anna parted her legs to rub herself against Maggie, opening her mouth under the pressure of the other woman's lips. Everything about Maggie stoked her blood, kindled a dimension of arousal in her that no man had ever equalled. Not even Derek.

Anna drove her hands into Maggie's short hair as their tongues danced. Their breasts pressed together, nipples chafing deliciously. Maggie kissed Anna's lower lip, trailing her mouth over her jaw and down to her neck. She proceeded down Anna's body with little kisses, licks and nibbles that rained pleasure over her skin. Maggie dipped her tongue into Anna's navel, then slipped her hands between Anna's thighs to push them gently apart.

Anna let her head rest on the floor. She closed her eyes and gave herself up to the erotic expertise of the other woman. She had always been aroused by the idea of a man taking control, but she had never before experienced it with a woman. She suspected that if she wanted it, if she asked for it, Maggie would dominate her completely.

Arousal spiralled through her, widening like a tornado. She felt Maggie lower her head. Anna's body jerked at the sensation of the other woman's tongue on her intimate folds. She knew she was wet, and Maggie's murmur of appreciation elicited another wash of moisture. Anna's body tightened as Maggie began to explore her pussy, her tongue sliding leisurely around all the little pleats, her lips closing gently over her clit. Maggie's hands moved over Anna's abdomen until they reached her breasts. She cupped her breasts, her fingers tweaking the small nipples.

Anna closed her eyes and breathed deeply. She felt wholly covered by the woman and safe in a way that she had never felt before. She gasped with surprised pleasure when Maggie's tongue thrust deeply inside her. Maggie's murmurs vibrated into her and stimulated her blood. Anna moaned as her excitement began to intensify. Maggie continued fucking her with her tongue, driving her towards an explosive release. Anna lifted her legs as if trying to draw Maggie further into her.

'Yes,' she gasped, her fingers clutching Maggie's hair. 'Stick your tongue in me. Please.'

Maggie's tongue thrusts increased in pace as her fingers spread over Anna's clit. The combination of the two evoked another layer of excitement as Anna strained towards an orgasm. She came with a squeal, her body shuddering under Maggie's expert touch. Maggie drew herself up and kissed Anna hot and hard.

'Don't move,' she whispered.

Her muscular legs straddled Anna's thigh. Her pussy spread open and pressed against Anna. She felt warm and slick. Maggie placed her hands on either side of Anna's head and began to ride her thigh. Anna watched with fascination as Maggie drove herself towards her own orgasm. The other woman's face slackened with pleasure, her eyes drifting closed, her lips parted. Her skin flushed a pale red as her arousal began to expand. Her thighs tightened on Anna's leg. Anna's skin dampened with Maggie's sweet fluids.

Maggie leant over Anna, her hips working wildly against Anna's thigh. Her breasts dangled forward like pendulous fruit. Anna grasped the full mounds and began massaging them, leaning forward to take one hard point between her teeth. Maggie groaned her approval. She continued gyrating back and forth, then side to side, stimulating her orgasm with a single-minded determination that excited Anna all over again. Maggie's expression tightened, her eyes squeezed shut as an orgasm rocked through her body.

'Ah, so good.' She lowered her head to kiss Anna again, thrusting her tongue into her mouth. 'God, you're yummy.'

Anna slid her hands to the back of Maggie's neck. 'I could come again,' she murmured.

Maggie smiled against her mouth. 'Oh, you will, my lovely. You will.'

14

The wave surged underneath her. Freddie rose and planted her feet firmly on the board. The water crested over, breaking apart, spilling foam. It was a good wave, clean and smooth. She positioned herself and began riding down the face, curving left and right until the water began to level off. Freddie grabbed her board and started to head back for the breakers.

Just as she was about to turn, she caught sight of Gavin waving at her from the beach. For an instant, Freddie was tempted to pretend that she didn't see him, to paddle back out and keep catching and riding waves until the crash of the water drowned out her inner turmoil.

Instead, she headed for the shore. Gavin had nothing to do with Derek's asinine behaviour. Maybe he could even help her forget.

'Hey.' Gavin gave her his wide, artless grin. 'Waves look good this morning.'

'Yeah.' Freddie wiped drops of water off her forehead. He was wearing shorts and a T-shirt, which indicated that he wasn't planning to join her surfing. 'What are you doing here?'

'I stopped by your apartment, but you weren't there,' Gavin said. 'I figured you were probably here. How long have you been surfing?'

'A few hours.' Freddie glanced at her watch. 'You want to swim?'

'I don't have my wetsuit.'

'Not surf. Just swim. Wait here. I'll put my board in the car, and we'll go down by the pier.'

Freddie went to the parking lot and stashed her board in the back of her SUV. She stripped out of her wetsuit and rejoined Gavin on the beach.

'Come on,' she said. 'I'll race you.'

'How's the water?' Gavin asked.

'Cold. As usual.' Freddie flashed him a smile as she started jogging towards the pier. 'Maybe you can warm me up.'

'My pleasure.' Gavin caught up and jogged alongside her. 'But I actually stopped by to tell you I heard from Barbara. She didn't go to Vegas. She's in the Valley. Encino.'

Freddie didn't respond. The wet sand squished between her toes. Water splashed around her ankles.

'Hey, did you hear me?' Gavin asked. 'I said I know where Barbara is.'

'Yeah, I heard you.'

'Well? You want me to go with you when you arrest her?'

'No.' Freddie slowed her pace. 'I think I'm quitting.'

'Quitting?'

'The business,' Freddie said. She stopped jogging and picked up a broken sand dollar that was nearly buried in the sand. 'Bounty hunting.'

'Bail enforcement,' Gavin corrected.

Freddie smiled faintly. She tossed the sand dollar into the ocean and watched as it splashed into the water.

'You're serious?' Gavin rested his hands on his hips, his expression mildly concerned as he looked at her. 'Why would you do that?'

Freddie shrugged. 'It's not really for me.'

'But you're good at it. Even I know that. I thought you loved it.'

'I did. Once.'

'So what's the deal?'

'It's complicated,' Freddie said. 'I'm just not into it any

more. There's one job I need to finish, but, after that, I think that's it for me.'

'So what'll you do instead?' Gavin asked.

'I don't know. I could always go back to being a security guard. Or maybe I'll become a surfing instructor or something. I hear they pay lifeguards pretty well.'

'Being a lifeguard doesn't sound much more exciting than being a security guard,' Gavin said.

'Well, whatever.' Freddie tossed another shell into the ocean. 'I think I need a new career path. Come on.'

She headed into the water. The shock of the cold made her gasp. She waded out into the deeper waters and dived under. Salt water stung her eyes and numbed her mind. She held her breath for as long as she could before coming up for air. Gavin was wading out tentatively.

'You want to fool around out here, you'll be on your own,' he said. 'Not even Aquaman could get it up in this kind of water.'

Freddie grinned. She approached him and wrapped her arms around his neck, lifting her mouth for a cold salty kiss. Their bodies chilled further as the water began to evaporate on their skin. Freddie rubbed her breasts against Gavin's sleek chest. She tucked her hands into his wet hair and thrust her tongue into his mouth.

'Damn,' Gavin breathed. 'Maybe you won't be on your own after all.'

'I hope not.' Freddie slid her hand down his chest to find the bulge of his penis. She cupped her palm around him.

They were far enough from the beach to afford them some degree of privacy, but for once Freddie didn't really care who saw them. From now on, she planned to do whatever she wanted, consequences be damned.

Gavin's hands slid underneath her thighs as he lifted her legs around his waist. Freddie slid her hands over his smooth back, her tongue exploring the inside of his mouth. He tasted cold and sweet. He cupped her bottom, squeezing her cheeks, his fingers slipping underneath the elastic of her bathing suit.

Freddie gasped when Gavin began fondling the pleats of her sex. He was usually quite adept at finding the most sensitive spots. She ground her hips against his hand as if begging for more. His forefinger circled her clit and teased the taut opening. She thrust her pelvis back and forth as if trying to fuck his finger. She strained to find the core of her arousal, aching to feel the familiar heat stoking her blood.

Nothing. Her blood was cold. She pressed her mouth against Gavin's again, driving her tongue hard into him, one hand clutching the back of his neck. She massaged his penis, wanting to feel him swell against her hand.

'God, Gavin,' she whispered. 'Make me come.'

'I'm trying.' He pushed a finger into her with a thrust that was mildly painful.

'Ow!' Freddie twisted her hips to dislodge his finger.

'Sorry.' Gavin reached for her again. 'Here, let me –'

'No.' Freddie pushed him away and separated herself from him. 'Never mind.'

Gavin frowned. 'Hey, this was your idea. Not mine. Fucking in a freezing cold ocean isn't my idea of a good time.'

Freddie pressed her fingers against her temples and sighed. 'I know. I'm sorry. It's not going to work.'

'Look, don't worry about it. Let's go back to your place. We'll take a nice hot shower, get all lathered up. I guarantee that'll work.'

'No.'

'What the hell is the matter with you, Freddie? You're acting really weird.'

'I'm sorry.' Freddie reached out to put her hand against his cheek. 'I'm just having a bad day. Look, I think I need to be alone for a while, OK?'

'Yeah, sure. I'll call you tonight, then.'

'No, I mean alone,' Freddie said.

Confused frustration dawned in Gavin's expression. 'You're breaking up with me?'

'No. I just need some time alone.' Freddie couldn't figure out why men found it so difficult to grasp that concept. She started back towards the shore. 'I'll call you this weekend, OK?'

'What's wrong? What did I do?'

Freddie cursed herself for treating him with such callousness. 'You didn't do anything, Gavin, really. I'm just rethinking some stuff.'

'OK, well, I'm not going to sit around waiting for your call,' Gavin said with a scowl.

'I don't expect you to.' Freddie turned and went towards him again. She kissed his mouth and rested her forehead against his. 'Gavin, you're really wonderful. You've been great to me.'

'This sure sounds like a break-up.'

Freddie thought that it felt like a break-up, but she didn't tell him that. She pulled away and gave him a sad smile.

'I will call you,' she said. 'I promise.'

'Yeah, sure.'

Freddie felt him watching her as she swam back to the beach.

'You seen Freddie lately?' Gus Walker asked.

'No.' Derek's gut clenched unexpectedly. 'Why?'

'She hasn't checked in with me about a job she had,' the bail bondsman responded. 'I had a couple of new ones for her too, but she turned them down without telling me why.'

'I don't know why either,' Derek said, not without a hint of shame. 'When was the last time you talked to her?'

'A week or so. She told me she was going out to the desert again to try to bring in this drug dealer she was tracking. But she's not returning my messages and I can't get her on the cell.'

Derek frowned. Gus was right. Freddie was nothing if not professional. She always returned calls and emails within a reasonable amount of time.

'I'll look into it,' he told Gus.

'Haven't you *seen* her?' Gus repeated. 'I thought you two were joined at the hip.'

'You thought wrong.' Derek grimaced slightly as an image of him and Freddie joined in a completely different way appeared in his mind. 'I'll get back to you, Gus.'

'While you're at it, what the hell is going on with Anna Maxwell?' Gus asked.

Without responding, Derek snapped his cell phone shut and reached for his drink.

'Mr Rowland?'

Derek looked up. Cassandra Maxwell stood before him, looking every inch the elegant executive in a pale-pink suit with her hair in an immaculate twist. Derek had the sudden thought that Cassandra was the exact opposite of Freddie. It was a somewhat irrational thought. He should have thought that Cassandra was the opposite of Anna, but he suspected that the two women were more alike than either of them would have let on.

'Derek.' He stood and extended his hand. 'Nice to see you again, Cassandra.'

'Thank you.' She sat down across from him, placing her handbag on the table.

'What would you like to drink?'

'Scotch and soda, please.'

Derek lifted his hand to request the drink. As they waited, Derek studied Cassandra's face. She had refined features with vivid blue eyes and poreless skin. Artfully applied cosmetics enhanced what seemed like an innate sense of regalness.

'I'm assuming you still don't know anything about

your stepdaughter's whereabouts,' he said for the sake of appearances.

Cassandra took a sip of her drink and shook her head. 'No. I believe she has been in contact with her sister, but Erin claims not to know where Anna is. I see no reason why she should lie.'

'Why did you want to meet with me?' Derek asked.

'I'd like to know the current status of your search for Anna,' Cassandra replied.

'I thought you didn't care where she was.'

'Now that is not true, Mr Rowland.'

'Derek. Please.'

'All right, then. Derek.' She sounded as if she were tasting his name. 'We might have disowned Anna for her own good, but that does not mean that we no longer care what happens to her.'

'As long as what happens to her is prison.'

Cassandra gave him a level look. 'It's true that Anna deserves to go to prison. I have never doubted that. Neither has my husband.'

'Strange, then, that neither one of you has been willing to help find her,' Derek remarked.

'Only because we have invested enough time and effort in Anna,' Cassandra said. 'There comes a time when people must be responsible for their own actions. Don't you agree?'

'Of course.' Derek leant forward slightly. 'Are you?'

'Am I what?'

'Responsible for your own actions.'

Cassandra gazed at him for a moment. Something dark flickered behind her eyes, but did not crack her composure. 'Of course. Is there some reason I wouldn't be?'

'I don't know. But maybe your lover does.'

Cassandra blinked. Her expression didn't change, but her hand trembled slightly as she lifted her glass to her lips again. 'I don't know what you're talking about, Mr Rowland.'

'Derek.'

'I have no idea what you're talking about, Derek.'

'Sure you do. What's his name? Victor?' Derek's voice dropped an octave. 'What does he do for you, Cassandra? What does he do *to* you?'

Her full lips compressed in anger. 'How dare you?'

'Oh, I dare. I know how much you want to keep your affair a secret.'

'You bastard. What could you possibly have to gain by doing this to me?'

Derek reached into his pocket and pulled out a folded envelope. He pushed it across the table towards her. Cassandra looked from him to the envelope and back again.

'What is that?'

'Open it and find out.'

The tremble in her hands intensified as she reached for the envelope. She removed the papers and photographs. All colour drained from her face. She put the items down and reached for her drink.

'Where – where did you get these?'

'From a video I have of you two,' Derek said. 'It should have been a no-brainer, Cassandra, that, if you steal half a million dollars, you don't stash it in your lover's account.'

Cassandra turned the photographs face down on the table. Two bright spots of colour appeared on her cheeks. She reached for her Scotch and took a long swallow, as if attempting to steady her nerves.

'Or maybe you'd just anticipated that no one would find out,' Derek suggested. 'Were you that arrogant, Cassandra? Did you really think Anna wouldn't figure it out?'

Her skin was white as paper, her mouth thinned. 'What are you talking about? Have you spoken to Anna?'

'I might have.'

'If you know where she is, you'd better turn her over to the police. Otherwise you could be arrested yourself for harbouring a fugitive.'

'I think Anna is the least of your problems right now,' Derek replied. 'What do you think your husband would say if he found out that you stole the money from his company and gave it to your lover?'

Cassandra's full mouth compressed. 'What do you want?'

'What do you mean?'

'I mean . . .' Cassandra lowered her voice. Her blue eyes shot daggers at him as she leant across the table. 'I mean what do you want?'

'Look, I couldn't give a shit who you fuck and why,' Derek said. 'You want some guy spanking your ass, go ahead. Enjoy yourself. What pisses me off is that you stole the money and you're trying to get Anna to take the fall for you. And you're trying to keep Anna away from her father.'

'Anna did that herself,' Cassandra said coldly. 'Richard has always tried to help her. If she hadn't been a criminal in the first place, he might have been willing to give her another chance.'

'But because of you, he didn't.'

'You didn't answer my question,' Cassandra said. 'What do you want?'

Derek sat back in his chair. He was aware that he held the upper hand. Now it was just a question of how firmly he intended to use it.

'I want you to do whatever it takes to prove to your husband that Anna didn't steal the money,' he said. 'If that means turning yourself in, then turn yourself in. I want Anna off the hook.'

Cassandra frowned. 'Why do you care what happens to her?'

'I'm not into arresting innocent people.'

Cassandra grabbed the photos and the papers. She folded them in half and stuck them in a side pocket of her handbag.

'I will not have that little bitch ruin my career and my private life,' she said. The coldness of her voice didn't quite hide the underlying tremble.

'She's not the one doing it,' Derek replied. 'You are.'

'Take your best shot.' Cassandra stood, drawing herself up, her chin lifted. 'I dare you.'

Derek had to admire her chutzpah. 'I've never backed away from a dare,' he said.

'Then I don't expect you to start now.' She picked up her pocketbook and gave him a short nod. 'Good day, Mr Rowland.'

Derek watched her leave, admiring the curve of her hips and the smoothness of her walk. He swallowed the last of his drink and reached for his wallet. He was almost sorry about what he had to do next.

15

Freddie opened the drawer and looked at the layers of silk and lace. Her lingerie drawer had always been a secret pleasure, filled with soft, sensuous things that she wore next to her skin and that only a select few had the opportunity to see. There was something sly and sexy about arresting a fugitive while wearing a purple bustier or a pink lace bra and panties underneath her jeans and T-shirt.

She wondered what Derek thought of her wearing lingerie under her working clothes. He probably thought it was silly. A frivolous idiosyncrasy.

Or did he? He wasn't immune to her. She'd felt his sudden and huge erection against her hip when he had been pressed so tightly against her, when his mouth had descended so fiercely on hers. No, he wasn't immune.

Then again, a man like Derek wasn't immune to any woman, not just her. He had only been caught up in their physical closeness. It wouldn't have mattered who was lying underneath him at that moment as long as it was a pliable female body.

Yes, that was it, Freddie reasoned. That was the kind of man Derek was. She should have been relieved at the thought. Instead, a heaviness seemed to be weighting down her very soul.

She took a red lace bra and matching panties from the drawer and stripped out of her jeans and T-shirt. She slipped the bra straps over her arms, tucking her full breasts in the cups. The constraint pushed her breasts together and created a deep valley between the two mounds of flesh. She pulled the panties over her hips.

The French cut made her legs seem even longer, and the thin strap just covered the crease of her bottom.

Freddie looked at herself in the mirror. She reached up and unfastened her hair from its usual knot. The cinnamon locks tumbled around her shoulders. Sometimes she forgot that she could actually look like a woman. Gavin had just recently been the one to remind her that she could also feel like a woman.

She stroked her hands over her waist and hips. Her skin warmed to her own touch. Her hair felt soft and silky against her back. She circled her finger around one of her nipples as it budded up against the red lace. A tiny glow erupted inside her.

She smoothed her palms over her legs and into the warmth of her inner thighs, which were taut with muscles from surfing and running. She moved her hands around her hips to her bottom. Her skin was smooth, her rear cheeks firm. The strap of silk pressed between her cheeks and rubbed against the crinkled little hole with an oddly illicit sense of pleasure.

Freddie watched the movement of her own hands as if they belonged to someone else. She stroked her buttocks, the backs of her thighs, the small of her back, then around again to her taut belly and breasts. Staring at herself in the mirror, she dipped her fingers underneath the skimpy lace panties to touch her sex. Moisture coated her fingers. Freddie shuddered.

She let out a sigh and sank on to the bed, her eyes closing. An image appeared behind her eyelids, one of her entwined with Gavin, their mouths open in a hot kiss, his hands stroking over her body. The glow inside her expanded, filling her veins with heat. She pressed her fingers more firmly into her pussy, fondling the slick folds, rubbing her clit. Her breasts felt swollen and constrained by the tight bra.

Freddie pushed the straps off her shoulders and cupped one breast, toying with the hard nipple. She rolled on to her side and closed her eyes. Her thighs clenched together, trapping her hand. An ache began to coil around her lower body.

Gavin was still there in her mind's eye, his expression growing taut with arousal as she wrapped her hand around his cock and began stroking. His penis swelled deliciously in her grasp. Their legs tangled together as her body opened for him, encouraging his entry, wanting to surrender. The image blurred. Freddie pushed the panties over her hips so that they dangled around her thighs, giving her more access to her pussy while preventing her from parting her legs too widely. Her breath escaped.

The picture cleared. Where was she? Not in her bedroom. In some exotic room with silken drapes and a massive bed covered with a fluffy, silver-threaded duvet. An airy chiffon canopy covered the bed and fluttered in the breeze from an open window. The air smelled clean and fresh, perfumed with the slight aroma of flowers. Gavin was still there, but he wasn't alone. There was another man, one who was like the opposite side of a coin. Where Gavin was golden and artless, the other man was dark and worldly.

Freddie pressed her face into a pillow and groaned. Derek had never before appeared in her fantasies, never invaded the most intimate recesses of her imagination. But there he was, all hard edges and power, his gaze fixed on her naked body as if he wanted to devour her. His limbs were long and muscular, his solid chest covered with a layer of dark hair. Freddie ached to smooth her hands over his entire body, to stroke through the mat of hair and downward to the heavy cock that was already growing.

But she couldn't touch him. All she could do was lie there and stare at him, fascinated and not a little afraid. She knew what he could be like, how dangerous he could be when the situation warranted. And he was looking at her with a controlled kind of anger, as if it were wound like a spring inside him that might release any second.

'How many times has he fucked you?' Derek's voice was deep and cold.

Freddie swallowed. She was aware of Gavin's immobile presence. 'Just – just a few.'

'How many is a few?'

'Four, maybe. Five.'

'Was it good?'

'What?'

'Was it good?' Derek repeated. 'Did you like it?'

Freddie tore her gaze from him to look at Gavin. He was watching Derek with wariness. Derek moved suddenly. He planted his hands on either side of Freddie's head as he hovered over her and blocked Gavin from her line of sight.

'Don't look at him,' he ordered. 'Look at me. Did you like it?'

'I . . .' Freddie's tongue flickered out to moisten her dry lips. His eyes penetrated her, seeming to look into the core of her being. 'Yes.'

His expression hardened with anger. Freddie regretted her admission even as a thrill spiralled through her. Derek grasped her wrists and pinned them above her head as he had done the other day, but this time Freddie had no desire to resist. She watched as desire flared in his eyes, as he lowered his mouth to hers and kissed her with a force that was as punishing as it was arousing.

His knee thrust between her thighs. His body was heavy on hers. She wished he would release her so that she could touch him, move her hands over every inch of his powerful body, but his grip remained tight. He straddled her, his erection pressing insistently against her thigh, his skin so warm. His lips trailed from her mouth to her ear. He released one of her hands. Freddie moaned and moved to grasp his erection. She imagined that his penis would be long, beautifully thick, that it would pulse hot against her hand. Her pelvis arched up to him.

She gasped and tried to reach for Gavin.

'Get the fuck away from him,' Derek ordered.

'But I want him too.'

'You can't have him.'

Freddie glared at Derek. 'Since when do you make that kind of a decision?'

'Since I decided that you're mine.' He thrust into her hot and hard.

Freddie groaned, awash in the sensation of him inside her. He pumped into her, sleek and smooth, driving into her blood. Then the image shifted. She was on her hands and knees, her palms resting against the soft coverlet, her full breasts dangling below her. Derek was behind her, clutching her hips as he pulled her back towards him and sank his erection into her again. His hips slammed against her buttocks.

And Gavin was there, too, but in front of her, his erection projecting towards her mouth. She parted her lips. He slid his prick into her mouth, salty and delicious against her tongue. Freddie closed her eyes, working her hand faster between her legs. She was utterly full of hard, male flesh, her mind saturated with the feeling of being completely taken. She worked her lips and tongue over Gavin's cock as his hands dug into her hair, as Derek drove in and out of her and her body shook. Juices flowed between her thighs. Both men were gripping her body, permeating her very being with their drive towards release.

She felt Gavin begin to surrender first. His hands tightened in her hair, his prick moving with increasing urgency into her mouth. She sucked him hard, licking his shaft with her tongue, pressing wet kisses against the tip. He grunted, his body tensing, and then he pushed into her with a yell as semen spurted from him. Freddie shuddered with pleasure and drank every last drop, electrified by the idea that she was the one to provide both men with sensual ecstasy.

Gavin moved aside, slipping from Freddie's imagination so that only Derek was there. He pistoned inside her with increasingly long strokes before his own release filled her anew with a flood of seed. Then he pulled out of her and turned her on to her back as if he wanted to see her face. She stared up at his hard features, which glistened with a sheen of sweat. He was magnificent, all male power and energy. He stretched out beside her and gathered her body against his. His hand slipped between her legs and began working her clit.

'Come now,' he whispered, an edge of command to his voice.

Freddie trembled. She parted her thighs. His fingers were expert, touching her exactly where she needed to be touched. She buried her head against his neck, inhaling the male scent of his skin. His body was hot against hers. Every one of her senses was magnified to proportions she hadn't known existed. Suffused with the intensity of Derek's touch, her nerves erupted with rapture. She came hard against his hand, crying out with pleasure, clutching at him as he murmured his approval and drew every last tingle from her body.

The images in Freddie's mind began to fade as sensations slipped from her body. She drew in gasps of air, absorbing every pulse of pleasure. Just before she let herself escape into a satiated sleep, a final picture flickered of Derek leaning over her again, his lips on hers, his hands clutching her arms.

'You'll forget about him,' he hissed against her mouth. 'If it's the last thing I do, I'll make you forget about him.'

As sleep began to descend, it occurred to Freddie that Derek had already succeeded.

Richard Maxwell stared at the photographs. They were spread over his desk like a map of his wife's infidelities.

And what infidelities they were! He had to give Cassandra a grudging degree of credit. When she did something, even cheat on him, she gave it a hundred per cent. He picked up a photo of Cassandra leaning over the bed while her lover spanked her.

Richard's penis twitched. She looked amazing, no question about that, her tits dangling, her ass thrust up like a white moon. There was another picture of her hogtied with her back arched, her eyes covered by a blindfold, her mouth open in supplication. And more of her restrained by ropes that crossed her breasts and went between her legs. Richard dropped the photos and rubbed his eyes. He'd thought over the years that Cassandra was capable of an affair, but he never thought she'd go through with it to such an extent.

He stood and stacked the photographs into a pile. Although he couldn't quite understand why, he was less upset about the affair than he was about the stolen money. Maybe it was because an affair was a wholly different kind of crime.

He left his study and went upstairs to the bedroom. He opened the door with an odd premonition of what he would find. Several of Cassandra's things had been cleared from the dressing table. He went to the closet. Three of her suitcases were gone, along with many of her clothes.

Richard sank down on to the bed. He was numb inside. He loved Cassandra, but she had also been the reason his daughters had distanced themselves from him. Anna in particular.

After absorbing the fact that Cassandra had left, Richard reached for the telephone and dialled Derek Rowland's number.

16

Freddie stepped out of the coffee shop with a cardboard cup in her hands. Her eyes narrowed on the sight of the blue Mustang parked next to her SUV. A wave of anger began to build inside her. Derek stepped out of the car, his hands up in a gesture of truce.

'Wait,' he said. 'I'm here on Gus's behalf. He called looking for you.'

Freddie didn't respond. She unlocked the door of her SUV, her head down. Derek stepped around beside her. She sensed a responding anger suddenly emanating from him.

'Look, I'm sorry,' he said, his voice tense. 'I made a mistake, but it was just a goddamn kiss, Freddie.'

His words pierced something in her heart, causing her chest to ache. She couldn't look at him. She wished that her hair was loose so that it could conceal her profile from his irritated gaze.

'Yeah,' she said. The word sounded dusty and cracked. 'Forget it, then.'

'I have forgotten it.'

Freddie thought that few other words could hurt as much as the ones Derek was saying to her now. She turned her head to meet his eyes. His features were like stone, his eyes as cold as flint. She couldn't help looking at his mouth, remembering how his lips had felt on hers, how a kernel of unmitigated desire had struggled to break through her rage before she managed to contain it.

'Is Anna still with you?' she asked.

'What?'

'Anna,' Freddie repeated. 'Is she still on the boat?'

'Yeah. Why?'

Freddie shrugged, trying to conceal an intense bolt of jealousy. 'Just wondering. She convinced you that she's innocent yet?'

'Actually, yes, she has. Her stepmother is apparently on the run now.'

'So what's going to happen to Anna?' Freddie asked.

'She's going to try to talk to her father. If he'll even see her.'

'Well, I wish her luck. You too.'

Derek sighed. 'Freddie, what do you want me to do? I can apologise, but I can't take it back. I said it was a mistake. I'm sorry.'

'Yeah, me too.' Freddie climbed into the driver's seat and busied herself with adjusting the cup holder. She'd thought that distance from him might ease her desire, but instead it seemed to have strengthened it. 'I don't want you to do anything, Derek.'

'Then why are you acting like I committed a fucking crime or something?' Derek asked in frustration. 'Is this it, Freddie? Are we done?'

Freddie stared out the front window to the coffee shop. She knew Derek. If she said yes, that their friendship was over, he would walk away and never try to contact her again. She knew that. And she couldn't even begin to imagine what her life would be like without Derek. In the past two years, they had become so close that she felt as if he'd been a lifelong friend. She'd never had a friend like him before and she knew she'd be hard pressed to find one again.

She jerked her head towards the passenger seat. 'Get in.'

'What?'

'Get in,' Freddie repeated. 'I'm going back out to Rick Peters' trailer.'

Derek went around the SUV and climbed into the

passenger seat. Freddie backed out of the parking space and on to Santa Monica Boulevard. As she headed towards the 405, she reasoned that she would rather have Derek in her life as a friend than not have him at all. Maybe this fierce longing she seemed to have for him would fade. Maybe it was temporary, caused by the recent rockiness of their relationship. Maybe her feelings would die down once their friendship got back to normal.

And then maybe she'd sprout wings and orbit the earth. Freddie let out her breath in a long sigh. She was still stunned by how one little kiss could have affected her so deeply, as if unearthing something vibrant and alive, something that had been lying dormant for a long time. She would just have to bury it all over again.

She glanced at Derek. He was looking out the side window, his expression still set hard. She knew that kiss hadn't affected him the same way. In fact, it didn't seem to have affected him at all aside from causing regret.

She shouldn't be surprised. She knew Derek was very sexually experienced. A kiss that lasted all of ten seconds wouldn't have much impression on him compared with his other conquests. Like Anna.

Freddie suppressed another wave of jealousy. She'd never before cared much about Derek's women. She knew they existed in a wholly different part of his life than she did. But now she had first-hand experience of what it was about Derek that drew women to him so readily. And, if her fantasy was anything close to reality, then his sexual powers would be intense enough to be overwhelming.

Lust shuddered through her. She ignored it. She'd make this go away. She would have to.

'You still seeing Gavin?' Derek asked.

'No,' Freddie admitted, then immediately thought better of her response. 'I mean, not really. Well, sort of.'

'What kind of answer is that?'

'We're still seeing each other,' Freddie said, thinking

that it wasn't exactly a lie. She had told Gavin that she'd call him, even if she really had no desire to. 'He's a good kid.'

'He's a –' Derek stopped and shook his head. 'Never mind,' he muttered.

Wise move, Freddie thought.

She headed over the 10 towards the Inland Empire and the desert where Rick Peters was still living in his trailer. Both she and Derek were quiet during the length of the drive. The sky stretched tightly overhead, the sun burning a hole through the blue skin. As they passed the eastern cities of Riverside County and moved closer to the desert, the landscape grew more uninhabited with eroded cliffs and sand dunes smudged with cacti, wild flowers and yucca.

Freddie turned off the freeway near Coachella and drove to a dirt road that bordered an expanse of fields overgrown with dried grass and weeds. Aside from Rick Peters' trailer, only a few ramshackle homes populated the desolate area.

Freddie and Derek stepped out of the SUV. She went around to the passenger side. Two big mangy dogs ran up to the chain-link fence surrounding the trailer. They started barking and growling, baring sharp teeth. Freddie reached for the Dazer.

'Who the fuck are you?' A gravelled male voice came from the direction of the trailer.

Derek and Freddie exchanged glances. They both knew they were not prepared to work as partners, and that their lack of a plan was the antithesis of their usual method of operation. Freddie thought that Derek probably didn't even have his gun on him.

'You missed your court date, Rick,' Derek called. 'Come on out.'

'Fuck you.' Rick Peters appeared in the doorway dressed in a ratty bathrobe, his face concealed by a scraggly beard. He was holding a pistol at his side.

Derek put his hand out towards Freddie as if in protection. The barking of the dogs grew louder.

'Rick, call off the dogs,' Freddie said. She reached for her gun.

'Who sent you?'

'Your bondsman,' Freddie replied. 'You're a wanted man, Rick, you know that. You were supposed to appear in court last week.'

She heard Derek say something, but she couldn't make out his words over the barking and the sudden sight of Rick lifting the gun. Before she could aim her own gun, a bullet cracked through the air.

'Get down!'

Derek propelled himself towards Freddie and brought them both crashing to the ground. Dirt filled Freddie's nose and throat. Derek covered her body with his and wrapped his arms around her head to shield her. Another bullet shot past.

'Get off my property!' Rick yelled.

'Behind the car,' Derek said into Freddie's ear.

He snaked his arm hard around Freddie's waist as they hurried to crawl behind the SUV. A third bullet slammed against the fender. The barking sounded like hundreds of bullets splitting the desert air.

'We can come back,' Derek said, his breath hard against her ear.

'No. He'll run again.'

'He might not.'

'He will,' Freddie insisted. 'This is the third time he's run. I have to get him now.'

They waited another couple of minutes. Derek motioned for Freddie to stay where she was as he peered around the side of the SUV.

'He's gone in.' He held out his hand. 'Give me the gun.'

Freddie shook her head. Derek glared at her.

'Give me the gun!'

'No,' Freddie said adamantly. 'This is my case, Derek. My skip.'

Frustration filled his eyes. She saw his inner struggle before he lowered his hand. A small feeling of triumph rose in Freddie as she started to stand.

'Freddie.' Derek's voice was tight with concern.

Freddie looked at him. His eyes were darkened to charcoal, his mouth set in a hard line. Dirt smudged his jaw.

Without thinking, Freddie reached out and slid her hand around to the back of his neck. She rested her forehead against his, her lips only inches from his mouth, her eyes locked with his.

'Don't worry,' she whispered. 'I can do it.'

'I don't want you to.' His hand closed around her wrist.

Freddie pulled away from him slightly, their gazes still locked. 'You have to let me.'

A minute stretched between them, a moment that felt like an eternity, an instant during which they both knew that their relationship could change irrevocably.

Then Derek let go of her wrist. Relief and gratitude flooded Freddie. She wanted to kiss him. Instead, she clutched the grip of her gun and started around the side of the SUV. Derek was close beside her.

'He's going to try and go out the back,' he said. 'I'll be right behind you.'

Freddie stayed low and ran towards the fence. Derek aimed the Dazer at the dogs, who came to a halt at the fence. Both animals whimpered, digging their heels into the dirt and ducking their heads as they backed down.

'There,' Derek called. 'He's going.'

Adrenaline churned through Freddie. Rick clambered out the back door of the trailer and started to run. She knew she could catch him, but she didn't know what other kind of weapon he might have on him. She increased her pace as he dashed into the overgrown field beyond the house. For an older guy, he could move fast. She heard Derek pounding through the grass behind her, but she knew that he would not interfere unless absolutely necessary.

Freddie's shoes crushed dried weeds as she charged after Rick, closing the distance between them in a matter of minutes. Rick still had the gun in his hand. He turned and tried to fire while still running. The bullet careened wildly off course. Derek swore. Before Rick had a chance to aim, Freddie slammed her body against his. They fell to the ground.

'You're under arrest, Rick,' she shouted. 'Stop struggling.'

'Bitch, get off me.' He fought to free himself.

Freddie fumbled for her handcuffs. She yanked them from her waistband while trying to keep him still with the pressure of her legs. The cuffs fell from her hand. Strands of hair escaped her barrette and whipped around her face. Rick's elbow slammed into her gut, catching her off guard. Freddie pressed her gun against his neck.

'Hold fucking still,' she ordered.

He quieted at the feeling of the metal barrel and went slack underneath her. Derek appeared beside them, yanking Rick's gun away from him. Freddie found her cuffs and wrenched Rick's arms behind his back. She slapped the cuffs on his wrists and drew in a ragged breath.

'Get up.' She stood and grabbed his arm, pulling him to his feet.

'You OK?' Derek asked.

Freddie nodded and pushed her hair away from her face. They were all breathing hard. Adrenaline continued to course through Freddie, her heart pounding. She prodded Rick back towards the trailer. The sound of police sirens sounded faintly in the distance.

'You're going to jail, Rick,' Freddie said.

They returned to the trailer just as two black-and-white Coachella police cars came screeching down the dirt road. The cars came to a halt, and the officers emerged with their guns drawn.

'It's OK,' Derek called, holding up his hands. 'We're bail enforcement. This man is a wanted fugitive.'

The cops didn't lower their guns until Derek pushed Rick to the road. He and Freddie kept their hands up as they explained the situation. They showed the officers their badges and IDs before handing Rick over to them. One of the officers radioed in to verify their story.

'We'll meet you at the department to fill out the paperwork,' Freddie told one of the cops.

After they had everything straightened out, Freddie and Derek returned to her SUV.

'Want me to drive?' he asked.

'Sure.' Freddie handed over the keys.

He opened the passenger door and held it open for her. She paused before climbing in, turning to face him.

'Thanks,' she said. 'You know, for trusting me.'

Derek's expression was sombre. 'I've always trusted you, Freddie. You're the only person I do trust, if you want the truth. What I've never wanted is for anything to happen to you. If that makes me an ass, then I'm an ass.'

Freddie smiled faintly. Even though he could provoke her limitlessly, she thought there was no one like him in the world.

She reached out and dusted the smudge of dirt off his jaw. A hint of stubble abraded her fingers. Something thickened in the air between them. Derek didn't move. Freddie told herself to stop touching him. She slid her fingers over the ridge of his cheekbone, then up his temple to trace the arch of his thick eyebrow. Her forefinger moved between his eyes, over the bridge of his nose, down to the indentation just above his mouth.

She was seized by an urge to kiss him there. She let the pad of her thumb brush across his lower lip. His breath was warm. A tremble vibrated and spread through Freddie's blood. She wanted his mouth on hers again. More than that, she wanted his body on hers, in hers.

Her fingers shook as she slid them over his neck, resting them in the hollow of his throat. She couldn't meet his gaze, shaken by the quickness of her reaction to him. Her belly clenched with nerves. A brief unwelcome thought flitted through her mind that many women had probably touched him like this, that it was nothing new for him.

It was, however, new for her. She wished she could strip his shirt off and run her hands over his body, exploring every inch of his muscular chest and shoulders. She'd seen him without his shirt plenty of times while they were swimming or running, but she had never touched him. Not like this.

Freddie dared to believe that Derek's breath had increased in pace, but he didn't move towards her. She lowered her hand and rested it against his chest, her eyes on the pulse that beat at the base of his throat. His heart pounded against her palm, sending quivers up the length of her arm.

She stepped closer to him. Warning bells and alarms rang in the back of her mind, but she ignored them. She had to know. She had to know if her sudden and intense need for him had been an aberration. Or maybe it was just something she needed to get out of her system. Maybe they both did. The risk to their friendship was one she would have to take.

Still not meeting his gaze, she lifted her mouth to his. He didn't lower his head in response. Her anxiety heightened, but she knew she had to carry this through. She slid her hand around to the back of his neck and brought his face down to hers. Her lips touched his. A shiver of delight rained through her. His keys dropped to the ground with a clatter.

'Christ, Freddie.' Derek's voice was hoarse.

Freddie closed her eyes and tried to breathe. She moved closer to him. Her breasts brushed against his chest. Her nipples budded instantly. A low groan vibrated from Derek's chest. His hands moved to clutch her hips, his fingers grasping at the thick denim of her jeans. He pulled her against him. His body was hard and warm and, if she dared to acknowledge it, Freddie knew she would feel the expanding bulge of his erection.

Derek shifted, his mouth slanting more firmly over hers. That combination of triumph and relief rose in her again as she recognised his surrender. Her lips parted to allow his access. His tongue swept into the crevices of her mouth, stroking the corners of her lips, smoothing over her teeth. Warmth seemed to overflow from him into her. His strong hands dug into her hips, holding her against him. One of her hands tightened on the back of his neck while the other spread over his chest.

Yes, she could feel his heart beating faster now, throbbing hard against her palm. His hands slipped around to cup her bottom as he continued to plunder her mouth with his, backing her up against the door of the SUV. A gasp stopped somewhere in the middle of Freddie's chest. Her ears filled with the mingled sound of their breathing. Her blood surged, pooling in the increasing ache at the core of her body.

'Wait.' The word slipped between them, hot against her lips and taut with restraint.

Freddie opened her eyes, meeting Derek's gaze for the first time since she had initiated this. His grey eyes seared into hers. For an instant, she thought she had imagined the word, but then he said it again.

'Wait.'

'What?' Freddie was stunned by the depth of her need.

His forehead rested against hers. He closed his eyes as if he were struggling for control. His hands tightened around her waist.

'Not here,' he said.

'What?' Freddie dimly thought that was the only word left in her vocabulary.

'Not here,' Derek repeated. 'Not here, and not like this.'

His words penetrated her fogged mind. A swell of anger was tempered by her awareness of the undercurrent of his statement. 'Not here' meant somewhere else. 'Not like this' meant some other way.

Freddie drew in her breath in an attempt to calm her racing pulse. She tore her gaze from Derek's, suddenly embarrassed by her uninhibited display of want.

'You're right,' she muttered. 'You are an ass.'

He drew slowly away from her, pressing his mouth against the tender skin of her temple.

'Guilty.'

Freddie turned away, her face flushed with a combination of desire and embarrassment. Derek picked up the keys he had dropped and went around to the driver's side. Freddie climbed into the seat, even more irritated that he appeared to have regained his control in a matter of seconds while she was still fighting for her own.

She was aware that Derek was looking at her as he started the car. She turned the air conditioning on full blast, welcoming the rush of cold air against her face, and gazed out of the side window.

'Freddie.'

'I don't imagine you turn too many women down,' she remarked, making an effort to keep her voice cool.

'So why would I turn you down, is that it?' Derek asked.

Freddie shrugged. She hoped she was projecting a convincing aura of nonchalance.

'I would never turn you down,' he said.

'Don't do me any favours,' Freddie retorted. 'And don't think I'm willing to sit around waiting for – for you.'

'You wouldn't sit around waiting for anything,' Derek said. He turned the car around and headed back out towards the main road. 'Or anyone.'

Freddie tried to tell herself that it was for the best. She tried to convince herself that she didn't want to risk her and Derek's friendship for a brief fling that might very well not lead to anything more.

She tried and failed. The basic fact of the matter was that she wanted him. Physically at the very least, and maybe even on deeper levels that she was not willing to acknowledge.

'You want to go running this weekend?' Derek asked.

Freddie silently cursed him for sounding so matter-of-fact. 'I can't,' she lied. 'I have a date with Gavin.'

His hands tightened visibly on the steering wheel. '*All* weekend?'

'Maybe.' Freddie threw him a mildly condescending look. 'Is there a problem with that?'

'I thought you weren't seeing him any more.'

'You thought wrong. Besides, aren't you busy with Anna?'

'She's going back to her Hollywood apartment for a few days. She's leaving for San Jose on Friday.'

Freddie was surprised. 'For good?'

'I don't know. She's going to try to talk to her father.'

'Aren't you going with her?'

'I wasn't planning to.'

Freddie didn't press him for more information, even though a tiny glow of relief began to kindle deep in her soul.

Derek halted the car at a stop light. He glanced at her again, then reached out towards her. Freddie almost drew away, but Derek moved his hand around to the back of her head and unsnapped the barrette holding her hair back.

Released from the constraint, Freddie's thick hair spilled around her shoulders in a cascade of reddish brown. Derek pulled his hand away and stared at her. Uncomfortable under his scrutiny, Freddie shifted.

'What?' she muttered.

'I don't . . .' Derek cleared his throat. 'I don't think I've ever seen you with your hair down.'

'Don't be ridiculous. Of course you have.'

'No.' He shook his head. 'I'd remember.'

He was looking at her as if he'd never seen her before. He took a few strands of her hair between his fingers and examined them in the sunlight as if he were looking at something rare and precious.

Freddie grabbed the barrette away from him and reached to pin her hair back again. She nodded towards the stop light.

'Go.'

'What?'

'Go,' Freddie repeated. 'The light's green.'

In more ways than one, she thought with a shiver.

17

Anna entwined her arms around Maggie's neck. Their mouths came together with voluptuous sensuality. Maggie's tongue was warm, sliding smoothly against the inner side of Anna's lip. Anna shuddered.

'I'm going to miss you,' Maggie whispered. Her hands moved over Anna's naked body. 'Are you coming back?'

'I don't know. I'm going to stay at my old apartment for a few days before I go up north. My father agreed to talk to me, but that doesn't mean he's forgiven me for anything.'

'You didn't steal from him,' Maggie said. 'Cassandra did.'

'I haven't exactly been an angel,' Anna admitted. 'I've caused him a lot of grief.'

'Well, maybe this can be a fresh start for you.'

'Maybe.'

And maybe it would even lead to the kind of peace and self-assurance that Maggie had found. A strange sense of satisfaction filled Anna at the thought. In the last few weeks, she had come to a deeper understanding of herself than she ever had before. She gazed at Maggie, reaching out to stroke a finger over her cheek. The older woman had proved to be not only a good friend, but a model for the type of woman Anna hoped she could become.

She lifted her head to press her mouth against Maggie's again. She cupped Maggie's large breasts, rubbing her thumbs over the thick nipples. Arousal twined through her, centring in the burgeoning pulse between her legs. Maggie's skin was always so warm. She slid her palm over the swell of Maggie's belly before reaching the soft nest of curls. Maggie's body tensed with excitement.

Anna didn't know when – or if – she would see the other woman again. She moved her mouth over Maggie's cheek to the hot juncture between her shoulder and her neck. Somehow, though, it didn't matter. Just as Derek had been a luxurious but temporary presence in her life, so too would Maggie be.

Anna thought that her life was divided into two main parts – her rebellious early years and now, hopefully, a future of reconciliation and redemption. Maggie and Derek were for ever lodged in an overlapping fold between those two parts, a place of healing and warmth.

She slipped her hands between Maggie's full thighs and pressed them apart. Maggie's body lengthened with sensual pleasure. Anna touched the oiled core of the other woman before lowering her head. She pressed her mouth against Maggie's folds, feeling Maggie buck upwards at the sensation. Anna placed her hands on Maggie's hips to hold her still as she began to deepen her sensual ministrations. She stroked her tongue over all the secret creases, around the tight knot of Maggie's clit, dipping into the taut hole. Her lips dampened with syrupy juices. She tightened her hands on Maggie's hips as the other woman began to writhe with the increasing need for release.

Anna ground her hips against the bedcovers as her own excitement began to expand. She loved everything about Maggie's body, from her strong limbs to the soft roundness of her breasts and buttocks. She sensed Maggie's muscles tightening, knew innately that she was beginning to reach the peak of her sensual ascent. Anna pressed her tongue into Maggie's vulva, drinking in the sweet-salty flavour of her. She worked her lips and tongue with increasing fervour as Maggie moaned and pushed her hips up towards Anna as if attempting to impale herself on Anna's tongue.

Maggie came with a shriek, her juices flowing copiously to dampen Anna's lips. Anna continued to lick her, urging every last tremble of pleasure from the other woman's body before she rose and kissed Maggie on the mouth. Maggie's lips parted as she sucked in the taste of her own body. A hot shudder passed from her mouth into Anna.

Maggie smoothed her hands over Anna's compact body, over the small breasts and the curve of her waist. Her fingers slipped between Anna's legs, parting her thighs.

'So tell me what you think of Derek's fucks,' Maggie whispered.

Her words jolted a renewed arousal through Anna's blood.

'What I think of –'

'Mmm. Does he fuck you hard?'

'He did. Yeah. The man has a cock like pliable iron.' Anna pushed her hips towards Maggie as if encouraging the caress of her fingers.

'He does, doesn't he?' Maggie murmured, sliding her lips over Anna's neck as she began to massage her pussy. 'Feels exquisite in your cunt.'

'Oh, yes.'

Anna spread her legs wider to allow Maggie to slide two fingers into her. She shivered and closed her eyes, imagining what it would be like to feel Derek thrusting inside her while Maggie fondled her at the same time. The image caused her tension to break apart, raining vibrations of pleasure through her blood. She shuddered and cried out, clutching at Maggie as the other woman continued to lightly stroke her.

'I'm really going to miss you,' Anna confessed, wrapping her arms around Maggie's shoulders as their mouths came together again.

'You know where to find me if you need me,' Maggie said. 'I'm not going anywhere.'

Anna thought that it had been a very long time since she had been able to count on anything or anyone. Even though she had no idea if she would ever see Maggie again, it was decidedly comforting to know that she would always be here.

She eased herself away from the other woman and rose to get dressed. As she slipped her feet into a pair of sandals, she glanced at a sketchbook that rested on a table.

'Do you mind if I take one of the drawings?' she asked.

'Help yourself.' Maggie slipped a cotton robe over her shoulders and went to stand next to Anna. 'I'd be honoured if you keep one. Take two, if you'd like.'

'No, just one.' Anna leafed through the book and carefully removed one of her favourite sketches – a three-quarters image of her face. Maggie had somehow managed to make her look both strong and vulnerable, including a glint of resolution in her eyes.

'I don't know how you do it,' Anna said.

'All I did was draw what I see.' Maggie gave her a smile and kissed her again. 'Take care, Anna. And don't change yourself. Just parts of your life.'

Anna thought that she would try to take that advice to heart.

She left Maggie's boat and crossed the dock to *Jezebel*. Derek was outside in the hot sun, shirtless as he sanded down the deck. Anna paused to admire his sweaty torso for a moment before she approached him.

'Getting ready to paint?' she asked.

He swiped his forearm down his face. 'Yeah. Making it a non-skid surface first.'

'So I thought I'd leave this evening,' Anna said. 'I have things to do at my old apartment before I leave for San Jose.'

Derek put down the sander and nodded. 'OK.'

'You sure you don't want to go with me?' Anna thought that she could use the strength of his presence.

'I guess I can drive you up there on Friday, if you want me to.'

Although it was hardly an enthusiastic offer, Anna smiled with relief. 'I'd appreciate it. Have you heard anything more about Cassandra?'

'According to your father, she didn't leave a trace. He can't locate Victor Thane, either, so there's no telling where they might be. Out of the country, probably. Have you talked to your father yet?'

'Briefly. Just to set up the meeting.'

'You nervous?'

'A little. Mostly relieved, though. At least he can't dispute the evidence.'

'He might even be relieved too,' Derek suggested. 'Anything else you need?'

Anna smiled faintly. 'You've done more than enough for me, Derek. More than I ever expected or hoped for. I don't think I'll ever be able to repay you.'

'I didn't do it for the money,' Derek said.

'Then why?'

He grinned and gave her a wink as he bent to pick up the sander again. 'Weakness for pixies.'

'Freddie's not exactly a pixie,' Anna remarked.

Derek stopped and looked at her. 'What does that mean?'

Anna was rather pleased that her suspicions were proving to be correct. She had known since the beginning that her relationship with Derek was temporary, but she hoped for his sake that he would realise his relationship with Freddie was not. She thought he needed someone like Freddie, a strong woman who not only shared his interests but would bring out the best in him. Derek needed Freddie to balance out his rough edges.

'I don't think you have a weakness for pixies, Derek,' Anna said. 'I think you have a weakness for Freddie.'

'Don't be ridiculous.'

'I'm not the one being ridiculous.'

Derek turned on the sander and returned to his task. 'I'll take you over to your apartment as soon as you're packed.'

Anna smiled to herself as she went into the cabin. She hoped that it wouldn't be long before Derek and Freddie realised what she had known for quite some time now.

Derek stood at the edge of the beach. A strip of sidewalk separated the sand from the street. Palm trees rustled overhead. The beach was strewn with a few sunbathers, soaking up the rays as the midday sun heightened overhead.

Derek slipped on his sunglasses as he walked out on to the hot sand. He didn't expect to find Freddie here since she usually surfed early in the morning, but it was worth a shot. She hadn't been at her apartment or her favourite coffee joint, so, unless she was out on a job, the beach was the next logical choice.

He scanned the water and failed to see her, although there were several surfers out beyond the breakers. Derek headed in the direction of the Santa Monica pier. He hadn't bothered leaving Freddie a message since he doubted she'd return his call. He suspected she was still mad at him for interrupting an incredibly hot kiss.

Somehow, though, through the dense fog of his increasing desire for her, he'd known that, if they didn't stop, he'd end up stripping her down and taking her right there on the dirt road. Just as he'd wanted to do the first time. And he knew deep inside that he'd never forgive himself if he treated Freddie like that, regardless of who had initiated the whole thing. She deserved better. Much better.

Derek came to a halt. His gaze narrowed on couple walking along the water's edge. Freddie was dressed in shorts and a T-shirt, her sandals dangling from her fingers as the shallow tide splashed around her ankles. Her hair was pulled back into a knot. That bastard Gavin was next to her, his head bent towards her slightly as he listened to what she was saying.

Irritation tightened in Derek's gut at the sight of Freddie with another man. The two of them stopped. Then Freddie reached up to kiss Gavin, one hand resting on his arm. His hands went around her waist. Derek's irritation hardened into anger. He wanted to go over there and rip them apart.

Instead, he took a breath and reined in his jealousy. He turned and stalked back towards the street so he wouldn't have to look at them together. He'd had his chance. He knew it. Women like Freddie were rare enough. She wouldn't sit around waiting for him. She'd told him as much.

He returned to Redondo Beach and headed for his boat. Maybe when he got back from San Jose, he'd take *Jezebel* out for a few days on the open seas. God knew she was the only female who made any sense to him anyway.

'Hello, Derek!'

Derek looked up at the sight of Maggie strolling down the dock towards him. She looked as sexy as she always did, clad in a multicoloured bikini top with a sarong wrapped loosely around her hips.

'Free for dinner tonight?' Maggie asked. She stopped in front of him, resting her hands on her waist. 'Maybe a little dessert too?'

Derek tried to drum up some desire for her, but his emotions felt entirely flat. It wasn't that Maggie had lost an ounce of her sex appeal. It was just that the only woman he seemed to be interested in any more was Freddie.

'I don't think so, Maggie. But thanks for the offer.'

Her tanned shoulders lifted in a shrug. 'Your loss.'

'In more ways than one,' Derek muttered.

Maggie's gaze slanted towards *Jezebel*. 'Is Anna still here?'

'She's at her apartment,' Derek said. 'I'm taking her up to San Jose this weekend so she and her father can work things out.'

'Any word on her stepmother?'

Derek shook his head. He had a strange hope that Cassandra Maxwell and her lover would never be caught. Regardless of what she'd done, she was a woman with a wild streak, one who secretly defied convention. Derek couldn't help but appreciate that.

'Well, tell Anna to give me a call if she comes back to LA,' Maggie said. 'I enjoyed her company.'

'I will.'

Derek went aboard his boat and into the cabin. The place seemed oddly empty without Anna, but he was glad to have his privacy back. He planned to take on as many jobs as he could handle so that he could afford to outfit the rest of the boat. Then he'd take off on his worldwide journey and leave this whole mess behind him.

18

Freddie climbed out of her SUV and headed for the dock. The boats swayed in the harbour like dozens of fishing lures. She arrived at *Jezebel* and climbed aboard, reaching out to knock on the cabin door.

'Derek?'

The door swung open. He stood there dressed in jeans and a T-shirt, a frown on his face. Even with his unwelcoming expression, a surge of awareness crested inside Freddie at the sight of him. She held up the Dazer.

'You left this in my car,' she said. 'I thought you might need it.'

'Thanks.' He took the box from her and stepped aside, even though he was still frowning. 'You can come in, if you want.'

'Gee, thanks for the welcome.' Freddie stepped into the cabin and looked around. All signs of Anna were already gone. 'So, um, when are you leaving for San Jose?'

'Friday. I think Anna is planning to stay there.'

'In San Jose?'

'Yeah.'

Freddie tried to ignore a ridiculously intense feeling of relief. She had nothing against Anna personally, but she couldn't stand the idea of Derek with another woman. Even imagining them together caused a sick kind of jealousy.

'I see.' Freddie sat at the chart table and began idly folding a corner of a map. 'Are you planning to see her again after that?'

'I doubt it.' He was glowering at her. 'Why do you want to know?'

'Curiosity.' Freddie returned his frown. 'Hey, what're you so mad about?'

'No reason.' Derek leant against the closed door and crossed his arms. 'You planning to see your surf boy again?'

'Don't call him that,' Freddie said irritably. 'He was a good guy.'

'Was?'

'Yeah, was,' Freddie retorted. 'I broke up with him earlier today, OK?'

If she hadn't known better, she would have sworn that relief cleared Derek's expression. The crease between his eyebrows disappeared, and his entire body seemed to relax.

'Earlier today,' he repeated.

'We had lunch on Third Street and went for a walk on the beach.'

Freddie shook her head at the thought of how amenably Gavin had taken her break-up. He hadn't been happy about it and even tried to change her mind, but in the end they had kissed goodbye and parted ways. Freddie didn't doubt that he'd have another girlfriend within a week, if not sooner. He was that appealing.

'He was a good guy,' she said again. 'I'll miss teaching him to surf.'

'Why did you break it off?'

Freddie levelled her gaze on him. Because of you, dammit, she wanted to snap, but she was still stung by how he had interrupted her advance last week. She wasn't about to admit that she continued to have all sorts of simmering feelings for him.

'Because he wasn't for me,' she muttered. She tossed him a glare. 'And don't you dare say you told me so.'

'I wasn't about to.'

Freddie pushed the map aside and stood. 'I should go. Things to do.'

'What things?' He was still in front of the door.

'You know,' Freddie said lamely. 'Things.'

She stopped before him. His eyes were fixed on her, something hot kindled in their grey depths. God, Freddie thought as her breathing grew shallow. One look from him and she nearly melted into a puddle. The air seemed to compress. Nervousness twisted through Freddie as she recognised the desire building rapidly between them, as if their previously thwarted lust had sparked to life again. As if they both wanted to pick up right where they left off.

Freddie took a step backwards. Derek took a step forwards. He reached out and put his forefinger against the indentation above her upper lip, the same place where she had touched him.

'Philtrum,' he said.

'What?'

'This.' His finger brushed gently against her skin. 'It's called a philtrum.'

Freddie's pulse was already increasing from his light stroking. Her senses heightened to such levels that she could practically feel the shallow ridges of his fingerprint against her skin.

'That is a very strange name,' she murmured.

'It's from the Greek word for love potion.' His finger moved down to the bow of her lip. 'Ancient Greeks thought the philtrum was one of the most erogenous places on the body.'

'How do you know that?'

'I know a few things,' Derek replied.

He moved closer to her, his eyes still fixed on hers, his hands coming up to cup her face, brushing strands of hair away from her temples. For a moment, he just looked at her, studying her features as if he were memorising them, as if he were seeing her for the first time.

He was so close that she could see the dark ring that surrounded his irises, the flecks of black in the depths of his pupils. She didn't back away from him. Then he lowered his head and his mouth touched hers in the most unique and erotic of kisses, his upper lip resting against her philtrum, his bottom lip on her mouth.

Freddie drew in a breath as her hands reached for and found the front of his T-shirt. His mouth parted slightly, capturing her upper lip in an intimate caress. Undiluted warmth spread through Freddie. She curled her fists around his shirt as if he were the only thing holding her upright.

Derek's hands slid over the curve of her waist to clutch her hips. His lips moved over hers and pressed them apart, deepening the kiss, his tongue sweeping into the crevices of her mouth. A brief thought crossed Freddie's mind that this could still be a mistake, but then she sank under the onslaught of his kiss and the thought dissolved into oblivion.

Derek murmured something low in his throat. Freddie didn't hear the word, but the husky tone of his voice went straight to her blood. The taste and scent of him – salt and shaving cream – filled her head with an abundance of sensation. Her hands slipped down to the hem of his T-shirt, and she hesitated for only an instant before sliding her hands underneath. Her fingers touched his bare abdomen, flat and rock hard with muscle. And warm. So warm. His naked body would feel unbelievable against hers. She shuddered.

Derek's hands moved to the back of her head. He tugged gently at the knot of her hair before making a noise of frustration when it didn't yield. Freddie reached back to unfasten the knot, letting her hair fall over her back and shoulders. Derek drove his fingers into the thick mass.

'Better,' he murmured against her mouth. 'Much better.'

His hands slid through her hair, his fingers coming up to massage the back of her neck, tilting her head so that he had more complete access to her mouth. No man had ever kissed her like this, as if he wanted to devour her, as if he would be content to go on kissing her for the rest of eternity. Freddie moved her hands slowly over the ridges of Derek's abdomen to his chest.

'Would you . . .' She eased away from him slightly and swallowed. 'Would you take your shirt off?'

Derek pulled his T-shirt over his head and dropped it on the floor. Freddie gazed at him with new eyes, seeing him not just as her friend, but as her lover. His skin was tanned and taut over smooth muscles, a mat of dark hair arrowing down to the waistband of his jeans.

Freddie splayed her hands over his chest, the coarse hairs brushing deliciously against her palms. His hands settled on her hips and tugged her lower body against his. A tremble coursed through Freddie at the sensation of his erection. She wanted to touch him there, to cup the growing bulge in her hand, but a hint of anxiety continued to linger.

Derek's mouth covered her lips again. As if sensing her sudden hesitation, he took her hand and placed it against his groin. Freddie drew in a breath, arousal twining over her nerves as she slid her fingers over his hard length. She could practically feel the blood pulsing through him.

His hands moved to slide under her shirt, but then stopped. His mouth lifted a hair's-breadth from hers.

'What are you wearing under this?' he whispered.

Freddie flushed. She hadn't bothered with sexy underclothes this morning, dressing for comfort rather than appeal. If she'd known she would be in this situation with Derek, she would have gone all out with the silk and lace lingerie.

'Um, nothing very interesting,' she admitted. 'Sorry.'

'Can I see?'

Still flushing, Freddie stepped away and took off her

T-shirt. She was wearing a grey cotton sports bra that was extraordinarily comfortable, but that couldn't have been more boring to look at.

'It's not lingerie,' she said.

'No.' Despite his agreement, he was staring at her as if nothing could possibly be sexier than what she was wearing right now. 'You're incredible, Freddie.'

Freddie looked down at the bra, wondering if she was missing something. The tight cotton hugged her full breasts and created an appealing valley of cleavage. Her firm nipples were outlined against the material, but it was still just a stretch of grey cotton.

'And it's not exactly silk,' she told him.

'You don't need silk.'

Freddie's lips curved into a smile as Derek approached her again.

'Then why have I caught you looking down my shirt?' she teased.

'Just because I've looked doesn't mean you need it.'

Derek cupped the back of her head again and lowered his head to kiss her. A sudden spark of urgency lit between them. He pulled her closer. Her breasts crushed against his chest. The heat of his body seeped into her. His fingers twisted around the straps of the sports bra and pulled them over her shoulders, his gaze darkening as her breasts were bared. He slid his hands underneath the twin globes, lifting them as his thumbs flicked across her nipples. Freddie drew in a sharp breath as her sex swelled with moisture. Her lower body began to tighten with increasing pressure.

She let Derek guide her to the bed and bent to take off her shoes. She fixed her eyes on his face as he divested her of the bra, baring her breasts to the touch of his hands.

'Jesus, Freddie.' His words were hoarse and filled with desire. 'You are so damn beautiful.'

Pleasure swirled through Freddie as a responding need

began to cloud her mind. Derek rubbed his hands over her breasts with exquisite slowness, moving over her smooth belly. He hooked his fingers under the elastic waistband of her shorts. Before he removed them, he looked at her. His grey eyes were smoky and lit with fire like volcanic ash.

'OK?' he asked.

Freddie nodded, her heart racing. Derek pulled her shorts and panties over her hips, exposing the tanned length of her thighs and the dark curls of her mound. His gaze moved with hungry pleasure over her naked body. A rush of self-consciousness rose to flush Freddie's skin, but then Derek levered himself over her body and all embarrassment melted away.

Derek's breath was hot as his mouth moved over the juncture of her neck and shoulder to her breasts. His hair brushed deliciously against her chest as he bent to take her nipple between his teeth. A cry of pleasure broke from Freddie's throat, her body arching up towards his.

'Wait,' she gasped. 'I want – can I see you?'

He eased away from her only long enough to divest himself of the rest of his clothing. Freddie stared at the thick length of his stalk, her breathing increasingly shallow as she rose to sit on the edge of the bed. She settled her hands on his hips and tried to draw him towards her, but he prevented the movement.

'You don't have to,' he said.

'I know. I want to.'

She grasped the base of his penis and leant forward to take him into her mouth. His skin was hot and throbbing against the surface of her tongue. Freddie's eyes drifted closed as she moved her lips over his shaft. She stroked her tongue over the length, swirling it around the hard knob. Derek's hands tightened in her hair.

'Freddie.' His voice was slightly strangled.

She pulled away from him as he eased her back on to

the bed. His body covered hers, taut with urgency, his mouth moving over her skin. He kissed her breasts, his tongue sliding over the juicy crevices underneath, his fingers tweaking her nipples. Their breathing came faster and harder, mixing with the rising scent of sex. Derek's hands slipped between her thighs and pushed them apart. Freddie's heart beat ceaselessly in her head, her blood scorched with the sensation of them together.

His fingers moved into her moist folds with gentle exploration. Freddie moaned, her legs spreading to allow his access, her hands going around to stroke his back. His forefinger eased inside her, his thumb circling the tight button of her clit. He touched her as if he already knew what would please her the most intensely.

Freddie moved restlessly underneath him. Both her mind and body were filled with anticipation and the stunning realisation that this was really happening. It was Derek, her best friend, her confidant, the man who had been stirring up a desire in her for months. A desire she had only recently allowed herself to recognise.

'Derek, now,' she whispered, pulling him towards her, wanting him desperately. 'Now.'

He positioned himself between her legs, bracing his hands on either side of her head, his expression tight with the effort of retaining control. He slipped into her with one velvety stroke that set fire to her blood. A groan escaped him, his teeth clenching.

Freddie moaned, wrapping her arms around his back as he began to thrust inside her with a rhythm that matched the beating of her heart. Their bodies moved slickly together. Freddie gave herself up to him, hugging his hips with her thighs, her teeth sinking into his hard shoulder.

Despite her urgency for him, Freddie's excitement built with delicate slowness and simplicity. Derek stoked her arousal with every movement, eliciting the ease of her response. Her body trembled. She clutched him against her and descended into the fathomless pleasure they were creating. She wanted all of him.

Freddie's neck arched. Derek's lips touched the pulse beating wildly at the hollow of her throat. His hands moved down to grasp her moist hips, holding her tightly against him as vibrations began to shudder through her. A cry broke from her throat. She convulsed forcefully around Derek's shaft, drawing out his own potent response. He thrust into her with a deep groan, flooding her body with his seed as he had flooded her mind with his presence.

They lay gasping. Derek buried his face in the junction of Freddie's neck and shoulder. She closed her eyes and stroked her fingers down his back. His weight was heavy and delicious on her.

Freddie didn't know whether they slept. All she knew was that it wasn't long before Derek was touching her body again, awakening her arousal a second time. She turned to him and opened her eyes, urging him on to his back. She rose on to her knees beside him and stroked her hands over him. She touched every plane of his body as if she were a cartographer and he were a landscape she wanted to map.

She smoothed her hands over his thighs, down to the sinews of his calves and then up to the sharp ridges of his abdomen and chest. She stroked his biceps and arms, even traced the shell of his ears with the tip of her finger. Then she lowered her head and followed the same path with her tongue, thrilling in the shudders that passed through his body. Pleasure melted into more pleasure as she straddled and rode him until her blood erupted once again, and then he was behind her, taking her fiercely, his fingers digging into her bottom. Before the hour was over, he pressed his mouth against her sex and drove her to further sensual heights with the expertise of his tongue.

Freddie could not get enough of Derek and, it seemed,

he could not get enough of her. Their limbs entangled, their skin grew hot and damp. They drank each other dry, their bodies liquid and suffused with sheer pleasure. Freddie's blood streamed with a seemingly endless river of heat as she lost track of where she ended and Derek began.

Finally when the crimson rays of the setting sun began streaming into the cabin, they collapsed back on to the bed, spent and exhausted.

Derek eased away from Freddie, his chest still heaving. She rolled on to her side, reaching up to brush her fingers along the edge of his jaw. She looked at him for a long minute, the planes of his face glistening with a fine sheen of sweat.

He opened his eyes to look at her. Their gazes locked. A strange feeling of unease rose in Freddie unexpectedly, marring the intense satiation that had flooded her being.

'Now what?' she whispered.

For a moment, Derek didn't reply. Then he broke away from her, moving his legs so that he was sitting on the side of the bed with his back to her. He pulled on his boxer shorts.

Freddie reached for her clothes. Something shifted in the air. She thought unwillingly of Maggie, of Anna, of the women who were drawn to Derek with such uninhibited swiftness. She slipped into her sports bra and panties.

'I should get back home,' she muttered.

Silence descended between them like a wall. Freddie glanced at Derek's naked back. His body was rigid with tension.

'Maybe we could go for coffee tomorrow or something,' Freddie suggested, making an effort to keep her voice light. She put on her shorts and T-shirt, then looked for the discarded band to tie her hair back. 'Or there's a new Mexican restaurant over on San Vicente.'

He didn't respond. Freddie found the band and

reached to pull her hair into a ponytail. She moved to stand in front of Derek. His elbows were resting on his knees, his hands clasped loosely between them. He didn't look at her.

'Hey, look, it's not that big a deal, OK?' Freddie said. A tremble threaded her voice. She made an effort to contain it. 'I mean, we were both obviously curious, you know, these things happen. It's not as if we owe each other anything that –'

The words stopped in her throat when Derek lifted his head. Freddie went silent at the look in his eyes, a dark combination of need and something else that she did not recognise. Her heart did a strange little flip.

'Christ, Freddie,' Derek said, his voice so low that she almost didn't hear him. 'I think I'm in love with you.'

Freddie stared at him. He appeared to be as stunned by his own words as she was.

'You – you think what?' Freddie breathed.

'I'm in love with you,' Derek repeated.

The admission should have roused something warm and pleasurable, but instead Freddie felt something crack inside her. She wrapped her arms around herself. She couldn't look at him.

'Derek, I think –'

He stood before she could get the words out. Freddie took a step back. He grasped her shoulders and pulled her against him. Her body reacted at the renewed contact with his, but she tried to suppress the fresh wave of desire.

'I mean it.' His voice was deep and urgent. His gaze seemed to penetrate to the core of her being. 'I don't want to be with anyone but you.'

'That doesn't mean you're in love with me.' Her throat felt tight.

'Freddie, this isn't a one-time thing.'

Freddie pulled away from him with a frown. 'What, you're the only one who can decide that?'

A hint of anger darkened Derek's expression. 'What the hell is the matter with you?'

'Nothing! I'm only saying that we don't have to make a – a commitment or anything like that just because we had sex one time.'

'Who's talking about a commitment?' Derek asked.

'You're the one saying you're in love with me!' Freddie reminded him. 'Look, I appreciate the sentiment, but I don't –'

'It's not just a damn sentiment,' Derek interrupted. 'You think I said that because we fucked, don't you?'

Freddie almost winced at hearing their encounter whittled down to its crudest form. 'I know you're experienced, that you've had lots of women.'

'Experience doesn't mean I'm a cold-hearted bastard.'

'Derek, I'm just saying that you don't have to tell me something you think I want to hear.'

'And you think I'd do that?' Derek snapped. 'What the hell, Freddie? Have I ever done that to you?'

'No, but –'

'But what? And don't tell me you wanted to fuck just to see what it was like.'

'What other reason could there be?'

His features hardened an instant before he grabbed her again. His fingers dug into her shoulders as his mouth descended on hers. The kiss was as punishing as it was arousing, searing Freddie with the promise of future passion if she was willing to acknowledge it.

She gasped, her hands pushing at his chest as she struggled to break away from him again. Her heart filled with some indefinable mixture of emotions. Combined with her intense desire to be with him was an outright fear over how deeply he had the power to hurt her.

Freddie yanked herself away from him, breaking his strong grip. She drew the back of her hand over her mouth and glared at him.

'You've proven your point, all right?' she snapped.

'You know I'm attracted to you. You don't have to take advantage of that.'

'You sure didn't act like I was taking advantage of you,' Derek replied bitterly.

'What do you want from me, Derek? Do you want to have an affair? Do you want to try and get each other out of our systems? Do you want me to fill the gap between your last woman and your next one?'

A dark kind of understanding appeared on Derek's features. The lines of his body tightened with increasing anger.

'That's what this is about? You think I'd use you until someone better comes along?'

'That appears to be your MO.'

'Look, I don't take advantage of anyone,' Derek said coldly. 'I don't force anyone to do anything they don't want to do, least of all a woman. If you think that's what I'm about, then get the fuck out of here.'

'I don't think you use anyone,' Freddie responded. 'I don't think you take advantage of people. I know, however, that you have the ability to move easily from woman to woman.'

'And you think I'd do that with you.'

'I have no reason to think otherwise.'

'Freddie, I just told you I'm in love with you!' Derek snapped. 'You think I'd tell you that and go fuck another woman next week?'

'I don't know what you'll do, Derek!' Freddie cried. 'I don't know if that's what you tell every woman you're with.'

'Jesus, Freddie, if I'd known your opinion of me would sink this low, I never would have fucked you in the first place.'

'Stop being crude,' Freddie said flatly.

'What do you want me to call it? That's what I do, isn't it? Fuck? God forbid I should actually make love to a woman.'

He turned away from her, his shoulders tense. They were both silent for a moment before Derek sighed.

'For what it's worth, I don't tell that to every woman,' he said. 'As a matter of fact, I've never said that to a woman before you.'

Freddie believed him. She had believed him the first time he said it. He had never lied to her.

'I don't mean to accuse you of anything,' she muttered. Tears filled her eyes unexpectedly. 'I'm sorry, Derek. I know you so well, but, in this way, I don't know you at all. I don't know what to do.'

'And you think I do?'

'Maybe it was a mistake.'

'Sure as hell didn't feel like a mistake,' Derek said.

Freddie looked at his back, her mind swirling with a mass of emotions that she couldn't even begin to sort out. And yet one clear thought emerged. It hadn't been a mistake. Nothing that felt so right, so good, could possibly be a mistake.

'I should go,' Freddie mumbled again.

She went towards the door. Her hand shook as she reached for the handle.

'Freddie.'

Freddie turned back to Derek. Her heart clenched. He was standing there with his hair all messy, his torso bare to the waist, an expression of both regret and lingering irritation on his face. He lifted his hands, palms up.

'What?' he asked. The single word contained a hundred questions.

They looked at each other for a long minute. Freddie swallowed hard, her hand tightening on the door handle.

'I don't know, Derek,' she finally confessed. 'I don't know.'

She gathered all the strength she had in order to turn and leave the cabin.

19

Derek pushed on the brake pedal and muttered a curse of irritation. Traffic on the I-5 was clogged because of an accident, which had slowed their progress considerably. Flat farmland stretched out on either side of the interstate with hills creating grey smudges on the horizon. Red brake lights glinted in the sun. Derek had little patience with traffic in general, but now it was driving him crazy.

'Sorry about this,' Anna said from the passenger seat, 'but I really appreciate you coming with me.'

Derek sighed and tried to straighten out his thoughts. 'I know. Sorry.'

'Is it Freddie?' Anna asked with far too much perception.

'No.' Derek shot her a glare. 'No, it's not Freddie.'

Anna shrugged and fell silent. Derek tightened his hands on the steering wheel. Of course it was Freddie. It was always Freddie. It had always been Freddie.

Never before had a woman occupied his thoughts to the virtual exclusion of everything else. Even before he realised how he really felt about her, she had still dominated his thoughts. For the past two years, he had primarily just wanted to be with her. It was Freddie he'd called when he had a problem, when he wanted to go to the beach or get something to eat or go for a run. She was always the first one in his thoughts. He couldn't believe how dense he'd been about realising that he loved the woman. Although, he admitted, love had never exactly been his speciality.

Freddie continued to fill his thoughts as he inched

along the fast lane of the I-5. He was still ticked off at her assumption that she was just one knot in his endless rope of women. Not to mention her accusation that he told every woman he was with that he loved her. While he could – with both reluctance and a little shame – understand why she thought that, he was still mad that she believed he was capable of treating *her* that way. Didn't she know how different she was?

The traffic finally cleared near Bakersfield, and they continued the rest of the way at a reasonable pace. Derek stopped only to refill the car and grab a couple of sandwiches for himself and Anna. He was glad to help Anna one last time, but he also wanted to get back to LA as soon as possible. He didn't know what he was going to do or how, if at all, he could repair things with Freddie. At this point, he wasn't even certain that he wanted to, but he at least wanted to have the option.

Dusk was beginning to settle into the air when he pulled the rental car up in front of the Maxwell house. He looked at Anna.

She was wearing a tailored black dress that she had picked up in a Santa Monica shop, and she had even taken the time to have her hair dyed back to its natural brown colour. Without her piercings and her blood-red lipstick, she looked almost wholesome. Derek couldn't help being somewhat touched by the lengths she'd gone to before seeing her father.

'You OK?' he asked.

'Yeah.' She gave him a shaky smile. Her hands twisted together. 'Just a little nervous. Am I wrinkled?'

'You look great.'

'Anna?' The front door opened, and Erin came hurrying down the steps.

Relief flowed over Anna's features as she got out of the car to greet her sister. They hugged tightly before Erin pulled back and gushed over how well Anna looked.

'You know Derek Rowland, I think,' Anna said.

'Sure.' Erin gave Derek a warm smile and held out her hand. 'Nice to see you again, Mr Rowland. You've been more help to us than you realise.'

'Glad to be of service.'

Anna tilted her head towards the house. A crease appeared between her eyebrows. 'Is he home?'

'In his study,' Erin said. 'He's waiting for you.'

'Has he said anything?'

Erin shook her head. 'Not to me. I thought it was a good sign that he was willing to see you at all.'

The two sisters started towards the house. Anna turned once to make certain that Derek was following them. He did so reluctantly. He didn't want to interfere on this meeting, but he had agreed to accompany Anna as one last favour.

Richard Maxwell was standing by the fireplace in the study, looking tall and imposing with his steel-grey hair and tailored suit. Anxiety lined Anna's body.

'Anna.' Richard's deep voice fairly echoed through the study.

'Hello, Father.'

Richard's eyes slid to Derek. He frowned.

'I asked him to be here,' Anna said hastily.

Silence fell. Anna cleared her throat. Richard nodded towards a chair.

'Have a seat.'

Anna sat down. Derek remained standing by the door.

'I'm sorry,' Anna finally admitted. 'Sorry about every-thing that's happened. About everything I've done.'

Richard didn't respond for a moment, but then he nodded. 'I am, too, Anna. I'm sorry for what Cassandra did.'

Derek didn't fail to notice that Richard didn't apolo-gise for his own actions, but he knew that any kind of apology from the other man would have to suffice.

'What happens now?' Anna asked.

'What do you want to have happen?' Richard replied.

'I'd like for us to give each other another chance,' Anna said.

'I've given you several chances.'

'Father, you know that Cassandra was always in the way,' Erin put in. 'She's the reason Anna was arrested in the first place.'

A frown darkened Richard's face. 'Cassandra was my wife. I will not have you tell me that she was an obstacle.'

'She was,' Erin muttered.

'*Was* your wife?' Anna asked.

Richard crossed his arms over his chest. A hint of something that might have been embarrassment flashed in his metal-grey eyes.

'I've filed for divorce on the grounds of irreconcilable differences,' he admitted. 'I have no idea where Cassandra is, but I have little doubt that she is with her lover.' He looked at Derek. 'You're sure you don't want to reconsider my offer?'

'What offer?' Anna asked.

'I offered him a job tracking Cassandra down,' Richard explained. 'He turned me down.'

Anna looked at Derek. 'Why?'

Derek shrugged. The amount of money that Richard had offered him would help to finish outfitting his boat, but Derek didn't want the job. Cassandra Maxwell was a thief and a liar, but he couldn't help possessing a degree of admiration for her. 'Not interested right now.'

'So who's going to go after her?' Erin asked.

'I'll have to find someone else,' Richard replied. 'But frankly, I would rather not get the police involved.'

'That means she might never be caught,' Anna said.

Richard shrugged. Silence descended.

'I'm willing to try,' Anna finally said. 'I know I've been far from perfect. I know it's not all Cassandra's fault. I've been part of the problem. But I can try.'

'Trying isn't good enough, Anna,' Richard replied. 'You have to do it. You have to straighten out your life.'

'What do you want me to do?'

'Hold a job. Stop running around with worthless men. Take some responsibility for your life.'

Derek could almost see Anna's mind working. He knew as well as she did that she had already tried several times, and failed, to follow her father's advice.

'I'm prepared to offer you another job,' Richard told Anna. 'Here at the San Jose branch. Assistant to an executive in the marketing department. It's not an entry-level position, but it's not an executive position, either. You will have room to move up. Or down.'

Anna was quiet for a moment before she shook her head. 'No.'

'What?'

'No,' Anna repeated. 'I don't want to work in the corporate world. It's why I keep screwing up. I don't like it. I'm not good at it.'

'Then what do you intend to do?' Richard asked.

'I want to go back to college.'

'College?' Richard said as if he'd never heard of such a thing.

'Yes. I want to take some classes. Art, photography, film. That kind of thing.'

'What in the name of God are you going to do with classes like that?' Richard asked.

'I don't know,' Anna admitted. 'But I need to find out what I'm good at. That's been my problem my whole life. I don't know what I'm capable of because I've never discovered what I'm good at.'

'What makes you think you'd be good at something like photography?'

'I don't know,' Anna said again. 'I just know that I have to try. I'll work at Jump Start part-time to pay for tuition. You can even put me in an entry-level position as long as the schedule is flexible.'

'And what happens if you drop out again?'

'I don't intend to this time,' Anna said. 'But I need to at least try. I can promise one thing, and that's that I'll do the best I can. I need you – I need you to give me another chance.'

Richard looked out of the window. For an instant, Derek thought that the other man would refuse Anna's request, but then Richard nodded.

'All right, Anna. I'll give you another chance. And I'll ask you to give me another chance.'

A sheen of tears glistened in Anna's eyes. She stood and crossed the room to her father, placing her palm on his arm. They didn't embrace, but then Richard reached out to brush his hand over Anna's hair in a gesture that was surprisingly tender.

Erin looked at Derek and gave him a smile of gratitude. Figuring that Anna had begun to accomplish what she had hoped to, Derek stepped out of the room and closed the door behind him. He left the house, pulling his keys from his pocket as he headed back to the car.

'Derek!'

He turned. Anna came out the front door after him. She hurried down the steps.

'I wanted to thank you,' she said. 'You've done a lot for me.'

Derek smiled and tugged gently at a lock of her hair. 'You're welcome. I'm glad it looks like things will work out.'

'I hope so.' She bit down on her lower lip, her brown eyes tinged with a hint of sadness. 'I don't suppose we'll see each other again.'

Derek wanted to tell her that they would, but he suspected it would be a lie. Obviously Anna knew that, too. He pressed his mouth against her forehead as something almost regretful rose in him at the thought of not seeing her again.

'We're friends, aren't we?' Anna asked.

He nodded. 'We'll always be friends. You need anything, you come to me.'

'I will. Thanks.' She stood on tiptoe to kiss him, her lips lingering against his. 'For everything.'

Derek rubbed his hand over her shoulder and started back to his car. Anna's voice stopped him again.

'You know, I think she's worthy of you.'

Derek looked at her. 'What?'

She smiled. 'Freddie. She's worthy of you. She might be the only woman who is.'

Derek stared at her for a minute before Anna gave him a little wave and turned to go back into the house. He went to his car and sat in the driver's seat.

An image of Freddie filled his head. She was like a confection – all honeyed skin, chocolate-brown eyes and hair the colour of cinnamon. Thoughts of her were always at the back of his mind. Even before their hot encounters, it was her face, her voice, her smile, her body that seemed lodged somewhere deep inside him. He had hated being without her. He never wanted to be without her again.

She's worthy of you. Derek disagreed. Freddie was way beyond worthy of him. The question was whether or not he was worthy of her.

Freddie dug her toes into the hot sand. Delicious. The sun stroked over her bare legs and thighs, burning through the material of her one-piece bathing suit. Her eyes were closed behind a pair of sunglasses, her arms resting at her sides. She tried to empty her mind, to think of nothing but the luscious heat of the sun and sand, the gentle rush of ocean waves, the distant rumble of sunbathers' voices.

She tried not to think of Derek, but she failed. He was always there in the back of her mind, the heat of his body even more compelling and desirable than that of the sun.

She missed him. It had been only four days since their encounter, but she still missed him. She knew she had accused him unfairly, but the truth was that she was terrified. Accusing him of being shallow and manipulative seemed to be the only way she could protect herself.

'Excuse me.'

Freddie lifted her sunglasses and opened her eyes. Squinting against the glare of the sun, she looked at a well-built young man whom she had seen playing beach volleyball.

'Sorry to bother you, but one of our players had to leave,' he said. 'We're looking for a sixth to even out the teams. You look –' his eyes slid over her curvy body '– athletic. You up for a game?'

Freddie didn't respond for a moment as she looked him over in return. He was nice-looking with a good body and a shaved head that added to his appeal. She tried to find some attraction towards him, something that would indicate that it wasn't just Derek, that she was ripe and ready for a mutual attraction with any potential candidate. Instead, all she could think about was Derek.

'No,' she finally said. 'Sorry, but I don't think so.'

'Too bad.' Rather than leave, he plunked himself down on to the sand beside her hand held out his hand. 'I'm Jack.'

'Freddie.'

They shook hands. Freddie wished he would leave.

'You come here often?' Jack asked, then grimaced. 'That sounded like a line, didn't it?'

'Yes to both questions.'

Jack grinned. 'Well, since I'm on a roll, you want to get a coffee or beer or something?'

'No, thanks.' Freddie slipped her sunglasses over her eyes again. 'Thanks for the offer, though.'

'Sure. Maybe I'll see you around again.' There was the

rustling noise of his standing up and brushing the sand off his legs.

'Maybe.'

At least he could take a hint, Freddie thought. She closed her eyes and leant her neck on the rolled-up towel that served as a pillow. She had to admit that it was nice to occasionally be reminded of her own allure. The reminders meant that Derek wasn't the only man interested in her. She had options.

Of course, she didn't want to take any of those options. She wanted Derek. She wanted not just his body, but his mind and soul and all those secret places inside him. And she wanted to give the same to him.

'Hell!' The curse escaped her on a muttered breath. She knew Derek was heading up north with Anna at that very instant. She wanted to believe that their relationship had shifted to a platonic level, but she wasn't certain of anything any more.

She allowed a brief image of Derek to appear on the screen of her eyelids. His chest was broad and strong, tapering to a narrow waist and hard abdomen. His arms and legs were sinewy with muscle, and then of course there was his very tempting cock.

Freddie shifted her thighs as the sun spread long fingers over her legs. Heat pooled in her very core. She remembered Derek's body on hers, inside hers. A burst of arousal flooded through her. Her skin was hot. She parted her legs slightly to allow the sun to burn against her pussy. Her lips parted as she drank in the delectable sensations.

She lifted one hand and rested it against her full breast. Her nipple budded up against her palm. With a covert movement, she tweaked it quickly between her fingers. Shimmers of electricity spread directly to her sex. She could feel her body begin to surge like the crest of an ocean wave. She wanted him. She wanted to ride

Derek again the way she rode a wave, wanted to spread her legs over him and drive her body down on top of his. She wanted to control him. She wanted to be controlled by him.

A small moan escaped her lips. Her clit twitched in reaction to the increasing heat of the sun. Her toes pushed deeper into the sand. Golden grains covered her feet with earthy warmth. Arousal swirled around her belly. She brushed her hand over her abdomen, resting her fingers lightly against the swell of her mons. She wanted to press her fingers into her sex, but her self-imposed restraint only augmented her excitement. She furtively pressed her thighs together. Her sex throbbed.

She knew her thighs were strong. Years of running, surfing and rollerblading had built up the muscles of her legs so that they were sleek and powerful. What she didn't know was whether her muscles were strong enough to satisfy her physical needs. She pressed her thighs together more tightly. Her clit pulsed hard, sending vibrations over every nerve. The urgency tightened in her lower body. Freddie drew in a breath, smoothing her hand back up over her belly.

She turned on to her side. The sun slithered over the backs of her legs and bottom, moving up to warm her back. Freddie sighed with sheer pleasure. She increased the pressure of her thighs. She could feel the heat intensifying there, as if the sun itself were preparing to fuck her. She shuddered at the thought, imagining a long, smooth rod of flaxen light pumping into her body. Her breasts were hot and heavy, spilling to the side and creating a deep valley of cleavage. Her hard nipples pressed against her arm.

Freddie crossed her legs and tightened them together. Her heart began to pound with the effort. She held the pressure until her leg muscles began to quiver, then she released it. Her clit continued to pulse with heightening urgency. The pleats of her sex rubbed damply together.

She squeezed her legs together again, biting down hard on her lower lip as she felt her body responding on more concentrated levels. Her breath deepened. She repeated the movement again and again, squeezing and flexing her thighs together, urging herself towards the summit of her growing pleasure.

Freddie let out a soft groan and sank her teeth into the flesh of her arm. The sun was scorching. She heard the distant rumble of the ocean, like listening to a lover's voice echoing through his chest. She clutched her legs together again as the need grew stronger, her muscles tensing, her blood trembling. Her whole body felt as if it were striving towards release. She squeezed her eyes shut and gathered in her breath as she pressed her clit one last time, holding the position with all her strength until the wave finally broke through her body.

A small cry emerged from Freddie's throat as she continuing squeezing her thighs to ride out the vibrations. When the final sensations pulsed through her body, she let herself go limp. She breathed hard, allowing herself to bask in the feeling of being entirely slack and satiated after what had proved to be more exertion than she'd anticipated.

She could do it alone. She could be content with the heat of the sun, the various creative means of self-satisfaction, the crash of the surf, the occasional dalliance with a tempting beach bum. She could. She just didn't want to.

Freddie rolled on to her back again. The sun continued to massage her moist skin. She parted her legs to let the rays spread over her inner thighs. An unexpected hint of self-directed anger rose in her.

She had never been a coward. In just a couple of years, she had proved to be highly successful in a very male-dominated business. She'd taken down men who were three times her size. She'd surfed on twenty-foot brea-kers. She'd been threatened by guns, knives, violent dogs, even a pair of brass knuckles, and yet none of that scared her as much as actually admitting how deeply she cared for Derek.

Freddie sat up. She would be damned if she'd let this bring her to a standstill. She'd faced everything in her life head-on, and Derek would be no different. She had no idea how things would end up, but she never did. No one ever did. All she could do was take the risk and trust that her instincts were right.

20

Derek shaded his eyes from the sun and looked up at the mast. He'd tested the new sail several times and it worked beautifully. He'd finished prepping and painting the deck, and the new diesel engine had been installed a few days ago. Now he just needed a few basic supplies of food and first-aid equipment and he'd be ready to go. He had already set a departure date for the following week. All he wanted right now was to be alone on the open seas. Well, that was almost all he wanted.

He started stacking the empty cans of paint on to the dock. He should be thrilled. This was what he had been working towards for several years. This would be the fulfilment of his heart's desire, to sail and see the world without answering to anyone but himself or anything but the sea. Too bad he felt so fucking hollow inside.

He straightened and caught sight of Maggie's boat. He hadn't seen her in a few days. Maybe he should pay her a visit. He tried again to find some thread of desire for her, but there was nothing. He thought of Maggie and could see only Freddie. He thought of Anna and could see only Freddie. He looked at women on the street and always compared them to Freddie.

'She looks good.'

It was Freddie's voice. Derek looked up and saw her coming down the deck towards him. Dressed in shorts and a T-shirt, her hair pulled back, she looked the same as she always did. And she looked entirely different.

'Yeah.' Derek wiped his hands on his jeans. Nerves suddenly clenched in his stomach. 'Got a new sail.'

'Congratulations.' She paused on the dock beside his boat.

Derek stepped aside in an unspoken invitation for her to board. She hesitated, but then climbed on to the deck.

'You got all the repairs done too?' she asked.

'Yeah. Richard Maxwell gave me a sizable cheque. Said it was for taking care of his daughter.'

'That was nice of him.'

'It was enough to buy the rest of my equipment,' Derek said.

Freddie blinked. 'For your trip, you mean?'

'I'm leaving next week. Wednesday.'

'Oh.'

A hint of satisfaction rose in Derek over Freddie's obvious surprise. If she thought he'd intended to sit around waiting for her, then she was about to be disappointed.

'So, uh, how is Anna?' she asked.

'Doing well. She sent me an email last week. She's taking some courses and getting along reasonably well with her father. He dropped the charges, of course.'

'Are you planning to see her again?'

Derek's expression darkened. 'If you mean am I planning to fuck her again, the answer is no.'

Freddie winced. 'I didn't mean that. I'm sorry.'

'I haven't been with anyone since you, Freddie.' Derek didn't intend to be, either, but he wasn't about to tell her that.

Freddie looked at him, her chocolate-brown eyes wary. 'I'm sorry for what I said. I – Christ, Derek, I'm scared. I admit it.'

'Yeah. Me too.'

'You are?'

'Sure,' Derek said. 'What if things don't work out? What if we end up wrecking what's been the best relationship I've ever had? I don't want to lose you, Freddie. Not as a friend.'

'What about as a lover?'

'I don't want to lose that either, but, if you want it to end, then fine. I'll deal with it.'

Freddie gazed out at the harbour. The sun burnished her skin and brought out golden highlights in her hair. Derek thought he'd never seen a woman so pretty.

'I don't want it to end,' Freddie finally said. 'I'm scared, but I still don't want it to end. Maybe we can just try.'

'Being lovers?'

'And still being friends. I don't want to lose you either.'

'I'm not interested in trying,' Derek said. 'I'm interested in doing.'

'OK, then,' Freddie replied slowly. 'Maybe we can do more than just try.'

Something both hopeful and bittersweet crackled in the air between them, as if they were both realising in that instant that they were about to embark on something that would change their relationship for ever. It might ruin their friendship for good, or it might be better and more rewarding than either one of them could ever have imagined.

Derek was betting on the latter. He went to the bow and took hold of the mooring line tying the boat to the dock. Freddie had never sailed with him before. He had always considered it a solitary activity, and she had never asked to join him. Now, though, it seemed as if everything was about to change.

'Want to take her out for a few hours?' he asked.

'OK.' She still looked uncertain.

Derek went to start up the engine. He checked the direction of the wind before casting off the lines. He pulled in the fenders, shifted to forward and began to idle away from the dock. When they were clear of the other boats and could pick up a good wind, he adjusted the outhaul to tighten the bottom edge of the sail and began to hoist the mainsail. He lifted his head, as always feeling a small thrill at the sight of the gorgeous sail billowing with the wind. He secured the halyard, unrolled the jib on the foredeck and hoisted it. After ensuring that the lines were secure, he returned to the cockpit and checked the navigation equipment.

Jezebel headed into the wind. Derek sailed until the coast of California was a skein of land on the horizon, then he slowly lowered the anchor from the bow and put the engine in reverse to let the anchor dig in. When he was certain the anchor was buried and secure, he approached Freddie.

The boat rocked beautifully in the cradle of ocean swells. Freddie hadn't spoken since they had left the dock, but neither had she taken her eyes off Derek. He nodded towards the side of the boat.

'Want to swim?'

'I don't have a suit.'

'You don't need one.'

A hot flame glinted in Freddie's eyes. She turned away from Derek and pulled her T-shirt over her head. A thin strip of red lace crossed her back just below her shoulder blades. Derek's prick stiffened slightly. He wondered if Freddie had intentionally put on lingerie before she came to see him.

She hooked her fingers underneath her shorts and pulled them over her hips. Ah, God. A triangle of red lace barely covered the plump globes of her bottom. Her hips were round and full, her long legs shapely. Derek remembered with an inward groan how those legs had gripped his hips.

Freddie looked at him over her shoulder. She reached up to pull the band out of her hair, shaking the reddish brown mass loose around her shoulders.

'I've never seen you sail before,' she remarked.

'I know.'

'How do you do it single-handedly?'

'Things like autopilot and power winches help. And lots of practice.'

'You know,' Freddie said, 'it's pretty damn sexy.'

Before Derek could respond, Freddie dived over the side of the boat in a sleek movement. She disappeared under the surface, then came up with a gasp.

'Damn! It's cold.'

'I thought you were used to it.'

'I wear a wetsuit when I surf.'

'Maybe you should wear lingerie. Keep all the other surfers warm, anyway.'

He grinned down at her and stripped off his own shorts and T-shirt. Unlike Freddie, he also took off his undershorts before diving in. The water slammed against his body like a freezing brick wall. Derek surfaced and sucked in a breath.

'Fuck! I knew there was a reason I usually stay on board.'

Freddie chuckled and splashed some water at him. She swam a distance away and rolled on to her back, letting the swells of water carry her along. Even in the frigid water, Derek was still getting aroused watching her long body bob along the water's surface. Her nipples pressed firmly against the red lace.

He swam up beside her and took hold of a length of her hair. Freddie came up and began treading water. Her eyelashes were spiky and wet, her teeth almost chattering with cold. Derek gazed at her for all of an instant before he brought his mouth down on hers.

Warmth saturated him, invaded his bones, sank into his blood. The icy water melted into tepid waves. Freddie gave a little gasp that slipped into his mouth and heated him to the core. He put his hands around her waist and drew her to him, their legs entangling as they tried both to stay afloat and come together. Derek kicked backwards, not letting go of Freddie as he moved them back towards the boat.

He eased Freddie in front of him and helped her up the ladder. His erection grew stiffer as he watched her ascend before him, the wet lace sticking to every curve of her buttocks. Droplets of water ran over her like little diamonds. She turned to face him, watching him climb up the ladder, her brown eyes skimming over his naked body.

'Cold water didn't put you at much of a disadvantage,' she murmured.

'Only because you're here.'

He held out his arms. She stepped into them. The water on their skin evaporated from the heat of the sun and the reignited heat of their bodies. Derek pressed his groin against the wet silk of Freddie's panties. She drew in a breath at the sensation of his growing cock and lifted her face to his. Their lips met hard and fast.

Derek drove his tongue into Freddie's yielding mouth, feeling her surge to meet him. She fitted so damn perfectly against him, as if she had always belonged there and always would. He cupped her face and angled his mouth more seamlessly over hers as the fire grew hotter. His lower body constricted, his erection pushing insistently against her.

They sank to the sun-warmed deck as the boat rocked beneath them. Derek pushed his hand under the elastic of Freddie's panties, sinking his fingers into her warm, wet curls. She gasped and lifted her hips as if inviting his penetration. He watched her face as he probed gently into the pleats of her sex. A crescendo of want and increasing need passed over her features. She twined her arms around his neck and drew him down to her. Their tongues danced. Derek licked stray drops of water from Freddie's face and neck. He peeled the wet silk from her body, gazing hungrily at her full breasts crowned with

248

taut, crimson nipples. He stroked his fingers around one areola while clasping his lips gently around the other.

Freddie moaned with encouragement, her head sinking back on to the smooth deck, her hand delving into his damp hair. Derek splayed his palm over her belly, pushing her panties over her legs so that she was lying naked beside him. The sun caressed her honeyed skin like a lover, deepened the gold flecks in her eyes. Derek could have looked at her for ever. He didn't care what the future held as long as Freddie remained his and his only. He knew he could take anything except losing her.

'Derek?' A hint of concern darkened Freddie's eyes as she sensed his sudden unease.

'I love you.' He willed her with everything he had to believe him. 'I mean it. I've never said that to a woman before. I love you, and I want you. Only you.'

There was a split second of silence during which the world seemed to stop. In that second, Derek thought Freddie would voice all her fears again, but then she gave him a slow, beautiful smile that danced in her eyes and banished all fear.

'I believe you,' she said. 'I love you, Derek. I think I always have.'

Relief flooded him. He brought his mouth down on hers again, fiercely and with a passion that could come only from pure devotion. He silently promised that he would never let her go, that he would never hurt her and never allow anything to happen to her. Freddie would be his to love and protect. She always had been, but now they both knew it.

He pulled her against him, unsurprised when she nipped playfully at his lower lip and eased him on to his back. He knew she had a controlling side, and he was more than willing to let her give it free rein. The deck was hot against his back as Freddie looked down at him and curled her hand around his shaft. He made a strangled noise at the sensation of her warm hand. Freddie smiled and worked his cock to a full erection before she eased her body over his and guided him into her.

Her wet hair clung to her breasts and shoulders, making her look like a mermaid. Her body undulated with smooth movements as she began to ride him, her pussy gripping him like a vice. She was hot and moist all over, her skin glossy with a mixture of sweat and salt.

Derek's teeth came together as he attempted to retain control – not an easy task with her so tight around his cock and the sight of her naked body. He reached out and grasped her breasts, toying with the hard points. Freddie shuddered and put her hands on his thighs, pushing her breasts more securely into his hands. She began riding him harder, faster, her breath coming in rapid gasps.

'Oh, fuck, Derek. I can feel it. I'm going to come. I am ... oh, now. Now.'

Freddie's eyes squeezed shut, her hands clutching at his chest as she pressed forward to stimulate her clit. Her body throbbed powerfully, a cry of pleasure streaming from her throat.

Derek forced himself to wait until she was finished, until the tremors began to wane from her blood, before he gripped her waist and drove his hips upward. Freddie moaned, bracing herself against him as he thrust inside her. An explosion shot through his body and he came with a shout, pushing into Freddie as if he wanted to reach her very centre.

She collapsed on top of him, panting, her mouth open against his. Derek stroked his hands down her damp back to her bottom. He thought that he could die right now quite happily.

'Come with me,' he murmured, his voice drowsy.

Freddie lifted her head. 'What?'

'Come with me. On my trip.'

Her silence made him open his eyes. She was looking at him with confusion and uncertainty. He met her gaze unflinchingly.

'You're serious,' Freddie said.

'Damn right.'

'I can't –'

'Why can't you?' Derek interrupted.

'I just ... I have to work, Derek.'

'I have enough money to last us a while,' Derek said. 'But we'll work when we need money. Wherever we are. We'll pick olives in Greece. Catch fish in Bangkok. Sell conch shells in St Martin.'

'But my apartment –'

'A Santa Monica apartment a few blocks from the beach? You could rent it out tomorrow if you wanted.'

'I don't know how to sail.'

'I'll teach you. I'll be the skipper. You be the crew. And my personal love slave.'

Freddie smiled, but she still looked doubtful. 'You're really serious.'

'I've never been more serious.'

'What if we fight?'

'We'll make up.'

'What if we get sick of each other?'

'Then I'll sell you to the first rich Turkish prince we meet.'

'Derek.'

He stroked his hand through her hair and rested it against the side of her neck.

'Freddie, take a chance. You can never predict what's going to happen. But take a chance that it might just be the most fucking amazing thing you've ever done. We'll sail during the day, make love at night, catch fish, stop in exotic ports of call. We'll see the world. We can stay wherever we want as long as we want. We might even decide to live somewhere for a year or two. Buy a little beachfront cottage in the South Pacific. Eat coconuts and bread fruit. Make love three, four, five times a day. Come on, Freddie. Come sail around the world with me.'

Freddie gave him another slow smile and bent to press her lips against his. 'You're a romantic fool at heart, Derek. I never knew that about you.'

'Come with me. There's lots more to discover.'

'Yes,' she whispered against his mouth. 'As long as I can discover it all with you.'

Happiness swelled underneath Derek's heart. He put his hand on the back of Freddie's neck, holding her against him. Days and nights stretched before them, an endless span of time that held only the promises of love and adventure.

Epilogue

The waters of Mediterranean pulsed with azure and cobalt. A ramshackle cluster of buildings faced the Portovenere pier, washed with colours of pink, ochre, yellow and brick warmed by the sun. Fishing boats, dinghies, yachts and a cruise ship spread over the water. Both local residents and a few tourists wandered along the coast. On a hill above the village, a large stone castle sat like a nursemaid watching her charges.

Derek and Freddie walked over sun-baked steps and through narrow streets bordered by multicoloured buildings. Voices rose from a market taking place in the centre of town. Fruits, vegetables, flowers and local handicrafts were spread out on tables as if basking in the gazes of the customers. Tomatoes red as blood, flowers with their petals spread almost lewdly, thick wedges of cheese, plump mushrooms and garlic cloves, leafy green vegetables, warm bottles of olive oil.

Freddie stopped next to a merchant selling jars of honey that seemed to throb with a golden light. She scrutinised one of the jars and began speaking with the vendor in broken Italian. Derek watched her for a moment. She looked luscious in shorts and a tank top that displayed her ample cleavage. Her hair was pulled into a ponytail during the day, but every night she let it down for him so that he could spread his fingers through the thick mass. His groin tightened at the memory of Freddie naked, her hair loose around her breasts and shoulders, her eyes hungry for him.

Derek reined in his control. He went past Freddie, knowing well by now that she would be practising her

Italian for close to ten minutes. In the seven months that they had been at sea, she had made valiant efforts to learn local languages and customs as well as she possibly could. Derek grew more and more proud of her with each passing day. She had proved to be a quick learner and an adept sailor, but mostly he loved her for the way that she embraced each day and found pure enjoyment in everything they did.

They sometimes fought, but, as he had predicted, they always made up and had an incredible time doing so. When they needed time apart, they'd dock the boat and spend a day or two alone, meandering around little villages or major ports of call. When they returned to *Jezebel*, they were always happy to be together again. Derek could imagine no better life than being at sea with Freddie.

He paused and examined a selection of painted terra-cotta plates. The woman vendor held one out for him, but he shook his head politely and turned away. He found an empty stoop in front of a pastel-blue building and sat down to wait for Freddie.

As he scanned the marketplace, his gaze stopped on a curvaceous woman who was perusing a stall filled with leather goods – mostly jackets, shoes and belts. Wearing a loose cotton dress, she moved with an elegant precision like that of an aristocrat. Her blonde hair was fastened into a pristine knot at the back of her neck, her sculptured features partially obscured by a wide-brimmed straw hat.

Derek's gaze narrowed. He stood up and headed towards the stall. The woman selected a leather belt and brought it to the vendor for payment. She slipped the belt into her bag and left the stall. Her stride was silky.

Derek stopped. He was aware of an odd feeling of relief. He shook his head as if to clear his thoughts and turned back in Freddie's direction. She had just completed her purchase and held up the honey for him to see.

'Good for all sorts of things,' she remarked.

'Can't wait.'

'You OK?' Freddie asked. 'You look distracted.'

He reached out and pulled her against him, drinking in the smell of salt and sun that lingered in her hair.

'I've never been better,' he said.

In truth, he never had. Later that evening, he and Freddie returned to *Jezebel*, where they licked sweet, sticky honey from each other's body before falling asleep underneath a blanket of stars.

Visit the Black Lace website at
www.blacklace-books.co.uk

**FIND OUT THE LATEST INFORMATION AND TAKE
ADVANTAGE OF OUR FANTASTIC FREE BOOK OFFER!
ALSO VISIT THE SITE FOR . . .**

- All Black Lace titles currently available
  and how to order online
- Great new offers
- Writers' guidelines
- Author interviews
- An erotica newsletter
- Features
- Cool links

**BLACK LACE – THE LEADING IMPRINT
OF WOMEN'S SEXY FICTION**

**TAKING YOUR EROTIC READING
PLEASURE TO NEW HORIZONS**

LOOK OUT FOR THE ALL-NEW BLACK LACE BOOKS – AVAILABLE NOW!

All books priced £7.99 in the UK. Please note publication dates apply to the UK only. For other territories, please contact your retailer.

DANCE OF OBSESSION
Olivia Christie
ISBN 0 352 33101 1

Paris, 1935. Devastated by the sudden death of her husband, exotic dancer Georgia d'Essange wants to be left alone to grieve. However, her stepson Dominic has inherited his father's business and demands Georgia's help in running it. The business is *Fleur's* – an exclusive club where women of means can indulge their sexual whims with men of their choice and take advantage of the exotic delights Parisian nightlife has to offer. Dominic is eager to take his father's place in Georgia's bed and passions and tempers run high. Further complications arise when Georgia's first lover, Theo Sands – now a rich, successful artist – appears on the scene. In an atmosphere of increasing sexual tension, can everyone's desires be satisfied?

Coming in September

THE PRIVATE UNDOING OF A PUBLIC SERVANT
Leonie Martell
ISBN 0 352 34066 5

I love the sound of heels on a bathroom floor in the morning. It sounds like . . . Mistress.

Madame K, *femme fatale* and sexual subversive, 38, is an uncompromising deviant. She exacts her pleasures through the disciplinary art of male humiliation, where attention to aesthetic detail is lovingly realised, and punishment is not given lightly.

Simon Charlesworth, cabinet minister, 52, is undergoing a crisis. Party politics, domestic routine and thoughts of mortality have recently begun to crush his soul and he is desperately seeking something. He hungers for authentic experience and excitement – but he doesn't yet know what form this might take.

When these two very different personalities meet by chance one evening in a bar at Victoria Station, London, the wheels are set in motion for a descent into sexual excess and an exploration of the human condition at its most primal. Through a series of humiliating and extreme adventures Charlesworth achieves the divine oblivion of erotic ecstasy. But there is something in Madame K's past that is due to return. Something that could cost Charlesworth everything he owns.

THE MASTER OF SHILDEN
Lucinda Carrington
ISBN 0 352 33140 2

When successful interior designer Elise St John is offered a commission at a remote castle, she jumps at the chance to distance herself from a web of sexual and emotional entanglements. Yet, as she sets to work creating rooms in which guests will be able to realise their most erotic fantasies, she finds herself indulging in fantasies of her own, about two very different men.

Blair Devlin – overtly sexy and self-confident – is a local riding instructor. Max Lannsen – the Master of Shilden – is darkly attractive but more remote. All they seem to have in common is their hatred for one another. Then, when Elise's sensual daydreams become reality, she discovers that each man's future depends on a decision she will soon be forced to make. To which of them does she really owe her loyalty?

Coming in October

EQUAL OPPORTUNITIES
Mathilde Madden
ISBN 0 352 34070 3

David thinks his love-life is over when he is left unable to walk after a car accident. But then he meets kinky Mary, who finds the idea of a boy in a wheelchair too sexy for words. But is their affair just based on satisfying Mary's kinks, or something deeper? As David's scars begin to heal, soon both of them are having to face questions about what their attraction to one another really means.

DARKER THAN LOVE
Kristina Lloyd
ISBN 0 352 33279 4

It's 1875, and the morals of Queen Victoria mean nothing to London's wayward and debauched elite. Young but naïve Clarissa Longleigh is visiting London for the first time. She is eager to meet Lord Marldon – the man to whom she's been promised – knowing only that he's handsome, dark and sophisticated. In fact he is depraved, louche, and has a taste for sexual excess.

Clarissa has also struck up a friendship with a young Italian artist, Gabriel. When Marldon hears of this he is incensed, and imprisons Clarissa in his opulent London mansion. When Gabriel tries to free her, he too is captured, and the young lovers find themselves at the mercy of the debauched lord.

Black Lace Booklist

Information is correct at time of printing. To avoid disappointment, check availability before ordering. Go to www.blacklace-books.co.uk. All books are priced £6.99 unless another price is given.

BLACK LACE BOOKS WITH A CONTEMPORARY SETTING

☐ ON THE EDGE Laura Hamilton	ISBN O 352 33534 3	£5.99
☐ THE TRANSFORMATION Natasha Rostova	ISBN O 352 33311 1	
☐ SIN.NET Helena Ravenscroft	ISBN O 352 33598 X	
☐ TWO WEEKS IN TANGIER Annabel Lee	ISBN O 352 33599 8	
☐ SYMPHONY X Jasmine Stone	ISBN O 352 33629 3	
☐ A SECRET PLACE Ella Broussard	ISBN O 352 33307 3	
☐ GOING TOO FAR Laura Hamilton	ISBN O 352 33657 9	
☐ RELEASE ME Suki Cunningham	ISBN O 352 33671 4	
☐ SLAVE TO SUCCESS Kimberley Raines	ISBN O 352 33687 0	
☐ SHADOWPLAY Portia Da Costa	ISBN O 352 33313 8	
☐ ARIA APPASSIONATA Julie Hastings	ISBN O 352 33056 2	
☐ A MULTITUDE OF SINS Kit Mason	ISBN O 352 33737 0	
☐ COMING ROUND THE MOUNTAIN Tabitha Flyte	ISBN O 352 33873 3	
☐ FEMININE WILES Karina Moore	ISBN O 352 33235 2	
☐ MIXED SIGNALS Anna Clare	ISBN O 352 33889 X	
☐ BLACK LIPSTICK KISSES Monica Belle	ISBN O 352 33885 7	
☐ GOING DEEP Kimberly Dean	ISBN O 352 33876 8	
☐ PACKING HEAT Karina Moore	ISBN O 352 33356 1	
☐ MIXED DOUBLES Zoe le Verdier	ISBN O 352 33312 X	
☐ UP TO NO GOOD Karen S. Smith	ISBN O 352 33589 0	
☐ CLUB CRÈME Primula Bond	ISBN O 352 33907 1	
☐ BONDED Fleur Reynolds	ISBN O 352 33192 5	
☐ SWITCHING HANDS Alaine Hood	ISBN O 352 33896 2	
☐ EDEN'S FLESH Robyn Russell	ISBN O 352 33923 3	
☐ PEEP SHOW Mathilde Madden	ISBN O 352 33924 1	£7.99
☐ RISKY BUSINESS Lisette Allen	ISBN O 352 33280 8	£7.99
☐ CAMPAIGN HEAT Gabrielle Marcola	ISBN O 352 33941 1	£7.99
☐ MS BEHAVIOUR Mini Lee	ISBN O 352 33962 4	£7.99

BLACK LACE BOOKS WITH AN HISTORICAL SETTING

To find out the latest information about Black Lace titles, check out the website: www.blacklace-books.co.uk or send for a booklist with complete synopses by writing to:

Black Lace Booklist, Virgin Books Ltd
Thames Wharf Studios
Rainville Road
London W6 9HA

Please include an SAE of decent size. Please note only British stamps are valid.

Our privacy policy
We will not disclose information you supply us to any other parties. We will not disclose any information which identifies you personally to any person without your express consent.

From time to time we may send out information about Black Lace books and special offers. Please tick here if you do <u>not</u> wish to receive Black Lace information.   ❏

Please send me the books I have ticked above.

Name ....

Address ....

....

....

....

Post Code ....

Send to: Virgin Books Cash Sales, Thames Wharf Studios, Rainville Road, London W6 9HA.

US customers: for prices and details of how to order books for delivery by mail, call 888-330-8477.

Please enclose a cheque or postal order, made payable to Virgin Books Ltd, to the value of the books you have ordered plus postage and packing costs as follows:

UK and BFPO – £1.00 for the first book, 50p for each subsequent book.

Overseas (including Republic of Ireland) – £2.00 for the first book, £1.00 for each subsequent book.

If you would prefer to pay by VISA, ACCESS/MASTERCARD, DINERS CLUB, AMEX or SWITCH, please write your card number and expiry date here:

....

Signature ....

Please allow up to 28 days for delivery.